'Good God, w

The dragoon's cul
anger. 'If you can
don't ride one. A
animal, you could have killed yourself.'

Katherine pushed herself on to her knees.
'You ungrateful wretch,' she fumed. 'I've just
saved your life, sir.'

Dear Reader

We have Pauline Bentley back with a vengeance! REBEL HARVEST looks at the ramifications of the 1715 Jacobite uprising, which lead to paranoia in all sections of the kingdom. Just how can the heroine rescue her young brother from his folly without being noticed by the hero? Elizabeth Lowther takes us to Austria in 1904, where the heroine's efforts to be professional in her job are thwarted by the villain—will the hero believe her reputation has been wrongly maligned? BREATH OF SCANDAL has the answer. . .

The Editor

Pauline Bentley has long been captivated by history. Born in Essex, she trained as a legal secretary, but always came away from visiting castles or manor houses with the desire to write about them. She now lives in Sussex, is married with two children and a growing menagerie of dogs, and finds inspiration walking over the South Downs.

Recent titles by the same author:

WOMAN OF CONFLICT
SONG OF WYCHAVEN

REBEL HARVEST

Pauline Bentley

First published in Great Britain 1992 by Mills & Boon Limited

© Pauline Bentley 1992

Australian copyright 1992
Philippine copyright 1993
This edition 1993

ISBN 0 263 77989 0

Masquerade is a trademark published by Mills & Boon Limited, Eton House, 18–24 Paradise Road, Richmond, Surrey, TW9 1SR.

Set in 10 on 10½ pt Linotron Times
04-9301-82846

Typeset in Great Britain by Centracet, Cambridge
Made and printed in Great Britain

CHAPTER ONE

1715

KATHERINE WINTERS urged her mare to a faster gallop. Let her not be too late. A man's life could depend upon her actions in the next few minutes.

Ahead a rider crested the next hill and even from a distance she recognised the scarlet coat of a—dragoon officer?

Her green eyes were bright with determination as she scanned the track. The undulating South Downs were virtually bare of trees, but large gorse bushes covered their slopes, and in places the bracken was high enough for men to lie in ambush.

Katherine resolutely flicked back her long fair curls and touched her heels to the mare's sides. Fate was with her. There was no sign of her brother's conspirators.

Since the arrival of the billeting sergeant at Ferncombe Place that morning, she had been filled with dread. Of course the army suspected nothing of her brother's involvement with the Jacobites. How could they? It was ill fortune that the village inn was full and their officer was to be billeted with them. Ferncombe Place was the largest house in the village and to have refused would be to invite suspicion. Yet with an officer living in such close quarters it would present an even greater danger.

The anger she felt at her brother's Jacobite sympathies returned. Few rebellions succeeded. The Pretender's cause had surely been lost from the moment George I was crowned last year.

Somehow she had to save her brother Paul from the consequences of his plan. To attack an officer, so as to prevent him doing his duty, would solve nothing. Another would be sent in his place.

Katherine felt no fear at her recklessness. She had strong convictions, and no matter the personal cost she would stick by them. Her sense of justice would not let her do otherwise. Since their father's death last year from a hunting accident, she had fought convention, and village gossip, by living alone while Paul completed his Grand Tour. Upon his return, she had seen a change in him. At St Germain he had met James Edward Stuart—the man many drank to as 'the King over the Water'. Paul made no secret of his Jacobite allegiance.

It was a cause which would inspire any bold adventurer. Paul at seventeen was young and idealistic. Though Katherine sympathised with James Stuart and felt the late Queen's half-brother had been wronged, she accepted that King George was the appointed successor to Queen Anne. Besides, the Stuarts were an ill-fated monarchy. What good was it to England to be divided by another civil war in the Stuart cause? It was true German George was not popular, but since the persecutions in the reign of Mary Tudor Protestant England would never accept a Catholic on its throne. And the Pretender was a Catholic.

Her first loyalty was to Paul. At twenty, and three years his senior, it seemed she had spent all her life attempting to rescue him from the scrapes his reckless nature led him into. Today was no different.

This was his most dangerous exploit yet. Not only was her brother dabbling in treason, this could result in murder. And that she could not let happen. Paul must learn caution.

While the captain was billeted at Ferncombe, nothing of Paul's sympathies must become known to him. Katherine sighed. It was not an enviable task. What Paul believed in, he believed in with passion. The next few weeks could be difficult indeed.

The dragoon had crossed the narrow coombe

between the hills and his black horse was steadily picking its way along the track towards her. The hazy late September sun slid out from behind a plume of silvery clouds. As yet Katherine had no plan how to protect the officer. She crouched lower over her mare's neck and beneath her emerald velvet riding habit her body felt cold as she faced the hazardous task.

A flash of light from the bracken ahead warned her of danger. Her mouth was dry and the thud of her heart stifling. The sun's rays had glinted off a metal object. Was it a pistol barrel? At any moment the dragoon would be within its range.

Without thought of her own safety, Katherine kicked the mare to a gallop at the same time screaming out a warning.

'Beware, sir!'

She veered her mare to put herself between the captain and the marksman. Her brother's conspirators would never shoot her. She held tight to that belief as she plunged onwards, the gap closing between the two horses.

She had a brief impression of the dragoon's angular face beneath his three-cornered hat. It was tight-lipped and white with rage as he was forced to swerve to avoid being ridden down.

There was a distant report like a branch snapping followed by her mare's whinny of pain. Cassandra's ears were laid back, her head jerking downwards, to drag the reins from Katherine's hands. Neighing with pain and fear, the mare bucked. Katherine was thrown off balance, and instinctively kicked her feet free of the stirrups as she began to slide towards the ground. There was a blur of long grass rushing towards her, and a searing pain flared through her ankle when she thudded on to the ground. Unable to stop the momentum of her body, Katherine began to roll down the steep slope.

Blindly, she snatched at tussocks of grass and bracken to halt her tumbling. They came away in her hands and for several moments sky, sun and grass revolved crazily over her head, until she was pitched into the tortuous prickles of a gorse bush.

Katherine lay still, too stunned to move. When a figure blocked out the sun, she shook her head to clear her wits. Her back and legs smarted from the needle-sharp leaves of the gorse bush sticking into her flesh. Raising herself on a bruised elbow, she saw that her petticoats had tangled on the hooked talons of the bush, and her bare thighs were displayed almost to her hips. She tore the petticoat from the bush, ripping it in her haste to salvage her modesty. The sudden movement caused her to grimace from the pain of her bruised and battered body and her ankle felt as if it were held in the grinding jaws of a mantrap.

'Good God, woman!' The dragoon's cultured voice was clipped with anger. 'If you can't control a spirited horse, don't ride one. Apart from ruining a good animal, you could have killed yourself.'

Katherine pushed herself on to her knees. The throbbing fire in her ankle drained the colour from her cheeks, but her eyes sparked with indignation as she glared up at the dragoon silhouetted above her. She had met several officers in recent years, all of whom she disliked for their arrogant and overbearing manner.

'You ungrateful wretch,' she fumed. 'I've just saved your life, sir.'

Even as her temper soared, her agile wits were forming an excuse for her behaviour. No suspicion must fall upon Paul. 'These hills are the haunt of footpads, even outlaws. They have no love for a King's officer. A pistol was aimed at you.'

Angry at his censure, she ignored the hand extended to help her to rise. The moment her injured foot took her weight, she was forced to bite her lip against a wince of pain. Breathing shakily, she hobbled backwards to save her balance.

The unwelcome hand gripped her elbow, steadying her. Her glare swept upwards from a pair of gleaming black boots, over cream breeches moulded to strong, manly thighs, past the narrow hips, waist, broad chest and shoulders beneath the gold-braided scarlet jacket. The dragoon was a head taller than her own height of five feet six. He stood with his back to the sun, one hand resting on his hip. The breeze stirred the feathers trimming his hat, but his features were shadowed from her.

'Madam, am I to understand that although you careered into me like a madwoman you believe I am in your debt?' The anger was gone from his deep voice, replaced by what sounded suspiciously like amusement.

Katherine glared at him. It was a look of blistering fury which had many times sent lesser men scuttling for cover. The officer lifted a black brow with an insolence that seemed to be questioning her sanity.

'Madam is perhaps not used to finding herself in the wrong?' he drawled.

Katherine's tart reply checked on her lips. She could not remember the last time a man had countered her verbal attack. His hand remained firm upon her arm as he tilted his head to one side in frank appraisal. The audacity of the man! From the time she had been of marriageable age she had been unimpressed by the bewigged and powdered fops who would pay their attentions to her. Neither did she suffer fools lightly.

She widened her eyes, condemning him for his insolence. When she held the glittering stare in his black eyes, she saw them narrow in calculation. This man was no one's fool.

That would make his presence at Ferncombe Place doubly dangerous. His lean, angular face, for all its ruggedness, was strikingly handsome. But there was nothing in that uncompromising countenance to reassure her. That clean-shaven square jaw was resolute. The ebony eyes, sharp with intelligence, would miss nothing.

The full line of his mouth curved into an assessing

smile. 'You speak of outlaws quite calmly, ma'am. Why should you risk your life to save mine?'

'Because this side of the road is my brother's land. We are law-abiding if the outlaws are not.'

She looked past him to where his black gelding was cropping the grass. There was no sign of her grey mare.

'Your horse appears to have bolted, ma'am. She's an ill-tempered brute.'

'She's of the sweetest disposition, though does not lack spirit. Cassandra was hit by a bullet.'

The dragoon frowned and looked towards the road. The hill was deserted. Just discernible was the sound of retreating riders. She checked her anger. She was foolish to lose her temper because he did not believe her. She had achieved her aim. He was safe and no blame would fall upon Paul.

Incensed that the dragoon should presume to doubt her story, however, she wrenched her arm free of his hold and limped back from him. The agony in her ankle was receding, but it still throbbed painfully and her boot was pressing against its steady swelling. She turned her back on the soldier and sat down on the grass. The boot stuck fast as she tugged at it, and the movement brought a sob to her lips. Pulling off her gloves, she threw them to the ground, and took the dagger she always carried at her waist from its sheath. Lifting her riding habit to her calf, she began to saw at the stout leather of her riding boot. The rapid swelling of her ankle was becoming unbearable in the tight leather.

'Someone was certainly up to no good,' the officer commented drily. 'They've fled now.'

He bent one knee and knelt beside her. 'Is your ankle broken?'

The concern is his voice shredded her control. The fall had shaken her more than she cared to admit. 'I believe not, but it's swelling fast and hurts like Hades.' He took the dagger from her fingers and sliced through the length of the boot and gently lifted her foot free.

Katherine leaned back on her elbows, sighing at the relief from the pressure. The peace it brought was instantly shattered. The dragoon lifted her foot on his bent knee, his hands boldly stripping her silk stocking from beneath its garter and peeling it from her leg. Aghast at his forwardness, she slapped his hand aside.

'Enough, sir. You are too forward.' When she would have taken her foot from his knee the pain flared through it.

'Be still, ma'am. I mean you no harm, or disrespect.' His black eyes challenged her in a way that sent a shiver through her body. 'With your permission I would inspect the extent of your injury. It could be it will be more comfortable if lightly bandaged.'

Without awaiting her permission, he ran his hand lightly over her ankle and foot with competent assurance. She did not murmur when he touched the most painful place, but her ankle jerked from the spasm of her pain. He looked up at her, assessing her expression in a way she found disconcerting.

Now the danger of the officer being attacked was past, Katherine became aware of the isolation of the hillside. With her ankle throbbing and Cassandra gone, she suddenly felt very vulnerable. She picked up the dagger the officer had discarded, feeling safer as she replaced it in its sheath.

'Nothing is broken, but your ankle is bruised and badly wrenched.' He placed it gently on the ground and stood up. 'I fear it will pain you to walk upon it for some days.'

'A small price to pay, if it meant you passed unharmed across my brother's land. I'll have Paul search out these outlaws. They are a disgrace to the district.'

'That will be a task for my men, ma'am. We are here to ensure no unlawful disturbances take place.'

Katherine's unease mounted. By unlawful disturbances did he mean he was here to prevent the Pretender's landing? Had the authorities learned of the Jacobite plots? Guilt made her gaze slide away from his assessing stare. To her dismay she saw the extent of her dishevelled appearance. During her tumble her hat had come off and the pins scattered from her hair. It fell in sun-gold waves past her waist. To her further discomfort a flounce from her lace stock hung in tatters over her military-style jacket. Though she was not one to preen for hours before a mirror, she was too feminine not to feel shamed by her unkempt appearance. It made her tilt her head more defiantly.

'You're a brave woman, ma'am.' The officer made her a gallant bow, which she suspected was not without a touch of mockery. 'I salute your courage.'

When he again lowered his long body to crouch beside Katherine, she felt her breathing grow shallow. She had never been intimidated by any man; but there was something about the dragoon which made her feel distinctly threatened, and it had nothing to do with the danger he presented to Paul.

It made her study him closely. He was younger than she had at first thought. Perhaps no more than his middle twenties. He wore no white officer's wig, but as a concession to his military status his own long hair was powdered and tied at the nape of his neck with a black satin ribbon. From hours in the open his rugged complexion was tanned, adding to the aura of strength and masculine sexuality which was unlike anything she had encountered before. He was a man who made his own rules.

The knowledge exhilarated rather than perturbed her. She would take care not to underestimate him, but she did not fear him. She had long lived by her own code of honour and was confident she was bright enough to outwit any man.

He held out his hand to assist her to rise. This time she graciously accepted it and was surprised that its warmth seemed to permeate through her entire being. It made her defensive.

'Courage had nothing to do with my actions.' She

dismissed his compliment with her usual disregard for them. 'I was angry that the outlaws sought to harm a traveller upon our land.'

She tested her weight on her ankle and grimaced at the pain it brought her.

Without warning he stooped, placed a hand behind her legs and lifted her into his arms. Her eyes widened with outrage and her hand went to the dagger at her hip. It was pressed against the officer's side and could not be drawn.

Seeing her futile movement, he laughed. It transformed his stern contenance, the admiration in his eyes setting her pulse racing in the strangest manner.

'Were my intentions of evil motive, that puny blade would not halt them. I said earlier I mean you no harm. Though this should serve as a lesson not to ride the countryside without a groom in attendance. Since your horse has bolted, you must permit me to escort you to your home.'

Katherine nodded her acceptance. For the first time in her life she found herself tongue-tied in a man's presence. It was obvious she could not walk home, and since this officer would be billeted at Ferncombe Place it would be foolish to refuse.

The dragoon whistled his horse, who trotted to them. Katherine was lifted effortlessly on to the saddle and he stepped back, his manner at once formal. He raised a straight brow as his gaze held hers for a long moment. It took all her will-power to hold that penetrating stare. It was not just his nearness which was so disconcerting. There was so much at stake. He must not guess she had anything to fear from his stay in her house.

Suddenly the absurdity of their encounter struck her. A laugh shook her body until she could no longer contain it and it bubbled unrestrained to her lips. The dragoon looked at her, puzzled, which added to her mirth.

'My pardon, sir. . .' she finally found the breath to speak '. . .but we are both ruffled and puffed up like

agitated bantams. Yet have we not each done the other
a service this day?'

'Fighting cocks would have been a more flattering
comparison.' His lips twisted in a wry smile. 'Captain
Luke Ryder of the King's Dragoons at your service,
ma'am.'

'Katherine Winters, sir.'

'Are you comfortable, Mrs Winters? Your leg does
not pain you too much?'

'It is bearable, Captain Ryder. And it is Miss
Winters, if you please.'

A flicker crossed his eyes, showing his surprise that
she was unwed. Again she was struck by his handsome
looks. But there was a hard, almost ruthless set to his
features which warned her he would be a dangerous
man to cross. There was also sensuality in the full lips
and almond-shaped eyes—an intriguing combination.

'Which way to your home, ma'am?'

'Ferncombe village.'

'How fortunate. That is where I'm heading. We are
to be neighbours for a while, it appears, Miss Winters.'

There was a speculative light in his eyes which made
Katherine's chest feel tight. He took up the gelding's
reins to lead him forward.

'My home, Ferncombe Place, adjoins the village
green, opposite the church.' Her voice was deliberately
cool. 'I believe you are billeted there, Captain Ryder.
Your sergeant came to the house earlier this morning
demanding accommodation.'

'It seems I am to be doubly in your debt. You do not
sound as though you were in favour of offering hospitality to a King's officer.'

Katherine's heart began to beat rapidly and she
needed all her will-power to hold his forthright stare.
'I value my privacy, sir. But it is the duty of all law-
abiding households to billet soldiers when the need
arises.'

'We are all bound by duty.' He continued to look up
at her as he walked. 'Few men, let alone a woman,

would risk their own life if they saw another in danger. You are a remarkable woman.'

Katherine smiled. Behind its sweetness was a hornet's sting. 'Would you do any less, sir?'

'Indeed not!' He looked surprised. 'But I'm——'

'If you're about to say that you're a man,' she cut in sharply, 'then forget it. What was I supposed to do when I saw a man's life endangered—swoon?'

'I was going to say,' he raised a mocking brow, 'that I'm a trained soldier, used to dealing with such matters.' He favoured her with a long, assessing stare. 'Do you ever swoon, Miss Winters?'

'Never!'

She caught the sound of a cough from the officer which sounded suspiciously like an attempt to stave off a laugh.

'Captain Ryder!' she snapped, thoroughly out of patience with the man.

'Your servant, Miss Winters.' He did not look up and the brim of his hat hid his expression from her.

'It's a mile to my home,' she mastered her exasperation to say calmly. 'The day is hot. Your horse will bear the weight of us both.'

He tilted his head to regard her steadily and she faltered at the gleam brightening his eyes. Too late she realised how brazen her words must sound. 'Pray, don't misunderstand me, Captain Ryder,' she amended hastily. 'There's a time for propriety, and a time when it must be overridden by common sense.'

'Do you not fear for your reputation, Miss Winters?'

Katherine shrugged, her stare penetrating as she delivered her warning. 'Have I need, Captain? I think not, for all that army officers are generally accounted rakes. I judge a man by his actions, not what gossip would make of him. As to my honour, I would guard it as I would my life. Tattle-tongues will gossip whether there is cause or not.'

He swung up behind her, and as he leant forward to collect the reins his cheek brushed against her face.

The touch sent a quiver through her. For an instant she found herself staring into those dark, slanted eyes so disturbingly close to her own. He was studying her with an intentness which had the power to rob her of breath. When he smiled, revealing strong white perfect teeth, her heart did a somersault. To a stranger her outspokenness and unguarded stare would appear brazen. His grin broadened. He made no secret that he found her attractive.

To maintain a semblance of decorum she held herself rigidly away from the heat of his body, resenting the way he seemed to be taking charge of the situation—to his advantage.

No man had destroyed her composure before. She prided herself that she was always in control of any situation. Since her fifteenth birthday, both her beauty and her large dowry had attracted a score of suitors. None had moved her. When her mother died from smallpox when Katherine was twelve, she had become mistress of the household. Her father had made his fortune by shrewd investments, usually the import of exotic spices and goods from the East, or precious gems and gold from Africa. After his wife's death, Francis Winters had become a virtual recluse. He spent hours locked away in his library with his books and experiments, preparing long scientific theoretical papers which he sent to the Royal Society.

Looking after her father's interests and caring for Paul had given her a strong sense of independence, a freedom she cherished.

She was used to being her own mistress. It had been an idiosyncrasy of her father to educate her himself. From the age of six she could read and write. By ten she was fluent in French, Italian, Latin and Greek, and her knowledge of mathematics and theology equalled that of her brother. Few of her suitors had received such an education, yet they saw themselves as her superior. When she married—in the eyes of the law—

she would be her husband's property. Long ago she had decided she would be no man's vassal.

In the last year, having reached the advanced age of twenty, she found it no hardship to accept that she was likely to end her days a spinster. Her present suitor and neighbour, Viscount St Clere, was a friend she had known for years, but though she enjoyed his companionship she did not love him enough to give up her independence. Once Paul was married, she had decided, she would employ a widowed companion and take her own Grand Tour of the Continent. She suspected it would cause a scandal, but her hunger for travel and excitement was too strong to allow her to be trussed and tied by convention.

So why was she blushing beneath the close scrutiny of this stranger? Her every sense had become aware of the manly smell of his warm skin and the pleasant scent of orris-root rising from his clothing. With every stride of the horse, she was conscious of the touch of his chest against her back, the pressure of his thigh against her own. The heat of his body scorched through the thickness of their clothing. To combat the sensual touch, she fixed her eyes on the track ahead.

'Miss Winters, I would not be an unwilling guest in your home. I shall instruct Sergeant Hopkirk to find me accommodation elsewhere.'

'I have not said you were unwelcome, Captain,' she replied.

She turned to regard him. Aware of the hard muscles of the dragoon's thighs against her own, their bodies touching from shoulder to knee, she again shifted forward on the saddle. Unconsciously, her hand sought the reassurance of the dagger she carried and adjusted the sheath so that it no longer dug into her ribs.

Katherine sensed rather than heard his silent chuckle. Suspecting he again mocked her, she retaliated sharply. 'I assure you that, should the need arise, my aim with a dagger is as deadly as any man's. I'm not so foolish as to venture forth completely unprotected.'

'You mean you know how to use that weapon?'

'Would you care to test my skill?' She glared at him over her shoulder.

For a moment she wondered if he might do just that. As they rode his arm brushed against hers. The admiration gleaming in his eyes as he regarded her caused the strangest sensations to twirl through Katherine's stomach. She found herself unable to drag her eyes from his compelling gaze. He was different from any man she had met. Suddenly the dragoon's expression hardened, his voice clipped and authoritative. 'We are approaching the village green. I will dismount. I would not have your reputation jeopardised.'

The intimacy of the moment was gone and she felt like a child put firmly in its place. Self-consciously, she pulled her loose hair over her shoulder, braiding it into a more decorous style. Her hat was still somewhere on the hill, forgotten. Clearly the dragoon had a more unsettling effect on her than she realised.

'There's your horse,' Captain Ryder announced. 'She's limping.' He ran and caught Cassandra's reins.

'How badly is she hurt?' Katherine demanded.

The dragoon spoke softly to the nervous horse, calming her, before he ran expert hands over the grey's haunches.

As Katherine approached Cassandra, Captain Ryder finished inspecting the mare's bloodied side. There was a long red gash along her back.

'Your horse *was* shot. Your pardon, Miss Winters; I was not convinced you were telling the truth.'

Katherine widened her eyes, her tone affronted. 'And why else, pray, should I take it into my head to ride a stranger down? I assure you I am an excellent horsewoman.'

His tanned face darkened with a faint red tinge, but she was too concerned for her mare's welfare to feel any triumph that she had been proved right. With an expert eye she regarded her mare's wound, and was relieved to see that it was not deep and the bleeding had already stopped.

In silence they approached the watermill, its great wheel churning up the millpond as the miller ground the villagers' corn. The miller's wife and two daughters came to the door of their cottage, their expressions openly curious as they watched Katherine and the dragoon pass by, and they were not the only ones to follow their progress.

The captain ignored them, though Katherine could tell by the rigid set of his shoulders that he was aware of the villagers' curiosity and resentment. Katherine, like every family present, hoped that the soldiers would not be in the village long.

To break the uncomfortable silence she asked, 'Why did you not arrive with your men this morning, Captain Ryder?'

'There was a personal matter I had to deal with at Thornton.'

He did not elaborate further. Katherine's mouth tightened. Thornton was five miles away and infamous for its tavern, where half a dozen women openly plied their trade as whores. Not that Katherine was supposed to know of such places. But her brother frequently visited Thornton.

Captain Ryder looked up at her as they passed the Saxon church with its flintstone bell-tower. 'I had not heard there were outlaws in this district.'

Katherine felt her stomach tighten at being caught out in a lie. As usual in such circumstances she used attack as the best form of defence. 'It is well known hereabouts. Perhaps if you had spent less time enjoying such pleasures as Thornton had to offer you would be more aware of the degree of lawlessness in this district.'

'What pleasures would they be, Miss Winters?' Captain Ryder challenged, a hard note entering his voice.

This time it was she who blushed at the impropriety of her words. When he saw the colour flaring into her cheeks, the stern set of the captain's mouth softened.

'I spent an hour with the widow of one of my men,' he explained. 'He was killed last month during a riot in London. He was a good soldier. He left three children under the age of ten. I returned his personal possessions to her and what little money he had saved.'

'That was thoughtful of you, Captain.' Katherine was struck by his kindness—such women usually faced destitution in trying to bring up a family alone.

She stopped by the stone archway in a high flint-stoned wall. The ironwork gates were open. 'This is Ferncombe Place, Captain. I trust you will be comfortable during your stay.'

She watched his face as he regarded the four-gabled Elizabethan house, its sandstone walls and large mullioned windows reflecting the golden sunlight. She was proud of her home and was not disappointed at the dragoon's obvious appreciation of the beautiful architecture.

Before turning into the drive, Katherine looked pointedly along the road through the village. Some distance ahead, several dragoons sat on the grass outside the tavern drinking ale, while others more diligent were cleaning their weapons.

'My sergeant will report to me here, Miss Winters.' As they drew level with the front porch of the house, Grimshaw, the groom, appeared to take the horses.

'This is Captain Ryder, who will be billeted here,' Katherine explained. 'Has his servant arrived with his baggage?'

'An hour ago, Miss Katherine,' Grimshaw said gruffly, his bearded face beneath his almost bald head set with disapproval. 'Master Paul has returned. In a rare takin', he were. 'Is lordship arrived soon after. They'm in the library.'

At this further news Katherine's alarm increased.

What was St Clere doing here? His visits had increased of late and he had been more insistent in pressing his suit. It was true that during her father's life such an arrangement had been considered—the Viscount's first wife had died three years ago and there was no heir. Also St Clere was in financial straits. Her large dowry would enable him to put his estate in order and make it profitable again.

Of all her suitors St Clere was the one she was most drawn to. Not for his title—that meant nothing to her. And she knew it was more than her fortune that St Clere saw in her. She enjoyed his company. He was handsome, charming and far from old at thirty. But she did not love him. He was the most persistent of her suitors and it was beginning to wear thin the friendship she felt for him.

Captain Ryder handed Cassandra's reins to Grimshaw and came forward to help Katherine dismount. Ignoring her protests, he reached up to hold her waist.

For an instant she was held in mid-air. Their glances met. The sparkle of admiration she saw in his eyes made her heart pound. A smile, conspiratorial in its sweetness, touched his lips as he lowered her to the ground. Where his fingers gripped her waist, her flesh was tinglingly aware of his touch.

The pain jarring through her ankle as her foot touched the gravel brought an involuntary cry to Katherine's lips. Immediately she was raised into his arms, and found herself unable to suppress a misplaced chuckle at the obvious pleasure he showed at playing the gallant.

Now she was caught against his chest, her breathing slowed. She knew she should upbraid him for his forwardness, but somehow the words refused to form. Instead she raised her eyes to his face and cleared her throat. 'This is ridiculous, Captain, I am capable of walking.'

'You are in pain. Since you risked your life to save

mine, the least I can do is spare you further discomfort. Allow me to carry you inside,' he said.

Behind the polite façade of his words she sensed it was a command, not a request. To protest further would be undignified and cause a scene in front of the servants. And her ankle did throb most painfully.

The sound of his spurs echoed as he strode across the black and ochre tiled entrance hall. She nodded in the direction of a wide arch which led into the old-fashioned hall with its painted barrel-shaped panelled ceiling. Despite the heat of the day a fire burned in a huge marble fireplace. The room might look impressive but it was the draughtiest in the house. The captain carried her to a high-backed chair before the fire and lowered her gently on to it.

As he straightened, Paul strode into the room from the adjoining chamber. No one could suspect he had been out on the hill. His tan velvet suit was immaculate and his long brown hair tied neatly back in a queue. But the look in his hazel eyes warned Katherine he was furious, and when angry, Paul often forgot discretion.

Katherine spoke quickly before her brother said something disastrous. 'Paul, there's outlaws in hiding near the old hammer pond. Something must be done about them. They fired at Cassandra. She bolted and I was thrown. Captain Ryder saved me from a long walk home with a sprained ankle.'

'Outlaws, you say!' drawled St Clere as he sauntered from behind Paul into the hall. 'Katherine, my dear, how many times have I warned you not to ride alone? It's too dangerous.' As he spoke he looked meaningfully at Paul, warning him to say nothing more. 'We are indebted to you, Captain, for escorting Miss Winters home.'

There was a cold note in the Viscount's voice Katherine had never heard before. Henry D'Acre, Viscount St Clere was of medium stature and slight build, and wore a long, full-bottomed flaxen wig as befitted his rank. Now he looked at the dragoon with arrogant disdain.

St Clere crossed the room and placed a hand on Katherine's shoulder. It marked her as the Viscount's possession and Katherine resented it intensely. The atmosphere in the room became more charged by the second.

A glance at the captain showed Katherine he was unimpressed by St Clere's hauteur. The dragoon stood erect, but with one leg slightly bent in front of him, looking relaxed and at ease and in no way subservient to the nobleman. There was a look in his dark eyes which made Katherine grow cold.

A silent challenge had sparked across the room between the two men, the manner of which she did not fully comprehend. Whatever it was increased her fore-boding. The dragoon's stay at Ferncombe would indeed be fraught with danger for them all.

CHAPTER TWO

'You're too headstrong for your own good, Kat.' Paul's tone showed his irritation. 'What possessed you to ride without a groom in attendance? It's too dangerous.'

'I'll not be lectured in front of our guest, Paul,' Katherine responded with false sweetness. Her brother was being deliberately difficult. 'Where are your manners? I'm sure Captain Ryder would like some refreshment.'

'That's most kind of you, Miss Winters.' Captain Ryder stood at ease and despite her annoyance at his earlier boldness her interest in him stirred. From his bearing and relaxed manner it was obvious he came from a good family. She saw now that his scarlet jacket was of the finest wool, and the perfect fit over his broad shoulders and slender waist was the handiwork of an expensive tailor.

Paul rang for a servant, his petulance provoking Katherine. In appearance Paul was tall and confident beyond his years, but there were times, as now, when the immaturity of his years betrayed him. Intrigue needed the restraint and cool head of seasoned men.

She looked from her brother to the officer. Seeing Luke Ryder's formidable self-possession, she felt a *frisson* of fear. The tension was tangible between the men. If Paul was not careful he would antagonise the dragoon and make him suspicious. Neither was St Clere making matters easier. The Viscount was staring out of the oriel window, arrogantly ignoring the officer.

To lighten the mood Katherine turned to St Clere. 'My lord, by coincidence Captain Ryder is billeted with us. It seems there are rumours that the Pretender is to atempt a landing.' As she spoke she twisted her braid in her fingers, affecting a pose of innocent unconcern.

'There are always rumours, my dear,' St Clere answered easily. 'One pays little heed to them.'

Sanders, their major-domo, answered Paul's summons. He had anticipated their wishes and carried a silver tray with two wine flagons and a dish of cinnamon cakes.

While the servant poured their drinks and handed them round, Katherine said, 'Sanders, I believe Captain Ryder's servant has arrived. I left instructions for a room to be prepared in the west wing.'

Sanders bowed to her, his short round body stiff with his own disapproval that the dragoon was to stay in the house. 'There is no servant——' Sanders sniffed his disapproval '—but that sergeant brought the captain's baggage over an hour ago.'

'Thank you, Sanders. While Captain Ryder is a guest here you will inform the servants that they are to serve his needs,' she told him

Katherine hid her vexation as the major-domo left. She would talk to Sanders; after thirty years' service to her family he was a respected member of the household, but Katherine would not tolerate incivility to a guest.

Paul drained his goblet, replenished it from the flagon and made to refill Captain Ryder's cup. When the dragoon demurred, Paul regarded him sourly. 'A dragoon who won't drink—there's a rarity. The last troop billeted in the village were drunk every night, their captain included.'

'My men will not disturb the peace of your village, Luke responded curtly.

'Good to hear it!' said Paul, moving to the fireplace. He placed his boot on the firedog and Katherine was horrified to see its sole covered in mud and bracken fronds.

'Did you see any sign of the outlaws, Paul?' She looked pointedly at his boots. 'You were up on that side of the estate, weren't you, inspecting the crumbling wall by the old convent gardens?'

'No sign of them at all,' Paul replied. He drained his goblet and faced the dragoon. 'How long will you be in the district, Ryder?'

'It's difficult to say. I'll not intrude upon your hospitality longer than is necessary.'

'It's no intrusion.' Paul forced a tight smile.

Captain Ryder put his goblet down on a table and turned to Katherine. His dark eyes were filled with such concern that an exciting warmth spread through her body as she held his stare.

'You look tired, Miss Winters. If you will excuse me I must receive my sergeant's report.' His stern expression softened as he took her hand and raised it to his lips. Their heat lingered upon her flesh. 'I trust you have sustained no lasting injury?'

She smiled up at him, unable to resist a light-hearted teasing. 'It's not the first tumble I've taken from a horse and I doubt it will be the last. The pain is easing already. I would not delay you from your duty, Captain. We dine at eight if you would care to join us.'

The bold smile she had come to expect lit his face. 'I would be honoured, Miss Winters.'

Luke Ryder took his leave of St Clere and Paul Winters, but paused at the doorway to look back at the woman, strangely reluctant to leave her company. Even with her cheek smeared with a line of dirt she was beautiful. Beautiful and untamed—a fascinating combination.

Later, as he walked across the village green to join his men at the inn, he still carried the image of Katherine Winters in his mind. At the outset, believing her the spoilt, haughty creature her expensive riding habit had led him to expect, he had been antagonised by her anger. St Clere's possessive attitude to Katherine Winters rankled Luke. She was certainly beautiful enough to attract a viscount to pay court to her, and it was likely her dowry would be adequate for such a match. He shrugged. When his own sister Lucy had married, her marriage portion had been in excess of twenty thousand pounds, and she had married the second son of a baronet.

Luke's eyes hardened as he reflected upon the enquiries he had made about the inhabitants of Ferncombe once he had known he was to be billeted in the village. St Clere was the largest landowner, Highclere being only one of several properties he would inherit on his father's death and he took the title of Earl of Brent. The Winters' money came from trade, but not ordinary goods—selected imports for the noblest families in England. Ferncombe Place spoke of its owner's wealth and position in the community.

Though a soldier, Luke was at ease in such a place, for it was similar to his own family home in Somerset. As a younger son, he would, however, inherit nothing, and there was a spark of pride in him which rejoiced in that knowledge. What he achieved in life he would do so by his own hand. Not that he was a pauper. Army pay was poor, but he did not rely solely upon that for his income. There was an adequate legacy left him by his grandfather. And there was the brigantine he owned.

It was not often he dwelt upon his possessions, but he had sensed Paul Winters' resentment. He knew their kind. The young man considered himself Luke's superior because of his affluence, but Luke was Paul Winters' equal—perhaps not in riches but in family background. Ferncombe Place had spoken of wealth and good taste. Katherine had the self-possession of a woman of independent means. Was she then an heiress in her own right?

The thought made him shiver with disgust. From what he knew of her character she had none of the flaws of such a callous, fickle breed. He hated such creatures, and with good cause. But for one of their kind, his friend Hal Penrose would be alive now.

Luke clenched his jaw against the pain of grief which

still remained from his friend's death. Hal had been his friend from university; they had joined the same regiment together and were inseparable. Hal had saved his life in battle. Hal was the cool-headed one who in their earlier years together had tempered Luke's wildness. He was the most loyal, the most entertaining of companions, and Luke had felt closer to him than he did to his two elder brothers. His death had hit him hard. And an anger still burned deep within him at the way Hal had been wantonly murdered. . .

Luke harnessed his memories and returning grief. Heiresses! How they disgusted him. Hal had been worth a dozen of their heartless breed. And he had met many in his lifetime—none had made him change his opinion. They cared only for wealth and position. Hal had made the mistake of falling in love with one.

Cynicism now destroyed Luke's earlier pleasure in Katherine Winters' company. Was she such a one? Somehow he thought not, and he relaxed. She had risked her life to save him from the outlaws' bullet, and that was a totally selfless act. No heiress would be capable of that. Kate was different from any women he had met. Her sound practicality had astounded him, and her bravery was admirable. There had been no maidenly hysterics when he tended her foot.

That memory brought a more provocative one to his mind: the sight of her long, shapely legs revealed almost to her hips as her petticoat tangled in the gorse bush—a delectable sight which had quickened his blood.

Luke grinned wryly.

How had so fascinating a creature remained unwed? Clearly St Clere saw her as his possession. Was she his mistress? Somehow he believed not. For all Katherine Winters' fiery spirit, there was an air of innocence about her unconscious sensuality. With St Clere dancing attendance she'd not stay innocent for long.

The thought was oddly displeasing. St Clere's reputation was not unknown to him. The Viscount could rival the late King Charles for his number of mistresses. Also his name had been linked with the Jacobite cause.

Luke rubbed his chin. Had he by chance been billeted in a house sympathetic to the Pretender? Paul Winters had certainly been hiding something. He knew the signs.

Was Kate involved? The intimate shortening of her name sprang so easily to mind that it surprised him. Yet in their brief time together he did now think of her as Kate and not Miss Winters. He smiled to himself. He was certain that the attraction was mutual. What better way to discover the secrets of that household than by winning the confidence of Paul Winters' sister?

Later that evening Katherine sat in the winter parlour with her ankle resting on a footstall. She had endured the ministrations of the doctor, who announced that with rest it would be fit to walk upon in a day or two. Undeterred, she disregarded the doctor's advice and limped to her bedroom to change for dinner, refusing all help from the servants when she returned to the parlour.

'Damn it, Kate, we had the dragoon in our sights,' Paul said tersely. 'What did you have to interfere for? Now we're stuck with him for God knows how long.'

Katherine ignored his scowl. 'I saved you from your own folly, if you could but see it. For my trouble that fool doctor would make an invalid of me. Not that I intend to sit around doing nothing for so long. My sanity would desert me.'

Paul was unimpressed by her pique. He lounged on the settle across the room, sipping his brandy. 'As master in this house, I could have you confined to your room for the duration of that damned dragoon's visit. A fitting punishment.'

Katherine wrinkled her face at him. 'You would not be so cruel.'

'It's time someone took you in hand, Kat. I'll not have my sister behaving like a hoyden.'

'That's not fair, Paul.' Katherine was hurt by his accusation.

'Isn't it?' There was a new authority in his voice. 'I will be master in my own home.'

Paul's pride was hurt that she had disobeyed him. Katherine could understand that.

'While Captain Ryder is here, we must make the best of it,' she counselled. 'Surely for a week or two you can curb your Jacobite intriguing? The very fact that he has stayed here and found nothing could later prove to your advantage.'

'The man's a danger to us all.' Paul stared sullenly into his glass.

'Not if we are careful.'

Paul drained his glass and Katherine watched with misgivings as he refilled it. He looked over the rim of his glass, his manner challenging. 'You spent long enough with the fellow. What do you make of Ryder?'

'He's a cut above the usual soldier. He's intelligent and I suspect ruthless in pursuing his duty.' She leant forward in her chair to emphasise her words. 'There must be no meetings of your friends in this house while he's here. It's more than cards you occupy yourselves with when they come. Don't take any risks, Paul.'

'There'd be no risk if you hadn't interfered,' he retorted.

Katherine's eyes flashed with returning anger as she sat back to regard her brother. 'Was I supposed to sit by and let you commit murder?'

She rose to her feet, too angry to give way to the pain shooting through her ankle as she limped towards him. 'You've changed, Paul, since your Grand Tour. You were always impetuous, but never cruel, or cold-blooded.'

'It would not have come to murder,' Paul retaliated, his hazel eyes rounding with shock at the suggestion.

Katherine curbed the need to shake some sense into him. 'How can you be so naïve? This is no game, Paul. Treason leads but one way—to the gallows.'

She put a hand on his shoulder, feeling his tension through the gold brocade jacket.

'I'm not a child, Kat. Stop treating me like one. What would a woman know of such matters?' he protested.

The determination in his eyes warned her he now considered himself too old to follow her guidance. He was a man now and would follow his own path.

'It will lead to murder one day, Paul,' she said heavily. 'If the Pretender lands, it could even come to a massacre. Have you considered the consequences?' She spread her sapphire skirts and knelt at his side. 'Forget this madness, Paul. I'm not a fool. I know that when you were in France last summer you gave your homage to the Pretender.'

'If you mean did I have the honour to be presented to the Chevalier St George, then you are correct,' Paul blazed. He jerked his arm from her and stood up to pour himself another drink. 'James Stuart is our true King. Not that lump of German lard who sits on the throne.'

The coldness in her brother's eyes frightened her. Somehow she must make him see reason.

'I've no love for King George,' she answered as she raised herself from the floor to regard him steadily. 'But he's a Protestant and his right to the throne comes direct from Charles I's sister, Elizabeth of Bohemia. He was named by Queen Anne as her successor.'

'So the Whig Government would have us believe. What proof is there *who* Queen Anne named as her successor? King James Edward Stuart is Queen Anne's brother. His right is the greater.' Paul smoothed a hand over his brown hair. 'Or do you believe the tales that he was a changeling, smuggled into Mary of Modena's childbed in a warming-pan after her own child had been born dead?'

'Of course I don't believe that. No sane person would.'

Katherine touched her brow, seeking the words of

reason which would change his mind. She took a steadying breath and went on. 'Like his father, James II, the Chevalier is stubborn. He will not renounce the Catholic faith so England will have none of him. Better to accept that than risk your life for a lost cause.'

'A just cause, Sister. Never forget that.' A fervent gleam lit Paul's eyes and he seemed to grow in stature as he spoke so passionately of his beliefs. 'Are you asking me to turn my back upon all I believe in? German George has no love for England. He refuses to speak our language, and would bleed us dry to pour England's wealth into his precious Electorate of Hanover. He's a dull-witted martinet, with vulgar tastes and a mean spirit. I'll never forswear my loyalty to King James and deny my principles for such a man.'

With those words Katherine knew she had lost her argument. She shook her head, her fear for her brother's safety battling against her pride in his resolve. Paul did not need her censure, but her love and support. She held out her arms and embraced him. 'You make me feel ashamed. Whatever you choose to do, I'll not desert you, Paul.' She moved back to hold him at arm's length. 'Only take care. I love you dearly. You're all the family I have.'

His assured grin did little to cheer her.

'I knew I'd make a Jacobite of you, Kat. and, talking of family, it's time you married and raised one of your own. You know St Clere would make a deuced fine husband.'

She sighed. 'He would make some woman a remarkably fine husband, but not this one.'

'It's what Father wished for you. You've not forgotten the marriage contract he drew up before his death?'

'I'll not be bound to something I did not agree to,' Katherine asserted.

Paul shoved his hands into the pockets of his jacket, regarding her sharply. 'St Clere's been patient up to now, but he means to have you, Kat. He's every right to hold you to that contract.'

'If he did he will have a wife who hates him. I'm not ready for marriage,' she declared firmly. 'St Clere promised to wait until I was twenty-one for my answer. That's six months away.'

Paul stepped back from her and sat down, his mouth grim. 'You've not had your head turned by that dragoon? He seemed taken with you. You play with fire encouraging him.'

'I did not encourage him.' Katherine's temper sparked. It rankled that Paul had guessed that the dragoon intrigued her. 'Every moment Captain Ryder is in this house will be fraught with danger. If I was friendly to him, it was to foil your hostility. It would be foolish to rouse the man's suspicions that we were hiding something.'

'Such vehemence, Kat. You forget I know you well,' Paul snapped. 'For all your denial, it's plain you find the officer attractive. I've seen how ruthlessly you can set aside unwanted admirers.'

He studied her at length, then a slow smile spread across his elfin face. 'His interest in you can be used to our advantage. It's because of your interference that the man's lodging here. So you'd better ensure he's kept entertained and out of our way. We don't want him sniffing into affairs which don't concern him.' He laughed without mirth. 'Captain Ryder won't know what's hit him. You'll lead him a merry dance, Kat.'

'No, Paul, I'll not deceive him.' The idea was unacceptable to Katherine.

'You'll do as you're told.' Paul drank down another brandy and jabbed his finger at her. 'You got us into this mess. It could be his life or mine.'

Paul stood up, his figure weaving as he walked to the door. 'I'm dining at Highclere with St Clere.' He tapped his nose in a significant gesture. 'We have some notable guests. Make sure you keep that dragoon entertained.'

Katherine watched with dismay as Paul strode out of the parlour. She had not reckoned on dining alone with

Captain Ryder. From the courtyard she heard Paul
ride out and at the same time there was a firm,
measured tread across the tiled hall proclaiming the
officer's approach.

Katherine smothered a groan of frustration. She did
not want the role of informer her brother would inflict
upon her.

Restless, she limped across the room, her gaze drawn
to the portraits of her ancestors on the panelled walls.
Every one of the men in the portraits had fought in
some conflict.

Faint-heart, her conscience mocked her reluctance
to deceive the dragoon. The Winters family fought for
what they believed right. Would she make Paul a lesser
man than their kinsmen? That same fighting spirit was
in her, but she channelled it in loyalty to her loved
ones. The door opened and Captain Ryder entered.

'Good evening, Captain,' Katherine welcomed him,
her misgivings pushed aside.

He had changed his military coat and over his white
brocade waistcoat and linen knee breeches he wore a
black velvet jacket edged with a silver leaf design. The
lace at his cuffs and throat was purest white and
delicately woven. But the most startling change was in
his hair. He had washed all the powder from it and the
blue-black locks were swept back from his face and
tied in a long queue at his nape.

She had thought him handsome before, but that
black hair against his swarthy skin was breath-stealing.
When his dark eyes smiled into hers, her heart gave a
capricious leap.

'Did I just hear your brother ride out? Is he not to
join us?' he asked.

Katherine heard the suspicion in his voice and felt
herself grow hot with trepidation. It was most improper
of Paul to leave her to dine alone with Captain Ryder.
She forced an unconcerned smile. 'He sends his apolo-
gies. Paul had a previous engagement. To maintain the
proprieties my maid will of course be in attendance.'

'I had not dared to hope we could dine in so intimate a manner.' He took her hand and led her to the cushioned settle. 'You should not be standing, Miss Winters. Your ankle must pain you still.'

'I find pain easier to bear than the boredom of inactivity,' she told him.

'A fate worse than death for a woman of your high spirits,' he quipped. 'And no doubt the poor officer whose life you saved, but is the cause of your confinement, is viewed with displeasure.'

Katherine lowered her gaze from the bold stare which sent her pulses racing. 'You presume much, Captain, to even consider that my thoughts were upon you.'

He put his hand over his heart. 'Then I am stricken to the core, Miss Winters. Your anger I could have borne with dignity, but your indifference leaves me bereft.'

'Only stricken to the core!' She almost choked upon her laughter at his exaggerated gallantry. 'Are you not mortified beyond redemption?'

His eyes sparkled as he responded to her teasing. 'Be assured, brave lady, I am suitably mortified.'

She bowed her head in amused acknowledgement. His sense of humour complemented her own and promised that the evening would be diverting.

'I am determined that my ankle will not stop me dancing at the reception at Highclere next weekend,' she said. His full lips compressed at the mention of St Clere's home, and, conscious of her task tonight, she hurried to add, 'Shall we dine, Captain?'

He held out his arm to escort her from the room and she placed her hand upon it. Even through the thickness of his jacket she could feel its firm, muscled strength, and though their bodies did not touch she was acutely aware of the power in his lean frame. She had always been excited by an edge of danger and she felt her blood race with anticipation now. She despised deceit, but the challenge to protect Paul by matching her wits against the captain was an exhilarating one.

They entered the dining saloon which was lit by a score of candles in the central chandelier, though the corners of the room were cast into shadow. The long table seated a dozen people each side and tonight their two places were set at either end with a high silver fruit stand and a tall arrangement of flowers in its centre.

Katherine took her place and waited for Captain Ryder to be seated. The maid's presence was reassuring, but unintrusive. It was the vast length of the dining table which was oppressive. Katherine's view of the dragoon was blocked by both the fruit stand and the flowers. Whenever Paul was at home they sat opposite each other across the width of the table, not isolated by twelve feet of polished mahogany.

Sanders served the soup and stepped back into the shadows. They ate for some moments in silence.

'You have a charming house, Miss Winters. It's Elizabethan, isn't it?'

'Yes, it is.' Unable to see the dragoon as she spoke, Katherine leaned to one side to peer around the flower arrangement as she answered him. 'It was built in 1590 by my great-great-grandfather. Our family have lived here ever since.'

She straightened and dipped her spoon into the bowl before asking, 'Do you come from this part of the country, Captain Ryder?'

Their roles were reversed as he was now forced to lean sideways to look around the fruit stand to answer her. 'My family home is in Somerset.'

'A beautiful county,' she remarked. 'How long have you been in the army?'

The captain again leaned across the table. 'Nine years or so.'

About to ask another question, Katherine again moved sideways and found herself looking into the captain's face as he leant across with the same intention.

'This formality is too absurd, do you not agree, Captain Ryder?' She laughed. 'Sanders, we cannot converse in such a manner; please set Captain Ryder's place closer to me.' She indicated the chair to her right.

'Is that not better?' she asked when the dragoon was again settled.

'Infinitely.'

The upward curve of his lips made her wonder whether she had not been too familiar. Uncomfortable beneath his dark, assessing stare, she said quickly, 'When Paul and I are alone we always dine like this. I'm not one to stand upon ceremony.'

'I assure you I appreciate it. It is not often we find ourselves welcome when we must billet in a village,' he told her.

While Sanders removed the empty soup bowls and replaced them with plates of steaming pheasant in a spiced cinnamon and orange sauce, the captain continued to appraise her, until Katherine could feel the heat rising in her cheeks.

Flustered, she lowered her gaze. In the past she had always found it easy to stare a man down, especially if she considered his gaze was impertinent or over-bold. But, holding the captain's look, she had felt an insidious warmth spreading through her veins, quite unlike anything she had experienced before. She began to feel that she was being drawn out of her depth, and she responded by lifting an arched brow in gentle rebuke.

'Not all officers are as courteous as yourself, Captain Ryder. It is obvious you are a gentleman, otherwise I would not be dining with you with only my servants in attendance.'

The smile did not waver; rather, to Katherine's dismay, it seemed to convey a wealth of sensual promise. 'You are an unusual woman, Miss Winters. You have a self-containment any man would envy.'

'I am my own woman. Few men accept that.'

He raised his goblet in silent salute to her. Again Katherine was the first to lower her gaze from his compelling stare. She ate a slice of the pheasant. It was one of her favourite dishes and tonight it tasted especially succulent, as the wine she sipped seemed to roll around her tongue with a sweetness and greater intoxication than before. She put aside her goblet; the wine was lethally potent if it made her so light-headed after a few sips.

'You spoke of a reception at Highclere,' Captain Ryder remarked smoothly. 'Are there to be many guests?'

'When St Clere entertains he does so in grand style.' She looked closely at him, searching for signs that he was suspicious it could be a cover for a Jacobite meeting. His handsome face showed only polite enquiry. 'St Clere is a wonderful host,' she went on. 'As a guest in our house, you must attend, Captain.'

Thick black lashes lowered like a visor over his eyes. 'My duty permitting, I'm sure such an evening could be most enlightening.' He sat back in his chair, the teasing light gone from his eyes. 'There's talk in the village that you are to wed St Clere. He certainly was very possessive of your company this afternoon. Yet he allows you to entertain me alone this evening.'

The coldness of his tone startled Katherine into retaliation. 'I had not thought you a man who paid heed to gossip, Captain Ryder.' Her tone matched his in coldness. 'St Clere is a neighbour and a friend. There will always be speculation.'

'You do not deny it?' His eyes sparked with anger. 'Were you told to entertain me tonight as St Clere was expecting a messenger? A very special messenger from France? St Clere was a prominent Jacobite in the last months of the old Queen's reign.'

Katherine threw her napkin down on to the table and stood up. 'I'll leave you to finish your meal alone. I will not be insulted in my own home. Nor will I have my friends maligned.'

He was on his feet barring her path as she made to move past him. The candles overhead flickered in the upsurge of draught from their angry movements, and the wavering shadows heightened the formidable ruggedness of the officer's face.

'I ask your pardon, Miss Winters. I spoke out of turn.' He glanced towards Sanders, who had picked up a carving knife in defence of Katherine should the need arise. 'Please finish your meal. Your loyalty to your friends is commendable, though in St Clere's case perhaps misguided.'

'You are presumptuous, sir. Please stand aside and allow me to leave.'

'Not until you accept my apology,' he said. He smiled, and its provocative warmth melted her antagonism. Katherine stood very still, refusing to acknowledge that he held sway over her. His smile broadened.

'Miss Winters, for a woman of such perception you must be aware of the esteem in which I hold you. We have known each other but a few hours and, misplaced as it was, I resented St Clere's prior claim upon you.'

Sanders gave an outraged snarl. 'Have no fear, Miss Katherine, I shall summon the other servants and have this man removed at once.'

'No, Sanders,' Katherine said quickly. 'Captain Ryder meant no offence. We will continue our meal.'

She found her legs were unsteady as she returned to her place at the table. Common sense told her she should leave, but something far stronger called upon her to stay. And it had nothing to do with her brother's warning to keep the dragoon entertained throughout the evening.

She smoothed the napkin over her satin gown and when she looked across at Luke Ryder she could not keep the laughter from her voice. 'That, Captain, was the most outrageous apology I have ever heard. And the least said about it, the better. However, while you are a guest in this house we shall agree not to discuss politics.'

'No woman should trouble her pretty head over such

weighty matters. There are other more entertaining ways to pass the time.'

Katherine clenched her knuckles until they went white. She leaned forward, her eyes flashing with returning anger. 'Such weighty matters concern us all. Because I'm a woman, it does not mean I'm blind to the mess men would make of this country for their own gain. Many people believe James Edward Stuart has been cheated of his birthright by a petty German princeling who cannot even speak our tongue.'

The moment she had spoken she realised he had deliberately drawn her. She widened her eyes, meeting his accusing glare with defiance.

'Those are treasonous thoughts, Miss Winters.' There was a dangerous edge to his deep voice. 'Or do you see a handsome and charming Stuart prince as a romantic cause to uphold?'

To regain her poise she fidgeted with a wide diamond and pearl bracelet on her wrist. 'Trust a man to believe a woman could be swayed by romantic ideals!' she finally managed in a controlled voice. 'It is a cause which would turn England into a battleground. I'm not so hen-witted I would make a romantic ideal out of a doomed Stuart cause.'

'That is wise, Miss Winters, since for the last year a Hanoverian has sat upon the throne.'

Katherine felt the heat drain from her body; his words sounded like a thinly disguised threat. It stirred her turbulent temper.

'I do not need a lesson in history, Captain Ryder. King James II was indiscreet to openly flaunt his Catholic faith. His Protestant daughter Mary was welcomed by the people. A pity that Mary and William died childless, as did Queen Anne. But James Edward Stuart is Mary and Anne's brother. I admire him for upholding his Catholic faith when England has shown she will be ruled only by a Protestant.'

'God's truth, woman, must you twist everything I say? I serve the King who you show so little respect towards.

You speak treason.' White furrows of anger cut deep into the captain's bronzed countenance. He made a visible effort to control his temper, though his voice was glacial. 'The country is in a state of unrest. There have been riots on both King George's and the Pretender's birthdays. Would you see a return to the troubles which split the country during the last century?'

With difficulty Katherine remembered she was the hostess and this man her guest. 'You are of course entitled to your opinions, sir—however high-minded— as I am to mine. If our present King has no love or respect for our country, is it so surprising that we have little love, or respect, for him?'

His scowl was ominous. Having made her point, however, she knew when to concede. The tempestuous flame was doused in her eyes and her lips drew back in a disarming smile. 'I forget my manners, Captain Ryder. You touched a raw nerve. I have a great love for my country and resent that its sovereign sees it as a poor substitute for his beloved Hanover. We are a proud people, the English, but that does not make us insurrectionists against the Crown.'

When she continued to hold his glare she saw the anger fade from his eys. A light flared into the ebony depths and they again sparkled with a persuasive warmth.

'You were right to banish talk of politics between us. I crave your pardon, dear lady. As a soldier I have sworn an oath of allegiance to King George. He is our crowned and accepted King. As to the rights or wrongs of it. . .' He paused and spread his long, slender hands, his smile enticing. 'Shall we agree to differ?'

The force of his charm directed unerringly upon her was impossible to resist. 'I should not have provoked the disagreement,' she answered graciously. 'I would not expect a man of honour to defile his oath of allegiance.'

That speculative ebony stare pierced through to the core of her, but this time she refused to lower her gaze.

The admiration in his eyes warmed her body like the caress of a summer breeze. It stole away her breath and still she would not back down and look away.

He leaned back in his chair, his elbow resting on its low back as he continued to appraise her, but now a secretive smile touched his lips. He picked up his goblet and raised it in salute to her.

'We will speak no more of politics, Miss Winters. I would drink instead to your indomitable spirit and beauty.'

Katherine found herself mellowing beneath the admiration in his eyes. It was impossible to be vexed with him for long. She laughed, parrying his compliment with light-hearted banter.

'Why do men always resort to flattery when they feel they are in danger of losing an argument with a woman?'

Luke smiled and, reaching across the table, raised Kate's fingers to his lips. 'Men are all fools in the face of beauty.'

She shook her head, her neck arching back as she laughed. The loveliness and animation of her set Luke's blood aflame.

'And women would be the greater fools if they believed such flattery.' She subjected him to a forthright stare. 'You are no fool, Captain Ryder.'

'Perhaps I am then bewitched,' he said softly.

A becoming flush tinged her flesh pink. She was proud and passionate, more fascinating than any woman he had previously known. His gaze was drawn to the pulse vibrating in the long, slender neck, the candle-light deepening the contours of her bare shoulders in the wide neckline of her evening gown. Several fair curls had escaped their pins to nestle provocatively against her brow and neck.

When she leaned forward to rest her chin on her knuckle, the swell of her breasts was tantalisingly revealed, leaving his imagination to envisage their luscious fullness. The sensuality of her pose was as unconscious as it was seductive.

Luke had watched every expression pass through her magnificent eyes. She was imperious in her anger, a siren in her teasing, and now, though her smile was warm and unaffected, there were shadows of remorse darkening those green depths. She was hiding something from him. Had it to do with her brother, or St Clere? Was she covering up for that brother of hers?

He should be angry at her duplicity. Instead he felt regret. He could not allow himself to be used, even by so fascinating a woman.

A known Jacobite spy had been captured not far from here last night. Unfortunately the man had hanged himself in his cell before he could be questioned. But St Clere was the suspected Jacobite leader in the district and St Clere's name was romantically linked with hers. Was she entertaining him tonight so that St Clere could plot in safety?

He studied Kate's lovely face. She was waiting for him to speak, her lips parted in alluring invitation. How innocent was she?

'It is long since I have enjoyed such pleasant company.' As he spoke he covered her hand with his. Beneath his fingers he felt the woman's pulse quicken.

'You are too bold, Captain,' she reprimanded, and attempted to draw her hand away. When he tightened his hold upon her wrist, her eyes widened, betraying the excitement she felt at his touch. A man could forget all honour if he gazed for too long into those seductive green pools. The wisps of stray curls which framed her forehead and cheeks made him want to reach out and kiss them aside. Her hand was warm beneath his and her closeness was intoxicating. Beneath the low neck of her gown her breasts rose and fell as her breathing became shallow.

He had meant to assert his dominance upon her, teach her he could not be dallied with, yet somehow everything had changed; there was an alchemy fusing between them of a depth he had never known before.

Sanders coughed and with a start Katherine blinked to dispel the enchantment which was weaving its web around her. She pulled her hand away and, taking a deep breath, recovered her composure. 'You forget yourself, Captain Ryder. No gentleman would so take advantage of my solitude,' she said.

'I am a soldier and a man; what I want I set myself to get, fair Kate. Unlike your neglectful Viscount, I would never leave such a prize to spend her evenings alone.'

'He is *not* my Viscount.' She could not contain her exasperation.

'I'm pleased to hear it. You and your brother would do well to stay away from St Clere's influence in these dangerous times.'

The enchantment of moments earlier fizzled into cold reality. She who always felt so much in control of herself now felt like a child, floundering out of her depth. She stood up, resorting to anger to cover her confusion.

'I care not whether Viscount St Clere is a Jacobite, a Catholic or in league with the Devil himself—he has proved himself a worthy friend. I wish to hear no more upon the subject.'

He raised a dark brow, reproving her outburst. 'Your loyalty is a credit to you—however misguided.'

'Then we have nothing more to say to each other.' She moved past him to the door. 'Goodnight, Captain Ryder.'

He was at the door before Sanders could reach it. With her head high Katherine walked past him, ignoring his courteous bow. There was an angry swish of her satin skirts as she ascended the stairs, aware that he was several paces behind her. Their ways parted on the first landing where the corridors led off to their separate wings.

'Kate—Miss Winters!' His voice was gruff and unapologetic.

She paused on the landing, which was lit only by a few candles. He came to stand level with her, his voice low. 'Take care whom you defend as your friend. Some may prove unworthy of your loyalty.'

He took her hand and raised it to his lips before she could snatch it away. Then, with an enigmatic smile, he turned on his heel and strode along the corridor of the west wing.

For several moments Katherine glared after his departing figure, an empty sensation settling in her stomach. He had called her 'fair Kate'—presumptuous man. Not only had he maligned her friends, but he had presumed to dictate to her about her loyalty. Her chin set obstinately. Captain Ryder was too assured.

Traitorously her heartbeat quickened at the memory of his impudence. Her attraction to the handsome dragoon must be smothered. Her duty was clear. It was to Paul that her only loyalty lay. If he presented a threat to Paul, Luke Ryder must be watched.

And it was obvious she was the only one to do it.

CHAPTER THREE

THE Great Hall of Highclere Manor was aflame with hundreds of candles, as Viscount St Clere led Katherine into the centre of the crowded room which had been cleared for dancing. It was their third dance together and St Clere had hardly left her side all evening. From the speculative glances Katherine found upon her she was aware that the matrons were gossiping behind their fans as to whether St Clere would choose tonight to make a formal declaration. It took the pleasure from the evening.

As Katherine stood at the head of the line of dancers she hid her misgivings. In the last week the Viscount's manner had become yet more possessive. Twice Katherine was sure that Paul had deliberately left them alone together, and she had been forced to evade St Clere's amorous advances.

A month ago his ardour had pleasantly stirred her senses; now it irritated her and she no longer felt comfortable in his company. Was he trying to force her hand? To achieve his own ends, St Clere could be ruthless in manipulating people to his will. Once she had admired his stratagem. Now it angered her. Her mouth set into an uncompromising line. She would not be forced against her judgement. St Clere had promised her that he would wait until her twenty-first birthday for her decision on the marriage contract. He must bide his time.

As the thought formed she knew she was being unreasonable. Much as she liked St Clere, she did not love him. A few months more would not change what she felt. In fairness she must tell him her feelings.

She looked across to where St Clere had turned away from her and was talking to Parson Goodbody. Perhaps

46

she was incapable of love, she pondered as she studied St Clere's attractive figure. St Clere was not merely handsome, she thought admiringly, he was beautiful. Yet he stirred in her nothing more than the wish for his friendship.

The musicians struck up the opening chord of the gavotte. Katherine lifted the split skirt of her jade silk gown and as she sank into a deep curtsy the candle-light glittered on the brilliants and gold thread sewn on to her cream petticoat beneath.

St Clere took her hand and led her forward as the formal dance began. 'I'm the envy of every man here. I've never seen you look more lovely, my dear,' he remarked.

The dance took Katherine from him as she circled the room.

'No woman has led me such a merry chase as you,' he continued as they came together. His hand tightened over hers. 'Let me announce our betrothal tonight, Katherine. In a month you could be my bride and mistress of this house.'

'I'm not ready for marriage, my lord,' she admonished with a severity she had never used to him before.

'Then it is time you prepared yourself for the eventuality. I have waited long enough, Katherine.'

The haughty command tipped the scales of Katherine's temper, but she controlled it, unwilling to provoke a scene. 'You have been very understanding, my lord.'

The dance took her away and as she moved down the length of the hall she was distracted by her thoughts. She felt guilty that she had not been honest with him sooner. This was scarcely the time, or place, to reject his suit. As his hand reclaimed hers, Katherine regarded him with unwavering directness.

'I do not deserve your kindness or consideration, my lord. I'm honoured by your proposal, and I treasure our friendship above all things—except my freedom.'

He gave a low chuckle. 'You shall have freedom enough—providing you are discreet, my dear.'

She was appalled at how badly he had misinterpreted her words. She knew St Clere had had his peccadilloes even while his first wife was alive. During his years as a widower he had become one of the foremost rakes in London, with several actresses claiming him as their protector. The dance ended and he led her to a quiet corner.

'You misunderstand me,' she stressed. 'Infidelity may be fashionable among your contemporaries, my lord, but I believe adultery to be the greatest insult a man can offer his wife.'

That she had spoken so openly had shocked him, but she did not care. It was time they were honest with each other.

'Katherine, I adore you.' His gaze was fervent. 'With you as my wife I would need no other women.'

'I would not ask, or expect, so much of you, my friend.' She drew a heavy breath. 'I do not love you. I'm sorry.'

His expression was incredulous. No one had ever refused him anything. He would not accept it now. 'My dear, when I inherit my father's title you will become a countess, yet you scorn me as though I were no more than a stable-lad.'

'There you are wrong, my lord. If I fell in love with a stable-lad, I would marry him.'

'And shame your class?'

'I would be true to my heart. Anything less would make me no better than a whore who sells herself for gain.'

Angry colour darkened St Clere's face. They were standing beside a casement window which was opened on to the terrace. Before she could protest, Katherine found her arm grabbed and she was propelled outside by the furious Viscount.

'Have you taken leave of your senses, my lord?' she rebuked him in stinging tones as she wrenched her arm free of his hold. Her eyes sparked with indignation as she glared at him. 'Have you no regard to my reputation?'

'If a lost reputation is what it takes to win you as my bride, so be it.'

They stood in the full light of the open window, and St Clere pulled her into his arms. His mouth crushed down upon hers, smothering her cry of outrage. Her body was rigid within his embrace, her mouth clamped firmly against the invasion of his tongue. His fingers dug into her spine as his lips ground over hers, seeking to subdue her to his will.

When finally he drew back, she was trembling with outrage. She stepped away from him, drawing her handkerchief from the sleeve of her gown. With deliberate slowness she raised it to her top lip and wiped it across it. The smug satisfaction drained from the Viscount's face. She continued to wipe her full bottom lip, obliterating the taste of him from her mouth. Then disdainfully she screwed the expensive lace into a ball and tossed it aside.

'I'm not one of your paramours, my lord. Nor will I be shamed into marriage by such knavery. Go take your impudence and your title and be damned. I shall have none of you.'

She kept her head high, aware of the shocked hush which had fallen over the gathering from within the hall. She could feel the burn of a score of eyes on her. Turning on her heel, she walked back into the house.

An embarrassed cough and clearing of throats greeted her entrance while a rapid fluttering of fans accompanied her walk across the floor. Her sight was glazed with unshed tears of humiliation, and flames of heat licked upwards from her neck to scorch her cheeks. St Clere had treated her like a doxy—shamed her before their neighbours. Pride lifted her head higher as she strode onwards, the only sound in the hall the angry rustle of her silk skirts.

All at once everyone began speaking. No doubt St Clere had returned to the room. No one would think

the worse of him, she fumed. She must find Paul and
leave at once. She would not stay here and face the
humiliation St Clere had deliberately brought to her.

A tall figure in scarlet was crossing the room to
intercept her, and Katherine felt her eyes sting with
mortification that Captain Ryder should have witnessed
her shame.

'Bravo, Kate. That was a splendid show. A lesser
woman would merely have slapped St Clere's face for
his audacity. You showed everyone here the lecher and
knave he truly is.'

'I will not be mocked,' she seethed. 'Stand aside and
allow me to leave, sir.'

'And admit defeat?' he chided. 'Where's your fighting spirit? Leave now and you will be in the wrong,
your reputation will be lost. Stay, and you prove that it
was St Clere who overstepped the bounds of propriety.
Hold your head high, sweet Kate. Show this gathering
you are mistress of your own destiny. Dance with me.'

The musicians had struck up another tune. She put
out a hand to refuse him and saw that it was shaking.
'I could not dance.'

Her hand was taken and squeezed gently. 'Of course
you can. You've done nothing to be ashamed of.'

He held out his arm for her to take and, as she
encountered the admiration in his eyes, her courage
returned. A tremulous smile parted her lips as she put
her hand on his scarlet sleeve and allowed him to lead
her on to the dance-floor. There was a stir of comment
as they passed the row of seated matrons, the agitated
waving of their fans showing their disapproval.

A fair curl dislodged from her elegant *coiffure* by St
Clere's rough handling coiled over her bare shoulder
to rest on the curve of her breast. Katherine twisted it
up and secured it with one of the diamond star-pins
which held her hair in place.

'That's the spirit,' Luke Ryder acknowledged her
defiant gesture.

Her hand was taken in a warm, firm grasp as she

faced her partner. The dance was a stately one, the movements slow and sensuous as their bodies moved backwards and forwards. On the edge of her vision Katherine saw St Clere watching them. He beckoned a servant, who ran towards the minstrels' gallery.

Moments later the rhythm of the music unexpectedly changed. A cry of surprise went up from the dancers at the energetic strains of a country dance. Many of them left the floor and Katherine saw St Clere move away to the card-room. Country dances were never played at Highclere—the Viscount considered them fit only for servants and labourers.

Several of the younger couples had taken their places for the country dance, unaware of the insult St Clere had intended. Katherine linked her arm through the dragoon's. She had always enjoyed the country reels at the local fairs and was not about to let St Clere's censure spoil her pleasure.

They swung round in time to the rhythm, clapped hands and stamped their feet, until Katherine began to get breathless. She whirled inwards towards her partner, and in the closing bars of the dance Luke Ryder caught her about her waist and lifted her above his head.

Several men around them staggered under the weight of thir partners, but the grip which held Katherine remained firm and unwavering. Overcome with laughter, she gazed down into the captain's eyes, and the ebony depths smouldering with desire sent a searing jolt through her. Her breath caught in her throat. Where his hands held her her body tingled with awareness, and her stare was held captive by that fierce, hungry gaze as she was slowly lowered to the floor.

A second dance began. She moved to its rhythm in a daze. The room blurred—the sound of the music dimmed. A dark, unpowdered lock of his hair had fallen forward over his brow, giving his handsome looks a carefree, roguish quality which set her pulses racing.

Trance-like, she was conscious of the heat of his hand, strong and commanding as it held hers. When his thumb grazed across her palm, a gasp rose from her throat at the sensuous thrill which travelled along her arm. All at once it seemed as if her world centred on the man who was holding her, and the wild pounding of her heart drowned the sound of the music. There was a dryness in her throat and when she moistened her lips with the tip of her tongue her partner's mouth, so devastatingly close to her own, parted in a provocative smile.

Her body seemed to float as she pivoted away from him, and a delicious glow of anticipation warmed her blood. Through the remainder of the dance it seemed a madness possessed her. She had eyes only for her partner. And the way he looked at her left her light-headed with an indefinable yearning.

The dance separated them. As she circled the room, her glance seeking the figure of the captain from across the hall, the frozenness of St Clere's stance by the doorway penetrated her torpor. Alarm snuffed Katherine's pleasure. Tight-lipped with fury, the Viscount was glaring at Luke Ryder.

St Clere was a renowned duellist. He would never forgive her for refusing his suit. If he saw Captain Ryder as a rival it would take little for the Viscount to provoke a duel. And from what she knew of Luke Ryder he was not a man to back away from a fight.

To Katherine's relief she saw Paul appear at the Viscount's side. Her brother spoke quickly and, with a last glower in their direction, St Clere followed him from the hall. Her fears returned with greater intensity. Only one thing would take Paul from the gaming tables and stop St Clere from challenging Captain Ryder. . . there must be a Jacobite agent in the house. This party was a ruse to detract suspicion from one man among so many guests.

Shaken by the knowledge, Katherine gave a strained smile as she returned to her partner. The captain was looking at her strangely, his expression inscrutable, and it added to her unease and confusion. He must have seen St Clere watching her, and from the arrogant tilt of his chin she sensed his anger.

At the end of the dance Katherine flicked open her fan, waving it to cool the heat on her skin. Captain Ryder gestured to a servant holding a tray of drinks, and, taking two glasses of amber wine, handed one to Katherine.

'Shall we take these over to the window?' he asked.

Katherine nodded her assent.

A light breeze from the gardens cooled her bare shoulders as she sipped her wine.

Captain Ryder stood stiffly at her side. 'Many of the guests believed St Clere was to announce your betrothal tonight.' There was a cold edge to his voice which extinguished the enjoyment Katherine had felt during their dance. His expression was derisive as he continued, 'The scene I witnessed between the two of you on the terrace was hardly conducive to that. Or the manner in which you danced with me just now.'

The last of the warmth was gone from his eyes and they glittered like black ice. 'Perhaps the proposition St Clere offered you was less than honourable. Did he fail in your expectations? From the way he watched us, his desire for you was obvious. Did you accept my offer to dance to make him jealous?'

She could not believe what she was hearing. He made her sound like an adventuress.

'If you think that of me, Captain Ryder,' she answered with measured coldness, 'there's no point in continuing our conversation.'

She thrust her wine glass into his hand and made to move past him.

'Only the guilty run away, Miss Winters.'

His caustic comment halted her. Katherine angled her head so that her gaze was sidelong. It was flecked with venom. 'Only a knave pays heed to witless gossip,' she retorted.

'You play a dangerous game, Miss Winters!' The
captain's face was hard, showing the cool authority
which governed his control. 'Your relationship with St
Clere is the talk of the district.'

The room seemed airless as she choked on her pain
and rage. Was that what he thought of her? A scheming
baggage with no morals? No wonder he had asked her
to dance. It explained the bold way he had held and
looked at her. She had played into his hands, and now
her reputation was truly lost. With each thought her
temper climbed until her mood was defiant and dangerous at the injustice of such gossip.

Katherine lifted her head, bracing herself against his
censure. She shook back her cascading curls with a
proud gesture of disdain. 'Were I a man, I would call
you out for your insults.'

Sweeping her full skirts aside, she spun round and
walked with all the dignity she could summon from the
room.

Luke watched her go, the sight of her stiff, proud
figure piercing his self-control. Were it not for the
speculative glances turned on them both he would have
gone after her. Her reputation had suffered enough
this night without him damaging it further. He had
come here tonight to discover something of St Clere's
Jacobite plots, not become embroiled with the man's
intended wife.

But Katherine Winters was not a woman to be easily
dismissed, or forgotten. The dance had proved that.
She had been all woman, seducing him from duty with
the invitation of her smile, beguiling him with the sultry
promise in her lovely eyes. She bewitched him, making
him forget duty and the reason of his visit here. He put
down his wine glass and walked on to the terrace. Kate
Winters was a distraction he could not afford.

Katherine was halfway up the stairs leading to the
room set aside for the women's convenience when she
heard Paul's voice coming from the saloon at the back
of the house. She retraced her steps, and as she pushed

open the partially closed door she saw St Clere and Paul disappearing through the open window into the gardens. A third figure accompanied them. As they vanished into the darkness, she was startled to hear Paul address the stranger in French.

The fools, they would be caught! How could they take such risks with Captain Ryder in attendance? Her throat went dry. But then Paul believed that she was keeping the officer occupied. By losing her temper with the dragoon she had left him free to roam the house and gardens. Much as it irked her, her duty was clear. She must swallow her pride and ensure the dragoon was kept away from the garden.

She returned to the hall to scan the guests' faces, but there was no sign of Captain Ryder. She hurried to the dining-saloon where the food for the refreshment to be taken later in the evening was laid out on several tables. He was not there either. Panic filled her breast. If Captain Ryder had gone into the gardens, he might discover the conspirators. She had to warn Paul.

To avoid the curious gazes of the guests who had spread into the saloon, Katherine returned to the back room to make her search of the gardens for her brother. Lifting her skirts, she sped down the terrace steps and moved into the shadows of the box hedges.

She avoided the illuminated pathways, knowing that Paul would have sought greater privacy in a darkened corner of the grounds. She paused by the sundial where several paths met, and scanned the moonlit paths. The high hedges set in symmetrical patterns were a virtual maze. Her brother could be anywhere.

Undaunted, she continued her search, her progress slowed by her aching ankle. She had not noticed it while she was dancing, but now it throbbed, adding to the tension which was ploughing through her. By the time she reached the fountain her patience was thinning. She mentally cursed her brother's scheming as she rubbed her aching ankle.

Gradually the sound of falling water soothed her

agitation. If she could not discover where Paul was, it was unlikely that Captain Ryder would be able to do so. And, of course, it was possible that the Frenchman was an innocent guest. Somehow, though, she doubted it.

She put out a hand and let the falling water trickle through her fingers. Tonight had been a disaster, and it was her fault.

How could she have been so wrong about the dragoon? That brief, heady moment during the dance had been no more than a flirtation for the officer. Yet at the time she had sworn there had been a bonding of spirits—an empathy of mind and body. Romantic fool, she scolded herself. It had been nothing. A trick of the candle-light—nothing more.

Her thoughts broke off as she saw a movement on the path ahead. There was no mistaking that tall, dark figure or that purposeful stride. Captain Ryder was prowling the gardens.

Instead of approaching the fountain, she saw him turn off to the right and be immediately hidden by the high hedges. Katherine's heartbeat quickened. If she double-backed and took the next path on the right, she would encounter the captain and must try to divert him. In her haste to intercept the dragoon she rounded the far corner of the hedge at a half-run and collided with a solid figure. Strong arms slid around her body to catch her from falling.

'Kate!' The captain's deep voice was cold and formal. 'Have you come out here seeking St Clere?'

Katherine's heart contracted with alarm. Attempting a calmness her thudding heart did not echo, she countered, 'St Clere is with Paul in the gaming-room as far as I know. I wanted some time by myself.' She removed his hand from where it insolently remained on her waist. 'Is that so surprising, considering the insults I have suffered tonight?'

'If your relationship with St Clere is not as they say, the man should be brought to account for the harm he's done your reputation,' he persisted with a stubbornness which annoyed her.

His angry tone puzzled her and she was suddenly conscious that he was standing very close to her. The tall hedge against her back blocked her retreat, but she refused to be intimated either by his nearness or his anger.

'You mistake the matter, Captain Ryder. His lordship's intentions were honourable. It is I who am at fault. I'm not ready to bind myself to any man—either in marriage, or otherwise. St Clere will not accept that. And I am heartily tired of being the butt of every gossip in the county.'

In the moonlight, his eyes gleamed with a hard light. 'Many women of your years would not forsake an offer of marriage, let alone lose the chance to become a countess.'

'I do not see marriage as my salvation,' she replied heatedly. 'I would certainly never marry for position.'

The captain tipped his head to one side, watching her with thoughtful concentration. Disconcerted by his change of mood, Katherine stared into his face, but it was in shadow, concealing his thoughts. Neither of them moved, and though the hedge sheltered them from the breeze Katherine shivered.

Luke moved closer and across a hand's-breadth of space she could feel the warmth of his body permeating her own.

Again he seemed to fill her mind and vision. Always his nearness disturbed her. Alone with him, she knew herself at a disadvantage. Her only defence lay in attack.

'Are you married, Captain Ryder?'

She felt him tense, and could not suppress a soft laugh at his reaction. 'Such a question never fails to put a man on his guard. Yet you showed no hesitation in quizzing me about St Clere.'

'You have the most provoking habit of twisting my words.' The amusement was back in his voice and

Katherine relaxed. 'No, sweet Kate, I'm not married. I've seen too many laughing maids grow thin and haggard, and good men become drunkards, trying to keep a family alive upon army pay.'

'A worthy excuse, sir.' Her voice sharpened. Was that a warning that he was not the marrying kind? She suddenly realised she knew very little about him, and she wanted to know more. 'To have purchased your colours, Captain Ryder, puts you above such as those men.'

'I'm the youngest of three brothers. As such I needed a career, but unfortunately it caused a breach with my father. He decided I should become a naval officer, since we own a shipping line. I wanted the army. My grandfather purchased my colours and when he died he left me a modest legacy. Until recently I had no other income. I have since acquired a brigantine—the *Sea Serpent*.'

'Acquired, Captain? Your phrasing intrigues me.'

His white teeth shone in the moonlight. 'A friend's father owned the vessel. He was in financial trouble. I raised the funds to buy a half-share in the *Serpent*. Two years ago when my partner died I bought his share from his widow.'

'You would not be the first younger son to take a woman of fortune to wife,' she persisted, her curiosity getting the better of her.

'No man shall say of me that I married for wealth or power.' He moved closer, the moonlight showing his dark brows drawn down sardonically. 'My wealth I shall create with my own hands, and my position in society will be determined from my own efforts—not upon a woman's purse-strings.'

It was her turn to be taken aback by the vehemence of his tone as he went on curtly, 'I'd not shackle myself to an heiress for all the gold in England. They're an empty-headed, spoilt breed, too full of their own importance.'

Katherine was thankful that her own face was in

shadow. He had accurately described countless of her acquaintances who were restless and bored in the country.

'Your words hold the bitter ring of experience, Captain.'

'An officer is considered fair game to brighten such creatures' useless lives,' he rapped out. 'They have no thought but for their own pleasure. It amuses them to encourge an officer's attentions. But should the man presume to fall in love with them they cry off at so unsuitable a match. Good men have been killed in duels because of those heartless jades.'

The hollows of his lean cheeks deepened with anger before he went on with equal ruthlessness, 'Yes, I speak from experience. My closest friend, Lieutenant Hal Penrose, was caught in such a trap last winter. Only it wasn't a duel which took his life. It was a gang of drunken mohocks, led by the heiress's brother. She had led Hal on, amusing herself with his devotion. When he declared himself she laughed in his face. The next night her brother and his associates broke into Hal's rooms. He was alone, for I was on duty that night. They dragged Hal out into the street. After they had half beaten him to death, they put him into a barrel and rolled him about the streets. The barrel got away from them. My friend was crushed beneath the wheels of a carriage.'

No wonder he distrusted heiresses, she thought, appalled by his story. 'You have just cause to despise such women—though not all heiresses are so callous.'

'And what of the other side of the coin, Captain? At least one local heiress has fallen prey to a fortune-hunter. And officers do have a reputation for loving and leaving the ladies. The daughter of a neighbouring family eloped with her army lover, and when her dowry was withheld he abandoned her. She was disowned by her family and finally, destitute, alone and pregnant, she drowned herself.'

'There are good and bad on both sides,' he said gruffly.

How true. Katherine had always been wary of her suitors, many of whom had been attracted by her large dowry. St Clere would never have offered marriage were it not for the wealth she would bring him. Did the captain not know she was an heiress? It would be nice to meet someone who was ignorant of the fact—to truly know that they cared for her and not her money.

'I must return to the house.' Her voice sounded strange and husky to her ears. 'My brother will be looking for me.' She lifted the hem of her skirt to move away.

He was faster, blocking her passage as he put a hand to her chin and turned her face into the moonlight.

'Captain Ryder, I must ask you to let me pass.' She was shocked at the breathlessness of her voice, and her heart was beating so fast that it threatened to stifle her.

'My name is Luke,' he said with soft insistence. 'You have an honest face, Kate. Deception does not sit easily upon you. What are you hiding from me?'

Images of Paul and the Frenchman flashed through her mind. 'Please, Captain. My absence from the dancing will be noted. I should not be here alone with you. My reputation has suffered enough this night.'

'I would not see you hurt, sweet Kate. But are you being honest with yourself?' His hand moved along her neck, sending ripples of tingling heat through her body. He laughed softly. 'Why did you follow me, Kate?'

How like the conceit of a man to think that! So he had no idea Paul was in the gardens. Relieved, she began to relax, but she knew she could not leave him in the garden to wander at will. To her surprise the lie came readily to her lips.

'I think you know why I came into the garden, Captain. I regretted our quarrel.'

'Sweet Kate.' His warm breath caressed her cheek.

She swallowed; he was too forward and familiar, but her rebuke remained unspoken, all her thoughts centred upon him. Upon the touch of his hand the heat of his body now pressed against her, the outline of his lips so close, so perilously close, that she felt on the point of swooning.

In fact if he did not kiss her she was certain she would swoon, from pure longing. His hands moved to her shoulders, his thumbs making slow circles over the bare skin above the low neckline of her gown. A tremor of anticipation flowed through her body. His touch was mesmerising. She knew she should pull away and reproach him for his boldness, but her limbs seemed strangely languid, making movement impossible. There was only the awareness of his touch, of his commanding presence which threatened to overwhelm her.

Her breathing became shallow. She was unaware that her lips parted in invitation as she stared wordlessly into his tense, handsome face.

Then, with a soft sigh, his arms were around her. She was held in a strong embrace, her lips pliant as they were captured and held in his demanding kiss. Her hands pressed against his chest and she felt the quickening beat of his heart. It echoed the wildness of her own. As his mouth moved with expert thoroughness over hers, the warm sweetness of his breath tasting faintly of wine mingled with her own. There was a heat in her blood which drove away sanity, turned her bones to liquid fire so that she clung to him. Her hands glided over his back, delighting in the play of his hard muscles as he gathered her even closer in a tight embrace.

Sensations new and voracious impelled her to venture further along a sensual voyage of discovery. She felt more alive than at any time in her life, her body restless with an indefinable yearning which drove her to mould her form into the contour of his hard thighs. Even the few kisses she had permitted St Clere had not prepared her for the devastation Luke was causing upon her senses. She had not dreamed a kiss could rob one so entirely of one's reason. Her body simmered with a new and delightful heat. Every sense was heightened until she felt she was floating above herself. Her lips were hungry beneath the insistence of his mouth. A pulse throbbed deep in her stomach as his tongue teased and tantalised, probing the warm softness of her mouth. Her arms tightened achingly about him, binding him closer as she thrilled to his deepening kiss.

His breath expelled softly as his lips travelled from her mouth to nuzzle against her ear. 'Kate. Sweet Kate,' his voice resonated with passion.

She was losing her grip upon reality. His mouth moved over her neck and shoulders and her head rolled back, her body a millrace of new and exquisite sensations. She felt the touch of his hands on her shoulders and the coolness of the night air as he eased her gown down over her arms. Then his mouth was upon her breast and she gasped, moaning softly as she held his head against her, besieged by emotions so powerful that she began to shake, and would have fallen had he not held her tighter.

'Kate, my adorable Kate. Let me come to you tonight.'

The words penetrated her stupor, and she was shocked to find herself half naked in this man's arms. She pulled back from him, holding her dress over her breasts, her eyes widening with shock.

'No. I never meant. . .' Her voice broke as she backed away, reason triumphing over the havoc he caused to her senses. 'You should not have done that,' she accused shakily. She was appalled that she had permitted him such liberties. 'No gentleman. . .'

'I warned you, Kate, I live my life as I see fit. Not as custom demands it. I thought you the same.' He stepped closer but made no attempt to touch her again. 'I want you, Kate. Do you deny what lies between us?'

'There can be nothing between us, Captain Ryder,' she forced out. 'I want nothing from any man other than respect and friendship.'

'My name is Luke.' He disconcerted her by changing tactics. 'Between friends are not first names more informal?'

'I suspect that the friendship you envisage between us would not be possible.'

'Because you fear for your virtue?' His laugh was bitter and sardonic. 'Or because of your brother's misguided loyalties to the Stuart over the water?'

Katherine gasped. So he had guessed. Just how much did the captain know? Her head spun. She could not think straight with her clothes in disarray and him grinning at her like that. She turned her back on him and adjusted her gown. When she faced him again she was composed.

'You are impertinent, Captain.' She tossed back her head to confront him coldly. 'Since you are a guest in my house, we must on occasion meet. I trust when we do you will remember that you are a gentleman, and forget my moment of indiscretion. Now if you will excuse me I wish to return to Ferncombe.'

To her surprise he chuckled, amused rather than angered by her rebuke. He bowed to her.

'What are you scared of, Kate? It's time you became a real woman. There's blood in your veins, not water. I shall prove it to you.'

She turned then and ran towards the house. Every word he said was true and she despised herself for her weakness. She was not running away from him, she was running away from herself.

Wishing to avoid any of St Clere's guests, she entered by a side-door which led into the deserted library. Taking a moment to calm her agitation, she rang for a servant and asked him to tell her brother she wished to leave. Again alone, she leant against the bookshelves and closed her eyes, then opened them quickly. Luke Ryder's face was branded in her mind and her swollen lips were still tender and burning from his kiss.

Luke. She repeated his name and realised with a start that she made it sound like a caress. She put a

shaking hand to her head. Something had happened to
her during the dance tonight. However much she tried
to deny it, fight against it, rail at it, she knew she was
no longer the same woman.

Katherine drew a strangled breath. From this
moment onwards she must fight harder than ever to
retain her independence. The handsome dragoon was
a force she had not reckoned upon.

He was also a threat to all she held dear.

CHAPTER FOUR

'KAT, I don't believe you could refuse St Clere,' Paul stormed as he marched into the courtyard where Katherine was already mounted on Cassandra for her morning ride. 'It's madness. Has your head been turned by that dragoon?'

'Would it be so terrible if it had?' After a sleepless night when Luke Ryder had dominated her thoughts, Katherine was edgy and defiant. She looked across at Paul as he settled himself on his gelding. His complexion was pale and his eyes bloodshot from a night of excesses.

'This is no jesting matter,' Paul sneered. 'Dragoon officers aren't the marrying type. Not unless there's a hefty dowry in it to make it worth their while. Which in this case there is. But you're bound to St Clere.'

'Not of my own free will,' she reminded him pointedly. 'And Captain Ryder is not a fortune-hunter if that's what you fear.'

Paul scowled. 'I know that look, Kat. You're always most defiant when you're on the defensive. You are interested in Ryder. Good God, don't you see the danger that puts our plans in? Forget him. St Clere's the man for you! You're just piqued with St Clere for his behaviour last night. You drive him too far with your prevarication.'

'I was honest with him. He knows my mind. When I see fit to wed I will choose my own man.' Katherine sighed. The argument was pointless. She regarded him seriously, but her eyes sparkled with a teasing light. 'As ever you jump to the wrong conclusion. I admit I enjoy Captain Ryder's company, which is as well since I have been fored to entertain him so often these last days. There is no more to it than that.'

'I wish I could believe you.' Paul glared at her. 'You certainly overset St Clere last night. Fortunately I managed to pacify him. He's joining us for our ride today.'

Katherine hid her dismay. She was still angry with the Viscount for his callous treatment of her, and was about to make her excuses to cancel her ride when she saw St Clere cantering along the drive. When he drew level with her, he swept his hat from his hand in a gallant gesture and bowed so low over his saddle that the curls of his blond wig touched his knee.

'My dear Katherine, I crave your pardon for my conduct last night.' When he straightened he subjected her to his most disarming smile. 'You are the last woman in the world I would wish to offend. Can you find it in your heart to forgive me?'

'We have been friends a long time my lord.' She conquered her anger. It was not often St Clere admitted he was in the wrong. Her voice remained cool as she added, 'I did not deserve such treatment from you. But I accept your apology.'

'I do not deserve such generosity. I acted like a jealous fool. You know I adore you. I've brought you a gift to make amends.' He held out an oblong jewel case and opened it for her inspection. Inside was a diamond and ruby bracelet.

'I have forgiven you, my lord. I need no gift to appease me. It would be improper for me to accept it, since I am neither your betrothed nor your mistress.'

'I live in hope of the former, dear Katherine.'

Katherine gave him a level stare. 'I will not change my mind, my lord. I will not marry you.'

He bowed his head so that his cocked hat hid his expression from her, but she could see the tension in his body as his hands tightened over the reins. St Clere looked to where Paul had tactfully ridden a discreet distance away, so that the Viscount would make his peace with some privacy.

There was a brittle gleam in his eyes when his gaze

returned to Katherine. 'Then why not accept the bracelet and become my mistress? I mean to have you, Katherine.'

Katherine tilted back her head and laughed. She had been parrying the Viscount's outrageous proposals for three years, and refused to be shocked by his words. 'You are incorrigible, St Clere. You have mistresses enough without adding me to the pack.'

'None to compare with you.'

She shook her head. 'I have no wish to be a man's possession.'

'That was not the impression I got while you were flirting with that dragoon last night.'

Katherine's head came up. 'I had good reason. Would you have preferred him to have encountered your French guest?'

'You saw him?' St Clere's eyes became wary.

'Yes, fortunately before Captain Ryder did. I managed to divert the dragoon. The captain is no fool. I've no wish to see my brother arrested for treason.'

'And was that the only reason you flirted with him?'

Katherine sighed. No good would come by rousing one of St Clere's affronted rages. She widened her eyes in feigned innocence. 'Why else, my lord?'

'Come, you two sluggards.' Paul was irritable at their delay. 'Do we ride today or not?'

Relieved at her brother's interruption, Katherine urged her mare to a canter and kept ahead of St Clere as they rode through the village and out across the fields. When they passed through a wood and skirted the hammer pond of an iron foundry, it was impossible to talk above the noise of the furnace. The rhythmic thud of the great hammers resounded through the trees like a giant's heartbeat, leaving the area deserted of birds or game.

Katherine shivered; the beat of hammers sounded sinister to her strained nerves. From the hot, spitting fires of the Wealden foundries some of the finest cannons in England were forged.

Katherine studied Paul, who rode some way ahead. He was dressed more soberly than usual in a coat of brown worsted and cream knee breeches. For all his restrained apearance, the rigid set of his face showed her the tension which had been apparent since his return from France.

She faced St Clere, her fears for her brother overriding her antagonism towards the Viscount. 'It is your affair if you invite Jacobite spies to your home, but must you include Paul?'

'Paul is no longer a boy. He does what must be done,' St Clere said sharply. Then, seeing her concern, added less harshly, 'I've no wish to lose my head upon Tower Green, or see your brother swing from Tyburn. But King James's cause is just. It must be upheld.'

'At what cost, my lord? The English army is behind King George.'

'I do not expect you to understand, my dear.' His patronising tone rekindled Katherine's resentment towards him. 'Our plans are well laid. The Rising will begin in the north. England will come out for James Stuart. We will triumph.'

The track narrowed, and they were forced to pull over to the side while a wagon of cut trees pulled by four horses rumbled past from the opposite direction.

'Paul is impetuous but not foolhardy,' St Clere assured her. 'Your brother can be cautious when the need arises. Don't worry about him. He knows what he's doing.'

'Treason is no easy bedfellow. His risks are greater than yours. You have influential friends in high places,' Katherine pointed out.

She rode on in silence, locked into her dark thoughts. She wished she had St Clere's confidence. But even he could not predict the outcome of a rebellion.

A mile further on they were again forced to halt at the side of the track to give precedence to a troop of approaching dragoons.

At her side, Katherine saw St Clere stiffen and her

pulse quickened as she recognised the leading horseman.

Lines of tiredness were etched in Captain Ryder's sun-bronzed face. Sergeant Hopkirk had called him away from Highclere before Katherine left the reception, and had not returned to Ferncombe all night. His scarlet uniform was splattered with mud, the shine was gone from the thigh-length black boots, and a layer of brown dust also covered the black gelding's body. From the weary droop of the horses' heads they had been riding for hours. Katherine felt a prickle of fear. What could have kept the troop searching the countryside all night? Had the Frenchman, or an accomplice, been taken?

As the troop drew level Captain Ryder reined in and signalled for his men to continue. He bowed to Katherine, his dark eyes cool and assessing as he greeted her party.

Katherine capped her anxiety. She must appear relaxed, or her imagination would be Paul's undoing. It did not help to realise that St Clere was watching her every move. He had his own suspicions regarding her relationship with the dragoon.

'Looks as if you've had a long night of it, Ryder,' Paul said with relish. 'More trouble with the outlaws, was it?'

'There's been no sign of them since my arrival. We were patrolling the coast.'

'Aiding the excise men, were you?' St Clere scoffed. 'I could have saved you the trouble. You've been chasing shadows. The smugglers rarely use these beaches. They're too open. 'Tis a different story over Rye way. Regular runs are made there, so I hear.'

Luke Ryder's dark eyes narrowed with contempt as he regarded the Viscount. 'There's more than smuggled brandy that can be landed on these shores when the wind blows fair from France.'

Katherine swallowed. The unspoken threat was obvious in his voice. St Clere returned Luke's stare, his blue eyes blazing with hatred. Paul sat frozen in the saddle, his features stiff with strain.

To ease the growing tension Katherine turned a dazzling smile upon Luke.

'Your duty is an unrewarding one, Captain. You have my sympathy.'

'It has its rewards, Miss Winters.'

The warmth of the smile he gave her brought the heat creeping into her cheeks.

'Katherine always did have a soft heart for the underdog!' St Clere declared, his hand closing over his sword-hilt. Luke Ryder followed the movement, his face setting with grim satisfaction at the challenge.

'My sister—soft-hearted?' Paul snorted, obviously amused by the exchange. 'There's more barbs on Kat than upon the sweetest rose.'

The captain's gaze was hooded as it rested upon Katherine. It lingered upon her mouth, and her lips tingled with remembrance of his kiss. She knew he was purposely reminding her of that moment, and as his gaze levelled with hers there was no mistaking the boldness in the gleam of his eyes. A soft gasp parted her lips. Anger and excitement vied with each other to leave her oddly disturbed at the effect even his glance had upon her.

He touched the brim of his cocked hat in salute to her. 'Without its thorns, a rose is just another flower. Beauty spiked with danger can be an irresistible combination.'

He nodded curtly to Paul and St Clere, and as he drew level with Katherine his lips curved into a smile which conveyed both a threat and a seductive promise.

As she watched him ride away, she unwittingly put a hand against the frantic pounding of her heart. Despite the mud and travel dust, his figure remained impressive—one of proud assurance and calm self-possession.

When her glance returned to the Viscount she was taken aback by the anger in his eyes.

'I've a mind to call the man out for the way he looked and spoke to you,' he said.

'You'll do nothing of the kind,' Katherine retorted. 'You did harm enough to my reputation last night, my lord. I have no wish to become notorious by having a duel fought over me.'

'The officer attracts you, that is plain. But you must forget him.'

'Must I, my lord?' Katherine lost patience with his demands. 'I will choose my own friends. And I will not be dictated to.'

'Then you must be protected for your own good, my dear.' There was something in his tone which made her blood go cold. 'That man is a danger both to you and to our cause. Do not forget I regard the contract signed by your father as binding. I expect you to accept it with good grace. It's time the arrangements for our marriage were put in order. While Ryder resides under your roof, I'm within my rights to call him out. Now I have business in Chichester, Katherine. Good day.'

St Clere kicked his horse forward, dismissing her.

'You will do nothing to harm Captain Ryder, my lord,' she shouted after him. St Clere ignored her, and when she would have given chase to confront him she saw the Viscount leap the hedgerow and cut across a field. She found her passage blocked by a farmer's haywain and was forced on to the side of the track.

'I'm going back to Ferncombe,' she called after Paul, who was on the other side of the wagon.

She wheeled Cassandra round and set off for home. She had to warn Luke of St Clere's threat. Katherine was not frightened for herself, for she would never marry a man who threatened to bully her into submission. But she could no longer deny her attraction to the dragoon—her fears for him were too strong. For his own safety she must persuade him to leave Ferncombe. She would play upon St Clere's jealousy that he lodged at their home, for it would be equally fatal to arouse the dragoon's suspicions as to her brother's sympathies.

There was no groom to take Cassandra as she rode into the courtyard of Ferncombe Place, and Katherine remembered that today was market day. Grimshaw would have taken Tilly and Sarah the cook into town. Sanders would have gone too, for in his capacity as steward he would hire the new shepherd to replace Old Sam who had died of a seizure last month.

She dismounted and led Cassandra into the stable to rub her down after her ride. In the dim light she saw Luke brushing his black gelding. He had removed his scarlet jacket and rolled back his shirt-sleeves as he worked. He looked up at the clatter of the mare's hoofs on the flagstones.

'You have returned early from your ride.' He laid his arm along his gelding's back as he regarded her with a warm smile. 'The others did not come with you?'

Subject to that steady gaze, she felt suddenly awkward in his presence.

'I wanted to speak with you,' she said as she led Cassandra into her stall, and began to unbuckle her mare's girths.

Luke came to her side, lifted the saddle from the mare's back and placed it over the partition of the stall. In the close confines she was tinglingly aware of him. She turned her back on the sight of his broad shoulders and the way his close-fitting breeches were moulded over his slender hips and strong thighs. To cover her confusion she snatched up some clean straw and began to rub down her mare's back. Her hand was covered by Luke's long brown fingers, stilling their movement, then he threw a blanket over Cassandra's withers and turned Katherine to face him.

'What did you wish to say to me? For since last night there are a hundred things I would say to you.' He drew her away from the restless snufflings of the mare into an empty stall. 'Not least that you have been constantly in my thoughts, sweet Kate.'

His hands moved to her shoulders and she could see

the fine down of black hair on his strong forearms. His shirt was open at the neck and there was a sheen of perspiration on his brown skin. She felt her throat go dry. The madness he always wove about her senses was starting again. She took a step back; she must remain in control.

'We must forget what happened last night. In fact I have come to ask you to leave Ferncombe Place.'

'Was last night just a dalliance for you, Kate? Do you think now to dismiss me like a servant?' His voice was clipped with the cold menace she had heard when he had spoken of his friend's death last night. Did he think she had toyed with his affection and would callously cast him aside?

Luke's eyes burned into her flushed face. But he did not release her. 'I hadn't taken you for a tease,' he added.

'I have my reputation to consider,' she said, fighting to keep her voice even, for his touch was destroying her resolve. 'My father signed a contract agreeing to my marriage to St Clere. The Viscount intends our marriage to take place with or without my approval. That is a separate issue. In his jealousy St Clere vowed to kill you if we remain under the same roof.'

'Is he your champion?' His eyes blazed with contempt. 'Have you tired of the diversion I afforded you?'

'How can you say that?' Her voice was raw with the injustice of his words. 'I would not have you and St Clere fight. He is a renowned duellist.'

'St Clere's threats do not frighten me,' Luke asserted.

'I did not expect they would. But it would be foolish to antagonise him for no cause.'

'Are you sure there is no cause, Kate?'

His gaze was tender as he stared into her upturned face. He pulled her to him, his mouth descending on hers in a hard, demanding kiss that sent her senses reeling and she fought a losing battle against the subtle mastery which brought her to submission in both mind and body.

He held her tightly against him, kissing her with such sweet dominance that her lips parted, every nerve searing to the response he sought.

'Please, no,' she wrenched her mouth from his long enough to gasp. 'You must listen. . .'

'Hush, my sweet,' he said, his lips against her ear. His mouth was again upon hers, her denial silenced. She tried to push him away, but his kisses were devastating her will, subduing her until she was faint with pleasure. Her limbs refused to obey her, her flesh fired beneath this slow ravishment of her senses. It was as perilous in its intensity as it was enthralling. She was lost, incapable of fighting him, or fighting her own powerful emotions. Her hands locked about his neck, binding him closer.

She was drawn down on to the fresh-smelling hay. Her world careened crazily, and she could not hold back a soft moan of pleasure. She had no will-power left to resist him as he unfastened the bodice of her riding habit, his kisses warm and teasing as they skimmed her bare shoulder and moved down over the curve of her breast. It was only when she felt his hand move with assured insistence along her inner thigh that she tensed.

She tore her mouth from his and clamped her hand down hard over his, her cry desperate. 'No!'

His face was dark above hers and she saw the desire turn to anger in his eyes. 'Damn you for a tease!'

He captured her restraining hand and as she tried to wriggle from beneath him he pulled both her arms over her head. She was pinned under his hard, muscular chest, her breasts, covered only by the thin silk of her chemise, crushed against him. When she tried to move, he rolled on top of her, his thighs pressed like clamps over hers. Her pupils expanded with fear at the unmistakable evidence of his arousal.

'Let me go.' She struggled to be free, but his weight

pressed down harder. She fought back her fear, her eyes searching the glittering fury in his gaze. She was frighteningly aware of his manhood, hard and threatening as he lay above her. 'Please, Luke—don't. I didn't mean to tease. . .'

Luke laughed softly, his breath hot against her throat. 'Don't be shy, Kate. Coyness does not suit you, not with St Clere so avid a suitor.'

She drew a breath to cry out, but his mouth smothered her angry protest. Her head whirled from the onslaught of his kisses and she struggled against their intoxication.

'Luke! Stop!' she pleaded as his lips raised from hers.

His hands were on the delicate lace of her chemise, freeing her breasts. Her own hands now free, she thumped them on his chest, her voice breaking on a sob.

'Stop! Damn you for a lecher! I've known no man. I'm still a maid.'

His fingers stilled and he eased back from her, his face taut and distrustful. He stared deep into her eyes and what he saw made him believe her. He sat back on his haunches and rubbed a hand across his chin as she hurriedly straightened and fastened her clothing.

'You have the damnedest way of making a man lose his senses.' He stood up and held out a hand to assist her to rise. She regarded it warily. 'Take it, Kate. I'll not harm you.'

She took it and allowed him to pull her to her feet. 'My duty takes me to Chichester for three days. I shall tell Sergeant Hopkirk to find me other accommodation before I return.'

'It is for the best,' she said. Her gaze could not hold that piercing stare. She was embarrassed at her wanton response to his touch and kisses. 'It would be better if we did not meet again.'

'Is that what you want, Kate?'

The command in his voice brought her head up. His

dark eyes burned into her, making her stomach knot with longing.

'We hardly know each other. St Clere will have your blood if he suspects there is anything between us. Legally, I am bound to him.'

'You delude yourself, Kate. I think we know each other rather too well. Last night and today has proved that.'

From outside a dog barked and there was the sound of a horse and wagon on the cobbled yard.

'That must be the servants returning.' Her eyes were large and pleading as she stared up at him. 'Forget what happened. It cannot be repeated. St Clere is dangerous. I would not have your blood on my conscience. Please heed my words, Captain Ryder.'

'Did we not agree my name was Luke? And I promise you this—I leave here to protect your reputation. But we shall meet again. And the devil with St Clere and his threats!'

CHAPTER FIVE

LUKE RYDER rode away from the isolated cottage, his thoughts bleak. The morning mist still clung to the trees and the clouds were black, with a threatening storm against a grey, unwelcoming sky.

Since his return from Chichester, Luke had learned much of the Jacobite activity in this area. At Bosham Harbour a man answering Paul Winters' description, together with an older, dark-bewigged man, had been seen taking ship supposedly to Le Havre. From a more detailed investigation the features of the dark-wigged man fitted St Clere. It was Luke's guess that the ship could only be bound for France.

His antagonism towards St Clere ground deeper. The man was determined to bind Katherine to her father's contract of marriage, and the thought of Kate and St Clere together twisted like a knife in him. For all his noble title, St Clere was a lecher and an unprincipled scoundrel. Kate deserved better. But after the merry dance Kate had led himself Luke could understand how she had captured the jaded palate of a man like St Clere.

Memories of Kate crowded Luke's mind. There had been little of the coy maiden in the way she had ridden him down, or in the invitation in her green eyes during the dance and later in the stable. Yet he had not doubted her innocence when she denied him. But since then he had learned that she was an heiress, and his distrust for her kind was not easily put aside. Had she dallied with him for her own amusement? That was what rankled. A common dragoon captain would not be good enough for an heiress who had attracted the interest of a viscount.

His pride rose with his mounting anger. If she were

not an heiress he'd be tempted to tame that wild spirit and wed her himself. His turn of reasoning hit him with a jolt. It was true she had been rarely from his thoughts these last days—but marriage. . .

He rubbed his hand across his jaw. Were it not for her fortune. . .? His mind conjured the image of her lying beneath him in the straw, her eyes smoky with awakening passion. It was the image which had haunted him for days.

Army pay would scarcely support a wife in the manner to which Kate was accustomed. Still, he was not without assets. The *Sea Serpent*, which was presently being hired by a merchant in Rochester, was bringing him a comfortable profit. It was a worthy vessel. If he chose to captain her himself, he could soon begin to build his fortunes. Within seven years he could have three or four ships under his flag.

The sea had always been a passion in his life. It ran in his blood. Both his grandfather and father had owned a fleet of merchantmen. It had only been an argument with his father which had made him choose the army and not the sea as his future. The *Sea Serpent* could change that. And there was the legacy left him by his grandfather. It was enough to buy a house in a port like Rochester or Plymouth.

The idea expanded as he warmed to it. His disenchantment with the army was growing, but it was not until Kate had tumbled into his life that he had thought of a more settled future. Not that he suspected winning Kate would be easy. That was her fascination. She had more moods than the changing seasons. To master that proud spirit and beauty was an irresistible lure.

It would be but half the battle. There was the thorny question of her dowry. He wanted none of it. His pride rebelled that the world would brand him a fortune-hunter if he married Kate. First he must rise high enough to prove them wrong. Then he would marry her with honour.

But there were other complications. Her brother for

one. He would not hesitate to turn the information he had learned about St Clere over to the authorities. But, by accusing St Clere of being involved with the Jacobites, it would also implicate Paul Winters. Kate would never forgive him that. The weight of his duty settled heavily over him. Whatever the consequences, he would never forsake that duty.

The crack of a twig breaking close by snapped up Luke's head. Alert to danger, he drew his pistol from its saddle holster as he scanned the undergrowth. From both sides of the track six men ran out of the high bracken armed with cudgels. Surrounded, Luke raised his pistol, noting as he did so that they were all dressed in dirty smocks with large brimmed hats pulled low over their brows. Each had a sacking strip tied over his lower face.

The nearest grabbed at Crusader's bridle. Luke increased the pressure of his heels and the gelding responded by rearing up on his back legs. As the horse came down on all fours, Luke flicked back the firing hammer of the pistol and shouted, 'Stand aside or I shoot.'

As the men continued to advance, cudgels raised with menace, he fired. The pistol kicked against his hand as he aimed it at the man by Crusader's head. The attacker fell back, clutching his shoulder, blood seeping through his fingers.

'The bastard's shot Ferret. At 'im, men,' bellowed the heaviest-set man, who was clearly their leader.

Luke pushed his thick cloak over his shoulders, leaving his arms free as he drew his sword, determined not to go down without a fight. As a dragoon, he was in his element fighting on horseback, and though it was some years since he had been engaged in a battle he had lost none of his dexterity and skill. He lunged at a second man. There was a scream of pain as his sword point struck a rib-bone and was deflected from a mortal blow. A gash of crimson the length of a hand appeared

along his second assailant's chest and the man fell to
the ground.

Then the other three were on Luke. He kept a cool
head, his sword slashing to keep a fourth man hovering
out of reach. Unseen, a cudgel slammed down on his
knee from behind him, and the pain momentarily
halted the swing of Luke's sword-arm. At the same
time the man on his other side sprang forward, his
cudgel smashing down on Luke's sword hand. Luke
grunted with pain, his hand saved from being broken
by the thickness of his leather gauntlet. A second blow
knocked the sword from his numbed fingers. Luke
kicked out and his booted foot struck one of his
attackers on the jaw, his spurs gouging a bloody line
along his cheek.

The man spat out two teeth, his eyes above the
sacking bulging with rage. 'Get 'im, you blunderheads!'

Crusader shied, his ears laid back and eyes wild from
the smell of blood. Luke used the time to draw his
dagger from his belt with his uninjured hand. Trained
to protect his rider in battle, Crusader responded to
the expert touch of Luke's legs. Again in control, he
swung the gelding round, making Crusader side-step,
and when the horse's front hoofs came down on an
assailant's foot Luke felt a grim sense of satisfaction.
Another attacker was disabled. There was a crunch of
splintering bone and, howling with agony, the man
hobbled back, clutching his leg.

That left only three men standing. His blood surged
with the savage excitement of proving himself the
better man. The odds were more even. He felt calm
and detached, though his heart hammered at the
danger still threatening. A man was advancing on him,
swinging a heavy woodman's axe, and Luke swung
Crusader aside to avoid the lethal blow, but in so doing
did not see the cudgel aimed at the side of his head.

The blow stunned him. He reeled in the saddle and
before he could recover his balance and shake the haze
from his wits a second blow knocked him to the ground.

Pain exploded through his skull as Luke rolled away from Crusader's stamping hoofs. He came to his feet with the survival reflexes of a man who had fought for his life countless times, and, though his legs were unsteady, he crouched ready to attack, dagger extended.

The trees seemed to dance and sway before his vision. A blurred form launched itself at him, blotting out the skyline. Luke lunged with his dagger, but the man side-stepped, avoiding his blow. When Luke spun to follow his attacker, his head throbbed unmercifully, and a trickle of blood from his temple ran down into his eyes. Too late he saw the cudgel raised above him. He threw himself to the ground, saving himself from a blow which would have shattered his skull and killed him. Even so, the impact keeled him over, sending arrows of fire through his head. As he tried to rise an arm circled his neck, choking him. The dagger was torn from his fingers and his muscles screamed in protest as his arm was viciously twisted behind his back.

'Give 'im 'ell,' the leader spat out, his voice whistling through the missing teeth.

Luke was dimly aware of the three injured men supporting each other as they staggered away to tend their wounds. Then the pressure against his windpipe increased, torturing his scalding lungs as he gulped for breath. Still he refused to submit, and concentrated on surviving the attack of the last three men.

Gripping the arm pressed against his throat with his free hand, he twisted his body, seeking to haul his assailant off balance. But already another attacker was upon him. A fist slammed into his stomach, the pain doubling Luke over. Finally overpowered, he slumped to the ground and several kicks slammed into his back and ribs. His attackers were tired, their blows more vindictive than effective, muffled by the thick wool of Luke's cloak.

'That's enough,' one of the attackers grunted. 'Someone's coming. Get his money. It's supposed to look like a robbery. 'Sides, we weren't paid to kill him. Just warn 'im off.'

The attackers crashed through the undergrowth, the noise of their progress fading. Advancing closer was the sound of a trotting horse.

Luke groaned as he staggered to his feet and leaned against a tree for support. Gradually his surroundings stopped gyrating around him and the pain began to ease. Near by was the sound of running water. He stumbled towards it, pulling off his stock to soak it in the stream. The coldness of the water cleared his wits. Damned Jacobites parading as outlaws, he grimaced. He'd lay odds St Clere was behind this attack.

Katherine heard voices ahead in the wood and then the sound of figures running through the bracken. She put her hand to the dagger at her waist, the hair at her nape prickling with a sense of danger. It had been foolish to take a short cut through the wood when she was out riding alone.

A distant rumble of thunder sent a cold shiver of fear through her. She hated the weakness that made her shake with terror during thunderstorms. It was stupid and childish and time she outgrew the terror which she had been unable to conquer since that horrifying night——

She broke off the thought, refusing to dwell upon the past now. The crashings through the undergrowth boded ill. Better to turn and face the elements rather than proceed through the wood.

A whinny drew her attention and through the trees she glimpsed a black horse with scarlet saddle-trappings. Crusader was standing by the stream. She guided Cassandra towards the gelding, her heart beating faster at the prospect of meeting Luke Ryder. She had not seen him during the week since their encounter in the stable. Sergeant Hopkirk had moved the captain's possessions from the house and she did not know where he was now living.

Ferncombe Place seemed empty without the dragoon in residence. Paul and St Clere had gone away, ostensibly to a hunting party with friends, though Katherine suspected they were in France at the court of King James.

At least Captain Ryder's departure from the house made it unnecessary for her to lie to protect her brother. She had not expected to miss Luke so much. The evenings were the worst. She was used to dining alone, but she had come to enjoy the dragoon's companionship, and now the empty hours were interminable without his presence.

'Captain Ryder,' she called as she saw his figure kneeling by the stream. When he did not immediately rise to greet her, she felt a jab of alarm.

Something was wrong!

'Luke!'

He rose slowly and pulled his cocked hat forward over his face, but he did not turn to face her. His broad shoulders were hunched as though he was in pain. Her puzzled gaze took in the mud streaks on his long cloak thrown back over one shoulder, the piece of gold braid hanging in tatters. She slid to the ground.

'Luke, what's wrong?'

He turned then, his face shadowed by the front peak of his hat. 'What are you doing riding alone? Haven't you yet learned of the danger?'

The questions fired at her in a cold, clipped tone roused her temper. 'You're not my protector, Captain Ryder,' she began, but the angry words faded as she noticed Luke's pallor beneath his tan, and a tremor ran through his body as his hand went to his side. There were several rents in the scarlet jacket and it also was covered with mud-stains.

'You've been set upon!' She ran to his side, her fears for him dispelling her anger.

He stiffened as she put a hand on his arm. 'It's but a few bruises.'

She was close enough now to see the marks on his

face. His cheek was cut, as was the side of his mouth,
and his eye was swollen and beginning to blacken. He
coughed and she saw his lips whiten, his body braced
as he straightened his shoulders. She put her hand to
his cut cheek, her heart wrenching at the sight of his
injuries.

'What happened?' she asked.

His lips twisted into the beginnings of a sardonic
smile and ended with a grimace of pain.

'Someone wanted to warn me off. St Clere would be
a good guess.'

Her hand went to her mouth. 'Surely not!' The
distress in her voice was obvious. Her green eyes were
large, their expressive depths showing her horror and
concern at his suffering.

'St Clere sees me as a threat in more ways than one,'
he told her.

She took the wet, blood-stained stock from his
fingers and held it gently against the swelling on his
eye. She felt so helpless with nothing on her to soothe
his pain. 'I told St Clere there was nothing between
us.' Her voice shook. 'That you were no longer at
Ferncombe.'

She felt her anger rising at the injustice of the attack.
It was what she had dreaded. St Clere had not been to
her home since his ultimatum, but that did not mean
he had changed his mind. But he was an honourable
man—surely he would not stoop to having Luke set
upon?

'It's my fault this has happened. I'm so sorry.' Her
gaze clung to Luke's, her voice wretched.

He put his hands on her shoulders. The obvious pain
behind each of his movements broke down the flimsy
defences she had erected against him. He drew her
closer, his breath warming her cheek as his sable eyes
bored into hers.

'It was worth a few bruises to see the concern in your
eyes. Look into your heart, Kate. You talk as though

we're strangers. The gardens of Highclere changed that. Isn't it time you trusted me?'

How she longed to do just that. She could feel herself weakening, yet the years she had fought to retain her independence could not easily be put aside. He was her brother's enemy. She must not forget that. Now was not the time to allow her heart to govern her head.

Suddenly the wood was lit with a yellow flash, followed moments later by a boom of thunder. Katherine gave a yelp of terror, and buried her head against Luke's jacket as the ground vibrated beneath her feet. His arms closed protectively around her. As the last cannonade faded she became embarrassed at her weakness, but when she tried to pull away from him he held her fast.

'Nay, my sweet, you cannot escape me that easily. I never thought you one to be afeared of storms.'

'Not the storms, but the memory of——' Another flash of lightning ended her words in a sob. Her hands covered her eyes, her whole body violently shaking.

'Kate!' His arm around her was comforting, drawing her towards the horses. 'You'll be all right. There's shelter close by. Trust me!' The last of his words were drowned by another crack of thunder.

She kept her head against his shoulder until she felt Cassandra's saddle against her back. She drew back then, shamed by her weakness. But the terror which each storm brought was wild in her eyes, and she could not control her trembling as the first spots of rain fell.

She remounted and summoned her will to control her fear. Luke was with her. His strength was reassuring. He showed little sign of the agony of his injuries. His resilience put her to shame. She must think of him, the care his wounds needed, and not the horror of that night long ago.

'This way, Kate,' Luke shouted. Once astride Crusader, he veered his horse towards the edge of the wood.

The wind had risen and the first needles of rain stung Katherine's face as she followed Luke. They had covered several hundred yards before she realised that they were riding away from Ferncombe. She dismissed a twinge of dismay. The captain had said shelter was close, whereas her home was over a mile away. The storm would break long before they reached it.

As the thunder rolled over the surrounding hills she felt the roots of her hair prickle with static, and beneath her legs Cassandra's body quivered as the mare detected her mistress's fear. They left the wood. The sky had darkened so that she could only see a short distance ahead in the gloom. A zigzag of blue snaked to earth, striking a beech tree in the next field. For several moments its outline was haloed by fire, then a loud crack severed its trunk down the centre and the tree was engulfed in flames.

Cassandra shied and plunged forward with a shrill neigh. The mare was too terrified to respond either to the bit or the pressure of Katherine's legs. Katherine clung on grimly to Cassandra's mane as the mare galloped out of control, but with the sense to follow the ghostly shape of Crusader.

The rain became a torrent and the ground a swirling river beneath the flying hoofs. Without warning Cassandra skidded to a halt, propelling Katherine on to her neck. The horse flung back her head and snorted, protesting at the strength of the hand which was holding on to its bridle, and a flash of lightning revealed Luke's pale face at Katherine's side.

'Into the cottage,' he shouted against the growing violence of the wind.

Seeing the dim outline of an isolated dwelling several yards ahead, Katherine slid to the ground. When Luke took Cassandra's reins to lead both horses towards a flint-walled barn behind the cottage, she hurried after him. He was hurt. She could not permit him to tend the horses alone.

He made no protest when she began to strip off her

mare's saddle and harness. Outside the wind grew in violence and there was a steady roar as the rain pounded against the thatch above their heads. For several minutes they worked in silence, rubbing the horses' sweating bodies with straw. With the horses comfortably settled, Katherine paused by the barn door. The ground outside was flooded and the rain showed no sign of abating. A fierce gust of wind buffeted Katherine, robbing her of breath.

Luke's arm slid around her waist, steadying her. At that moment a bolt of forked lightning struck the next field, its deadly fire streaking along the ground, killing several huddled sheep while the rest of the flock scattered in terror. An involuntary scream tore from her lips and she turned her head away, burying it against Luke's chest. She had never been out in such a violent storm, and its malevolence frightened her.

'We'll have to make a run for the cottage,' Luke shouted as the thunder died to a distant growl.

She nodded. Together they sped through the wall of rain. After several paces her wet skirts wound about her ankles, tripping her. Luke's grip remained firm about her waist, preventing her from falling, but, hearing his sharp intake of breath as she collided against him, Katherine cursed her carelessness. Lifting her skirts high, she lengthened her stride to match his as they crossed the open space.

The cottage was a single-storey timber-framed building, and there was no welcoming light burning from within. Unmindful as to whether the dwelling was occupied or not, Luke opened the door and they burst in. Leaving her side, he went straight to a table and picked up the tinder-box to light the candle placed in readiness at its side.

'Shut the door,' he ordered as he strode across to the fireplace and set the flame to the prepared fire in the hearth.

Katherine did as she was told, taking note of her surroundings as she began to recover her breath.

Where were the owners? Unwilling to trespass, she stood by the door, ill at ease.

Beneath her feet the foundations shook at the boom of thunder overhead. The flickering flames from the fire beckoned her and she edged closer to their warmth.

'Your Sussex weather is as unsociable as its inhabitants,' Luke declared as he straightened with obvious stiffness.

'Where are we?' she asked warily.

He grinned wickedly, alerting her suspicions. She froze midway across the floor.

'This is the cottage I've rented,' he pronounced with obvious amusement at the dilemma she found herself in.

Wide-eyed with disillusion, she stared at him. Compressing her lips, she glared at him accusingly. He showed no remorse at his trickery, and to her alarm began to unbutton his uniform jacket. The tongues of fire from the burning logs threw his figure into sharp relief. Tall and dominating, he watched her, the harsh contours of his face as uncompromising as a satyr's.

Had he not warned her he was no gentleman?

He winced as he eased his wet jacket away from his shoulders. For him to show any sign of pain it must be severe indeed. Katherine's compassion for his injuries overrode her suspicions. The storm was making her edgy. What choice had they but to seek shelter? Common sense calmed her panic. Luke was wounded. It was hardly likely he planned seduction.

A study of the cottage showed Katherine that it consisted of a large room divided by a brightly coloured Flemish hanging at one end and an archway leading off into a darkened room at the other. Though sparsely furnished, it was neatly kept—and, apart from themselves, deserted.

Again, a splinter of unease jabbed at her. 'Have you no servant?' she asked.

The dragoon's full lips twisted. 'I value my privacy. There's little solitude to be found in the army. I manage well enough. There's a woman who comes in to clean and do my laundry.' His grin broadened. 'For the moment, Kate, you find yourself alone with me. Does that shock your sensibilities?'

At her icy glare he gave a crack of laughter which ended in a grimace and he turned quickly to prod the fire into life with his boot.

Katherine remained on her guard, but the evidence of his pain was in the hunched droop of his shoulders. 'Your injuries should be tended,' she said.

'They look more painful than they are. Nothing's broken. As a soldier I'm used to a few bruises.'

The lazy smile he turned upon her left her oddly breathless. Was he just being gallant not to worry her? Then she tensed as his appreciative gaze lingered upon the riding habit which the rain had moulded to her figure. Wounded or not, again his prepossessing figure dominated the cottage.

'Come nearer to the fire and warm yourself,' he invited.

Stubbornly she kept her distance. The cottage was lit by the soft orange glow of firelight and a single candle. The interior was seductive and far too intimate for her peace of mind. Luke stood in partial shadow watching her. His dark hair was unpowdered. The wind had ruffled the short locks at his temples and they curled over his brow, softening his rugged features. She took a step towards the fire, drawn by the magnetism of his presence.

Fascinated, she noted the way the captain's damp cambric shirt clung to his broad shoulders and sleek outline of his body. The material was almost transparent in its wetness, showing the dark patch of hair across his chest and the flatness of his stomach. With a start she realised she was staring at him, and her gaze slid away to focus on the leaping flames of the fire.

He moved to join her. When the firelight fell across his battered face it was a jolting reminder of the differences which lay between them.

She lowered her gaze, wondering whether he would think her forward if she offered to tend his wounds.

'You'd better remove your jacket before you take a chill, Kate. It will dry by the fire.'

His courteous tone did little to banish her growing unease. Her fingers froze on the fastening of her jacket. Beneath it her silk blouse would cling as revealingly to her figure as his shirt did to his.

He chuckled softly. 'I did not bring you here to seduce you, Kate. It was to save you from being half drowned by a storm.' He turned his back and disappeared behind the dividing hanging.

Why did she not feel reassured by his words? If only the memory of his kiss were not still branded upon her mind. It made his presence all the more menacing to her.

She pulled off her jacket and spread it over an iron-bound coffer which she dragged to one side of the fire. She sat down on a three-legged stool and stared bleakly into the flames. They were trapped by the storm, but she was far from defenceless, and the slight pressure against her side from the dagger was reassuring.

She heard him moving about the adjoining room and several times heard a stifled gasp. He could not possibly tend his wounds properly himself. Guilty that she had been so insensitive to his need, she picked up the candlestick and went to aid him. As she lifted the hanging aside a flash of lightning lit the bedchamber, and for once it was not the terrors of old it revealed, but a sight which in its own way was equally harrowing.

A curtained bed was in the far corner, but her gaze was drawn to Luke standing a few feet away from her. He had changed into tan breeches which hugged his slim hips and powerful thighs. He was stripped to the waist, his back turned to her as he cautiously rubbed some salve into a large bruise at the base of his ribs.

He turned, sensing her approach. The candle-light illuminated the room and his half-naked body, and the extent of his injuries appalled her. Several purple lumps and reddened lacerations distorted the lean contours of his back and ribs. The ride to the cottage must have been torture for him.

'Let me help you. Those cuts should be bathed else they will become infected.' Ignoring his glower, she took the pot of salve from his hands. 'Go and sit by the fire—the light's better.'

She moved ahead of him into the main room of the cottage. When he did not follow, she glanced back over her shoulder. He stood with one leg bent, his thumbs thrust into his waistband, the narrowed, dark eyes unfathomable.

'Stubbornness, Captain Ryder, will leave you unfit for duty,' she said.

Grim-faced and with every sign of reluctance he followed her to the fire and sat down on the stool.

Katherine went into the kitchen, found a bucket of drawn water and filled a kettle, which she took back into the main room to hang over the fire. The storm had rolled into the distance. While the water heated she examined his injuries, her concern for him so great that the distant flashes of lightning held no terror for her. Her fingers were gentle as they moved over his ribs. To her relief none had been broken or cracked. Even the bruises, though painful, were not as severe as she had at first feared.

'Those men were savages to beat you so brutally,' she said hoarsely. The injustice of the attack outraged her. 'I could take a horsewhip to them myself to teach them a lesson.'

'Such passion in defence of my person.' He sounded amused. 'I am flattered, Kate. But then you always were wilful.'

She sent him a withering glare. 'I do not like injustice, Captain Ryder.' She bent her head to concentrate on the task of cleaning the dirt from the cuts with the now warmed water. All the while she was aware of his gaze on her, compelling her to look up at him. She fought it and won.

It was a shallow victory because she was forced to pay greater heed to his body as she began to rub the salve gently across his back. Her fingers circled slowly over the hard muscles, her fingertips sensitive to every contour and the tantalising heat of his flesh. She discovered other old scars: a puckered bullet wound in his shoulder and a silvery groove from a sword-cut along his upper arm. The lubricant in the salve melted on the warmth of his skin and unconsciously her fingers skimmed over his shoulders with the tenderness of a caress. At Luke's indrawn breath, she looked up, fearful lest she had unwittingly hurt him.

His rugged countenance was tense. Thick crescent lashes partially shielded the black eyes smouldering with desire, the hollows of his cheeks taut with the intensity of his passion.

She drew back with a start, but his hand closed over her wrist, keeping it firmly clamped to his shoulder. Beneath her palm his skin burned. The flames from the fire played its seductive light over the firmness of his broad chest with its spread of dark hair, which tapered to the slenderness of an arrow down to his navel. Despite the bruises she was mindful of the threatening power of hard muscle.

There was an odd dryness in her throat and she said the first words which came into her head to break the silence between them.

'I still cannot believe St Clere was responsible for your beating!'

He raised a dark brow, his voice hoarse. 'St Clere understands what's at stake. The prize is high.' His eyes were now guarded, but a muscle cording in his neck warned her of the tight leash he kept upon his emotions.

Releasing her hand, he stood up, pulled a clean, ruffled shirt over his head and tucked it into his waistband. Then he folded his arms and perched on the edge of the table to study her for a long moment before adding, 'You play the innocent well, sweet

Kate. What are you hiding from me now? Your loyalties to the Jacobites?'

Katherine thrust down her pain, and, not trusting herself to speak, picked up the bowl and ointment to take them into the kitchen. She was halted by his scathing tone.

'Your silence betrays you,' Luke persisted ruthlessly. 'What are you afraid of? Your passionate nature—or me, because I wear King George's uniform?'

'That's absurd. I'm no Jacobite.'

'But your brother is.'

At that moment a flash of lightning lit up the room. It tinged blue his swarthy complexion, emphasising the bleak set of his mouth, and a fear, deeper than that of her own safety, or her terror of the storm, speared through her.

'You have a high opinion of yourself, Captain Ryder,' she accused coldly, and was relieved that her voice betrayed no sign of her inner quaking. 'I have nothing to fear from an officer of King George. My brother and I live quietly at Ferncombe.'

'Quietness steeped with intrigue.' He pushed himself off the table and caught her arms, a spasm of pain flickering across his face at the suddenness of his movement.

'I know your brother's involved with the Pretender's cause.' His black stare pierced her composure. 'Do you think I would deliberately act against him when I know the suffering it would bring you?'

She tried to pull away but his grip tightened. 'If you believe Paul capable of treason, why have you done nothing?'

He grinned sardonically. 'He and St Clere have covered their tracks well. Except that they are often in each other's company. The Viscount has been out-spoken in his support of the Pretender's claim to the throne.'

'That was before Queen Anne died.' She kept her stare level with his, refusing to rise to his baiting. 'St

Clere is our neighbour and has been a friend of the family for years.'

'And now St Clere would link your two families in another way—whether you wish it or not.'

Katherine's anger flared. The storm was returning with greater intensity, adding to the tension building within her.

'When will you learn to trust me?' It was spoken with the force of a command, not a question. He drew her closer so that their bodies touched.

'Why should I trust you?' She fought the temptation to do just that, and it brought a green fire leaping to her eyes. 'You're not a man to forget his duty. To withhold information about rebels would mean your disgrace.'

He grinned wickedly. 'So you admit you are hiding something?'

She stiffened in his hold. 'I admit nothing. You are twisting my words to suit your own ends.'

'Then it is time I was honest with you. St Clere is the leader of the rebels. It's him I'm after. I doubt your brother has done much more than drink to the health of the King over the water and spout hot air. Or that was all, before St Clere took Paul to France this week. St Clere is the danger to your brother, not I. He will lead him to the scaffold.'

'I have no idea of what you are implying. St Clere and Paul have joined the hunting party of a friend of St Clere.'

An uneasy silence stretched between them as they continued to glare at each other, both breathing heavily.

'Listen to me, Kate. I understand your loyalty to Paul. And I commend you for it. A Rising will not succeed. King George, although unpopular, has been accepted by the people.' His hands moved to her shoulders, his voice gruff. 'I don't want to see you suffer because of Paul's misguided allegiance.'

Those dark eyes so disturbingly close demanded that

she obey him. She wavered. How desperately she wanted to believe him.

A brilliant flash of lightning lit the cottage and the rafters creaked as though they bore the weight of a body. She screamed and covered her eyes with her shaking hands. Luke's arms went round her, holding her hard against the warmth of his chest. Her face was pressed against his shirt, the steady beat of his heart vibrating against her cheek. Its rhythm pulsated through her, taken up by the hard beat of her own. She could smell the herb of the unguent on his skin and the musky scent of his body which filled her senses. His hand stroked her hair, his breath warm as it fanned her brow, skimming down her cheek as he took her chin in his fingers and forced her to look up at him.

He took her face between his hands and with agonising slowness his mouth dipped towards her, so that her heart swelled, leapt, and drummed to a suffocating beat. He kissed her deeply, with passion. When she tried to resist, his mastery was such that her will was subjugated beneath the sensuality of his caress. Her eyes closed, a soft sigh rising from deep within her as her arms slid around his hard body, feeling the strength and power of him, his heat consuming her.

His mouth moved slowly over her lips until she was light-headed, and her mind swirled in an agony of longing. Her lips parted and she drank in the taste of him. A fire spread through her veins, turning her limbs to a searing powder until her legs were no longer capable of support. Of their own volition her hips swayed, pressing harder against him. Tiny shock waves of heat set her breasts tingling as his thumbs lightly grazed along their curves. Then, as his ardour mounted, he captured them in his hands, sending an explosive sweetness through her body.

When his mouth left hers to travel down her neck, her blood surged like a hot spring, and a tremor of pleasure rippled through her body as his lips nestled into the hollows of her throat. She arched against him, her fingers entwining in the cool thickness of his hair.

The virginal part of her mind was shocked at the liberties he was taking, but another fast-awakening, wanton part craved that the new and unimagined pleasure would continue.

An ear-splitting cannonade of thunder rudely jolted Katherine from the stupor possessing her. Was she bewitched, that this man could drive all reason, all decency from her mind? She tensed and wriggled in his grasp. Still his lips laid siege to her senses. A gnawing ache was building within her, demanding surcease. She was losing control. No man was her master. This was madness. It must end. Now!

'Stop!' Desperation gave her the will-power to pull back. She wrenched her trembling body free from his grasp. Suddenly remembering that he was her enemy, she wrapped her arms protectively about her shaking form. She hated him—hated herself for the ease with which he had cast aside her guard, stripped bare her defences.

'Stay away from me!' she warned, her hand going to her waist.

With a soft chuckle he captured her wrist before it could close over the handle of her dagger. He pulled her against him, his broad shoulders blocking her line of retreat. Not that there was anywhere to go. Even with his injuries he would be too fast for her. He had warned her he was no gentleman. Was he trying to trick her, or blackmail her with her brother's life to win her favours from her?

'So proud and so stubborn!' he mocked, his eyes boring into hers.

Katherine tried to jerk her hand away, but his free arm slipped around her waist, imprisoning her against him. Every part of her was aware of his strength and vigour, his masculinity. With negligent ease he was weaving a seductive web about her senses.

'There can be nothing between us, Captain Ryder,' she forced out shakily.

'You delude yourself, sweet Kate. There is everything that is fire and passion between us.' His arms settled possessively about her, pressing her against his long, hard frame.

His face looked as though it were carved from rock. Only his eyes were alive. They glinted with a fierceness that was like a sword thrust deep into her heart. 'Admit you feel as I do.' He laughed softly and reached for her. His hand remained firm on her wrist, preventing her from drawing her dagger in defence of her virtue. She had not the strength to wrestle with him; she had only feminine wiles to lure him with deceptive sweetness.

'I am honour-bound to St Clere. How can I acknowledge that it is your lips which excite me, not his?' she cried.

His eyes lit with a fierce light as he put his hands to the side of her face. 'Forget St Clere. There is no honour in him. Think only of us.'

In desperation to ward off the spell of his touch, her hand closed on the dagger-hilt and moved upwards in one swift movement. The point rested against his ribs and her voice rose an octave as she warned, 'Stand back.'

He did not even flinch. When he made no move to release her she pressed the dagger harder against his ribs. There was amusement and something far more pervading and soul-inflaming in his gaze which set her heart tumbling.

'Do you really intend to use that, my darling Kate?'

CHAPTER SIX

KATHERINE stared at Luke for a long moment. The dagger was held so tight that it bruised her palm, and his nearness was robbing her of the will to resist. But resist she must.

As she inhaled deeply, her anger and pride were the barricades of her defence. How dared he think her so easy a conquest? Her palm grew slippery as she adjusted her grip upon the dagger. She did not want to injure him, but if her honour depended on it—what choice had she?

With her free hand she pushed back from him, but his embrace remained unyielding. The darkly handsome face hovered satanically above her. He was watching her with lazy assurance, daring her to defy him, knowing that in the end he would be the victor.

What a fool she had been to think him honourable! She would not submit to his seduction. To her last morsel of strength she would fight him.

Even as her hand drew back to strike at his arm the awesome truth smote her. She loved him. She, who had declared no man would be her master, loved a man who had no scruples about making her his mistress.

From the golden sparks dancing in his eyes she knew he guessed something of her anguish. His confident laugh goaded her to fury. With a cry of outrage, she drew back the dagger to strike him. Her wrist was caught with ruthless ease as his mouth grazed her ear.

'Damn it, Kate, if you're not a hell-cat that needs taming. I want you. And I mean to have you. . . But as my wife.'

Katherine stopped struggling and stared at him. A prolonged flash of lightning made the cottage as bright as day. He, too, appeared taken aback by his words. Then the sound of his laughter was drowned by the thunder, and his eyes glittered with an intensity which left her breathless.

'Yes, my love—as my wife!'

Her dagger arm fell to her side. But, still wary, she continued to challenge him with her eyes.

'You spoke in haste. In passion, not love. You value your freedom too much to discard it upon a whim,' she protested.

'It's no whim.' His eyes burned into hers. 'I love you.'

Obstinately she shook her head, denying his words. 'You vowed you would never marry while serving in the army.'

'Minx, would you turn my words back on me?' His eyes shone with tenderness and warmth. 'I will buy myself out. It's time I captained the *Sea Serpent* myself. It will be a good life—an exciting life with you at my side.'

He paused to smile down at her, his voice deepening as he became caught up in the new world he was creating for himself. 'Together we will sail the seas.'

They stood, their gazes locked in silent combat. He was willing her to answer. Could she believe him? Their life together would be filled with adventure. She wavered, desperately wanting to believe him.

'The storm has wrought a madness in you,' she reasoned. 'Let's not talk of marriage now. You know nothing of me. Nor I of you.'

'I'm male. Six-and-twenty years old. Single. The youngest of three sons. My family home is in Somerset. My mother is French. My father is——'

'Enough,' she protested, laughing. 'You go too fast.'

Instantly his expression sobered. 'I'm used to grabbing at life as I find it. Such is a soldier's way. If I had time I would woo you as extravagantly as any Court gallant. I love you. That's all that matters. Should it not suffice?'

She was gathered close and his eyes searched hers—compelling her to obey him. With a racing heart she held his stare and the dagger clattered to the floor.

'Answer me, Kate,' he insisted. 'Say you'll be my wife.'

'I cannot. It's too soon.'

It had all happened so suddenly. Like a dream. The fervent light in Luke's eyes told her he loved her and the fight drained from her, replaced by a rush of happiness.

'Luke, you make it all sound so easy.' The bubbling excitement within her stilled. 'What of St Clere and my marriage contract to him?'

'You do not love St Clere. He must release you from a contract you had no agreement to.'

'It was my father's wish,' she said heavily. As she looked up at him, her heart swelled with a fullness that made speech impossible.

She loved him with every particle of her body and soul. Perhaps she loved him too well. He was a proud man. St Clere was not the only barrier to their happiness. What of her fortune? Luke had been so adamant when he vowed never to rise upon a woman's purse-strings. How could the simple matter of two people loving each other be so complicated?

Before she could begin to tell him of her fortune his hands slid over her neck to grip her shoulders. 'Do you love me, Kate?'

'With all my heart.'

The words spoken, she laid her head against his chest. She was committed. She lifted her head and heard him catch his breath as he saw in her eyes the emotion she no longer troubled to hide.

'I love you,' she said softly, 'but there are so many obstacles in our path.'

He grinned with a confidence that set her heart racing. 'Together we shall overcome them.'

Briefly she closed her eyes to shut out the passion shining in his gaze—then a wave of agony shot through her and her voice quivered as she blurted out, 'You know nothing of me!'

'I want you, Kate.' He kissed her with tender fervour and as she swayed against him, her fingers locking tight about his neck, he whispered against her ear, 'This is the only way I would have you answer me.'

'Oh, my darling, if only it were that simple.' She pulled back from him before his kiss overpowered her resolve. She looked deep into his eyes. 'I am that which you despise most. I am an heiress. It's my fortune St Clere would make his own, not me. He will not break the contract.'

Luke stepped back from her and rubbed a hand across the back of his neck. 'I don't give a damn about your money,' he ground out. 'You believe that, don't you, Kate?'

'Yes.'

'Then I will make St Clere see reason. Even if I have to fight him.'

'No, Luke.' She clutched at his shoulders in panic. 'St Clere is an accomplished duellist. I'll not have you fighting over me.'

He raised a mocking brow. 'Have you no faith in my capabilities? For shame on you, Kate Winters.'

He drew her into his arms. His dark eyes transfixed her with a mesmerising, persuasive stare, commanding her into submission. Then his warm lips were against the hollow of her shoulder as he whispered a throaty promise.

'You will be mine, Kate.'

Katherine sighed ecstatically. It was impossible to doubt that implacable assurance. Beneath the onslaught of his kisses, her neck moved back sinuously, her lips sowing kisses along his jaw. Her eyes were luminous with her need as her body seemed to flow into his.

The thunder rolled overhead but she was lost in a trance, her senses so filled with the scent and feel of him that her fear of the storm was surpassed by her longing.

The wind rattled the shutters and whined down the chimney, making the flames of the fire caper in an exotic dance. They lay on a blanket before its sensuous, golden warmth and Katherine stared up at Luke as he bent over her. She reached up to smooth a curl of dark hair from his brow and smiled into his eyes.

'I did not know it was possible to be this happy, or to feel such bliss, such a sense of belonging in a man's arms.'

'Then I shall not disappoint you, my love,' Luke murmured against her hair. 'This is but the beginning. There is so much more joy a man can bring to a woman.'

She could not contain a shiver of pleasure as she felt the strength of his body pressed against hers. He held her close, his kisses deepening as her mouth parted. But when his hand slid up from her waist to cover her breast Katherine again tensed.

'You've nothing to fear, my darling,' he whispered. 'I won't force you.'

'But I want you, Luke,' she said softly. 'It's just. . .'

'As I want you.'

His lips were enticing against her throat, his fingers subtly persuasive as they eased her shirt from her waistband. They moved with insidious skill across the delicate silk of her chemise which covered her ribcage. Their touch was exciting, coercing as he eased down the straps of her chemise. When he smoothed his palm over her naked breast she gasped, startled by the sensations spreading in hot waves through her body.

A delicious restlessness made her writhe beneath him, her emotions again spiralling out of her control. It was both frightening and exhilarating—yet it must not continue, her conscience dictated.

She levered her hands against his shoulder to make him stop. He remained poised above her, immovable, unyielding, his thumb circling her breasts, rousing them to an aching fullness. He kissed the hollow of her collarbone, then traced a line between her breasts. She gasped with pleasure, a subtle heat spreading through her loins.

Even as she began to shake her head in protest his hands wove their magic mastery, moving down beneath the waistband of her skirt and over her taut, flat abdomen. The denial became a movement of surrender. She moaned softly, her neck arching as she lifted herself closer to his hard frame.

Love conquered inhibition. Her shirt was discarded with masterly ease, her chemise drawn down to her waist. She could hardly breathe for the frantic beating of her heart, his lips possessing hers, his tongue teasing, probing the silken recesses of her mouth. She had never guessed love could be as all-consuming as this— that time could lose all meaning, spinning out and spiralling into an endless vortex, sensations building, rising, seemingly to suffocate, capable of drawing soft cries of ecstatic torment.

Katherine forgot her reservations and doubts—there was no room for anything in her mind but the waves of pleasure consuming her body as his mouth and hands caressed her. She abandoned herself to that pleasure, her legs parting as he stroked the satin softness of her inner thighs. A quavering breath sighed in her throat as his fingers slid into the heat and softness of her, driving deeper until she trembled and moaned, her hips moving in instinctive response.

Suddenly Luke's hand stilled. Katherine's eyes opened, her voice husky as she cried out his name.

Luke shuddered as he mastered the pain of his own desire. Any other woman he would have taken without compunction, slaking his own aching need, holding back just long enough for the woman to reach her own fulfilment. But this was Kate—the woman he loved, the woman he would cherish as his wife, become the adored mother of his children. Kate was different— special.

For her he would wait until they married in a few weeks' time. It was a matter of respect. And deep in his heart he knew it was also a matter of pride. He could not forget she was an heiress. He wanted to win her as his bride with honour, not by sordidly compromising her reputation.

Reluctantly he sat up and tore his gaze from the golden flesh so tantalisingly revealed by the firelight. Katherine stared at her lover, feeling bewildered and shamed. She looked at her naked breasts, her skirt pushed high, exposing her long legs to the thigh, and felt her cheeks begin to burn.

Luke sat as though carved from marble. The firelight flickered over his averted face. Desire had tautened the hollows beneath his cheekbones, and there was a shadowing of pain around his eyes. Abruptly he rolled away from her and sat up, resting his hands over his drawn-up knees as he stared into the fire.

Katherine watched him with disbelief. Her body burned from his touch; she wanted him more than she had wanted anything in her life, and he had withdrawn from her. What had she done wrong? Did he think her so brazen that he despised her?

'Luke!' Her anguish rang in her voice. 'Do you no longer want me?'

He turned to look down at her and a spasm of longing darkened his face. 'Not want you? You are my torment, Kate.' His voice was gruff. 'But not this way. In a few weeks we shall be wed. I love you enough to wait until then.'

She sat up and put her hand on his arm and felt the muscles contract at her touch. 'Then you are stronger than I. Your sacrifice is noble. But. . .'

'There speaks the siren.' He laughed down at her. 'No buts. . .you are temptress enough. I'm not made of stone. How can I hold you and not want you completely as my own? But I'll not compromise you. No man will say of us that you were forced to marry me to save your reputation.'

Her eyes sparkled with defiance and she tossed back her hair. 'I am mistress of my own reputation.' She held her arms out to him. 'Kiss me, Luke.'

He leaned forward and kissed her chastely on her brow. Then he flicked down her skirts and pressed her shirt against her breasts to cover them from his gaze.

'My glorious strumpet, cover yourself.' His lips curved into a tender smile.

She pouted rebelliously. Her body was still on fire from his caresses, an indefinable longing needing to be appeased. She admired his control, but the newly discovered sensuality in her would not be so easily silenced.

'Such a compromise of my reputation would solve many problems. I love you, Luke. The thought of marriage to St Clere is abhorrent to me. But the contract is legally binding. I can see no way out of it— unless we elope.'

'And have the world brand me as a fortune-hunter?' he said with angry heat. 'I would win you honourably, Kate.' He stood up to pace the room.

She sensed he had deliberately withdrawn from her, the strain of controlling his desire building a barrier around their teasing companionship.

He looked out of the window. 'The storm is passing. Once the rain stops we must leave. Are you hungry? There's some stew which just needs reheating.'

'If I cannot be made love to, I may as well feed one of my appetitites,' she retaliated in a teasing tone as she pulled on her shirt.

'You are a shameless baggage,' he laughed, responding to her bantering. 'Have you no compassion upon my chivalry?'

She wrinkled her nose at him and sighed. 'Truth to tell, I love you the more for it.'

Luke took her into his arms and pushed her shirt back into the waistband of her skirt before kissing the tip of her nose. 'I shall enjoy being the master of all your appetites, sweet Kate. Our marriage will never be dull. Now be a good woman and fetch the bowls from the kitchen, or my honourable intentions will be corrupted by your seductive wiles.'

She looked up at him through her lashes and smiled impishly. 'With you, Luke Ryder, I shall look forward to being a bad woman—a deliciously bad woman.'

With a delighted laugh, he gave her a playful pat on her behind as he sent her off into the kitchen.

They chatted easily as Luke prepared the food, and when it was hot he ladled it into two bowls. He offered one to Katherine and their hands touched. It was enough to set her blood afire. She lifted her eyes to hold his stare and her love for him was so fierce that she said tremulously, 'Luke, I'm so frightened I shall lose you.'

His eyes crinkled with an assured smile. 'That's not going to happen.' He kissed her brow. 'Eat your food.'

She did as she was told, its warmth and nourishment relaxing the tension. Then, the bowls put aside, Luke put his arm around her shoulders and drew her head down on to his chest. She closed her eyes, lulled by the steady beat of his heart against her ear and the strength of his arms around her. They did not speak but sat listening to the crackle of the fire and the drum of the rain against the windows. In the peace and security of Luke's arms she did not want to think of the problems which lay ahead. She had faith in Luke. Somehow it would all come right. It had to.

The fire and the food made her drowsy with contentment. She could be happy in a simple cottage like this with him. How perfect it would be. She could see it plainly, and a smile played over her lips as her eyelids drooped and she slipped into a dream filled with ideals for their future.

A stifled groan from Luke brought her awake with a start. The fire had died down and the cottage was in total darkness.

'Wake up, Kate!' he said, striking a candle. He made to take a pocket watch from his waistcoat pocket and stopped. 'We fell asleep. They stole my watch along with my money. But it must have been dark for hours. I've got to get you home.'

Katherine hoped to find Ferncombe Place in darkness. There was an oak outside her bedroom window and, as children, Paul and herself had often used it to escape the house in the early hours to go and explore the estate. She had no doubts now of her capabilities of climbing it, and her bedroom window was always left open. To her dismay there were lights in the entrance, old hall and parlour windows. Paul must have returned.

She turned to Luke. 'It would be best if I went in alone. I'll say I took shelter from the storm in a disused shepherd's hut and fell asleep.'

'You have a terror of storms. Will your brother believe you faced one of such magnitude by yourself? I won't let you face his anger alone. He has to know of our plans for the future. It may as well be now as later,' he told her.

From the stubborn set of Luke's jaw Katherine knew she could not dissuade him. If only they had not fallen asleep. Now it looked as though her reputation was compromised. Yet Luke had behaved with honour.

At the sound of their horses' hoofs on the cobbled courtyard Grimshaw came out of his room at the end of the stables. 'Thank heavens you're safe, Miss Katherine. The master is in a rare taking. St Clere's with him. They've been out searching the countryside these last two hours or more.'

It was worse than Katherine had imagined. She dismounted and with proud defiance put her arm through Luke's as they entered the house.

Paul and St Clere were in the old hall waiting for them. Paul's relief at seeing her safe faded as he noted Luke Ryder at her side.

'Good God, Kate! This time you've gone too far. You've brought disgrace to our name and upon St

Clere,' he raged. 'I'm astounded that your paramour has the audacity to present himself here.'

Luke stood stiffly at her side. 'You insult a woman whose honour is above reproach,' he said.

His fierce defence fired Katherine's blood with pride. 'I was caught in the storm——' she began.

'The storm ended hours ago!' St Clere bore down upon her, his face suffused with outrage. He glowered at Luke. 'I know your kind. You'd not be the first swaggering dragoon to turn a maid's head and bring disgrace upon her name.'

'Kate has agreed to become my wife,' Luke countered with icy calm. 'If you had any decency you'd release her from the marriage contract of a loveless marriage.'

'I'll see you in hell first,' St Clere bristled. 'You'll not get a penny of her fortune. You army fellows are all alike—younger sons, whoring and gambling away their allowances——'

'I'm able to support Kate!' Luke cut in. 'I'm not interested in her money.'

St Clere cast a disdainful glance over Luke's affronted figure. 'It's Miss Winters to you, you insolent whelp. Why, you couldn't even afford to pay her milliner's bill for a year,' he jeered. 'And what kind of a husband would you make? From the looks of you you've been brawling in a tavern.'

'Luke was ambushed and attacked by a band of ruffians,' Kate hotly defended.

'A likely tale,' Paul sneered. 'Dragoons are always drunk and fighting.'

Katherine looked at Luke, her heart aching at the insults thrown at him. There was a brittle gleam in his eye and his square chin jutted proudly. A muscle pumping in his neck showed the control he was exerting over his temper.

'Stop it, both of you,' Katherine raged. 'Luke was attacked. I saw the men ride off. Then the storm broke and we took shelter.'

'Where?' Paul demanded.

Katherine clamped shut her lips mutinously.

'At my cottage,' Luke announced. 'Because it was closest.'

'How many heiresses have been compromised by such trickery as you used on Katherine today?' St Clere scoffed. 'It won't work this time. I'm prepared to forgive Katherine her momentary indiscretion. I'm wise to the ways of fortune-hunters. I am Katherine's affianced husband—you'll never have her. I'll have you drummed out of the army in disgrace for this, Ryder. Katherine and I will marry in a month. Summon the servants, Paul. Have this vermin thrown out.'

Paul shouted for the servants.

'I'll not have my life planned for me,' Katherine declared. She had to stop this nightmare. Luke looked about to challenge St Clere to a duel, and that must be avoided. Her hand was still on Luke's arm and she squeezed it gently.

'Tempers are running too high for any reasonable discussion tonight. You'd better leave, Luke. Anything said now will only make matters worse,' she said.

Her eyes pleaded with him to go. His handsome face, battered from his beating, was stiff with pride. It tore at her heart.

'Go,' she urged in a whisper. 'I'll meet you at the cottage tomorrow afternoon. We will talk then. I love you.'

Ignoring St Clere's glowering form, Luke raised Katherine's hand to his lips. 'Will you be all right?'

She nodded. 'Paul is angry, but he's not spiteful. I shall keep to my room to give him time to cool down.'

Grimshaw and a burly young gardener answered Paul's summons. Her brother nodded to Luke. 'Get him out of here.'

Luke straightened, his head high, eyes cold and challenging as he rested his hand on his sword. The two servants hesitated. Luke marched past them to the door where he turned to deliver his ultimatum. 'This is not the end of the matter, St Clere. Kate has made her free choice. Accept it like a man. She *will* be my bride.'

St Clere stepped forward, his eyes snapping menace. 'She can't marry a dead man—remember that.'

The threat chilled Katherine's spine. She ran after Luke, and he paused at the sound of her step. 'Take me with you, Luke.'

'Not like this, Kate. I'll not have your name shamed.'

She gripped his scarlet sleeve. 'St Clere would make a dangerous enemy. It must have been he who paid those men to attack you.'

'The more reason that you do not fall into his clutches. The man has no morals or scruples. His threats do not impress me.'

'I don't want to lose you, Luke. Did you truly mean what you said? You do wish us to wed, despite St Clere's threats?'

'I meant every word, Kate.'

She walked with him to the door. 'Luke, kiss me to seal our betrothal.'

His warm mouth claimed hers in a swift kiss, his voice a promise in her ear. 'Until tomorrow at the cottage.'

He mounted Crusader and Katherine stood beneath the porch until his figure was swallowed up in the darkness.

When she returned to the hall both Paul and St Clere were standing waiting for her. Their faces were those of a judge passing the death sentence.

Paul looked at her with disgust. 'You have proved yourself too wilful for your own good. You will be locked in your room until your wedding to St Clere in a month. Should you continue this defiance you will be given no food and only water to drink. Think yourself fortunate St Clere sees fit to forget this indiscretion.'

She stared at Paul with disbelief. 'You cannot mean to force me against my will.'

'It is for your own good.' Paul looked away from her

incensed stare. 'Now go to your room—unless you would prefer Grimshaw to drag you there.'

'Paul! Why are you treating me this way? Do my feelings mean nothing to you?'

'Your welfare is my concern,' Paul pronounced with a pomposity which went far beyond his years. 'You forget I am head of this household. You will obey our father's wishes. Ryder is a fortune-hunter. You must be protected from him.'

'I love him.' Her face tightened with anger as she focused her freezing stare upon St Clere. 'Luke is the only man I shall ever love. I'm sorry, my lord. There are no circumstances in which I would consent to marry you.'

St Clere was very pale and there was a cruel curve to his lips as he replied, 'You are infatuated with this officer. You will come to your senses, Katherine. Your duty is clear.'

Never! Katherine vowed silently as she fled the room.

The next day Katherine sat in vigil at her bedroom window. The door was locked and she had been given no food. After midday she saw Paul ride out in the direction of Highclere. When he had disappeared from view, she opened the window wide. If Paul followed his normal routine he would not be back until dark.

Katherine scanned the grounds. There were no servants in sight and she stepped up on to the window-seat. She was dressed simply in a plain gown and a single petticoat. Reaching down, she gathered the back hem of her gown up through her legs and tucked it into the dagger belt at her waist. Her legs unhampered by the hanging folds, she squeezed herself through the narrow window.

Halfway through she froze, her shoulder jammed against the frame, her breasts flattened against the stone mullion. It had been several years since she had last used the window to escape her room. She was not

the slender waif she once had been; her womanly
curves could well betray her. She wiggled and changed
the angle of her body, pushing herself forward with her
hands.

Inch by inch she squeezed through the aperture and
put out a hand to clasp the sturdy branch of the old
oak. It was within easy reach and without hesitation
she stepped across into the sheltering foliage of the
tree. She climbed down to the lower branches, and
where several had been sawn away the stumps gave her
a secure foothold. Before dropping to the ground, she
again surveyed the grounds, her heart beginning to
race with the excitement of outwitting her brother and
the servants.

The way ahead was clear. She could not risk taking
a horse, for fear of discovery. Neither could she walk
through the village. There was a low segment of
flintwall beyond the orchard. Once over that she could
skirt the perimeter of the grounds until she was close
to the wood on the far side of the village. The risk of
being seen by a woodsman or farm labourer was
minimal, and once over the wall she would be safe
from discovery by their servants.

It could not have been easier. A fast run took
Katherine to the shadows of the formal hedges and she
was out and over the wall in less than a minute. The
two-mile walk to the cottage took longer than she
anticipated, and several times her injured ankle was
wrenched as it twisted on the rutted track. But the
sight of Luke drawing a pail of water from the well was
worth the rigours of her journey.

Luke put down the pail and held out his arms to
catch her to him.

'Where's your horse?' he asked with a laugh. 'Surely
you did not walk.'

'I did far more than that to get here.' She beamed at
him, pleased with her escapade. 'I had to climb out of
my bedroom window and down the oak tree. Paul

locked me in my room and thought to starve me into agreeing to marry St Clere.'

'Paul did what?' Luke looked murderous. His voice, raised in anger, shattered the peaceful setting of the cottage. 'That's iniquitous. The only way to settle this with St Clere is to call him out.'

'No, Luke. Besides, aren't officers forbidden to duel?' Katherine cried in dismay. 'You'll be disgraced. It need not come to that. I've thought about this very carefully. They would rule my life and I'll not stand for it. I'd rather die than be sold to St Clere without love.'

Luke stood very stiff and erect. Even without his military scarlet his commanding stance was that of a man about to ride into battle. Open confrontation was not the way. Would he agree to her plan? Her heart gave a twist. It was the only way. But she had a sinking feeling he would not like it.

She spread her hands on the fine linen of his shirt, feeling the powerful beat of his heart. 'I love you, Luke. But we must act quickly if I am to escape marriage to St Clere.' Her eyes widened with deliberate intent to beguile him. 'You do still want me for your bride?'

'As I want life itself.'

'Then there is a way.' Her voice was pure temptation. 'There's a parson at Paghurst. It's a small, isolated hamlet not three miles from here. He will marry us without question. . .for a price.' She touched a heavy purse hanging from her waist. 'I've twenty gold coins to ensure he does.'

At seeing Luke's mouth set in a disapproving line, she hurried on. 'Parson Rudd is a drunkard and a wife-beater. He's tolerated in the hamlet because they are a poor community. It's probable the villagers are involved with the smugglers. It would not surprise me if Rudd was also in their employ and allows them to use his church.'

'Why has he not been brought to justice?' Luke, as a law-enforcer, was prompted to ask.

'Because the smugglers rule by terror. But enough of that.' Katherine wound her arms around Luke's neck, her eyes sultry with promise. 'In less than an hour I could be your bride. Within two hours we would be back here and I would prove how very much I love you. . .' Her voice trailed off as she lifted her mouth to his.

When she drew back, the desire in his eyes was the answer she wanted. 'Once we are married, Luke, St Clere can do nothing.'

She raised a brow, provocative in her final test of his mettle. 'However, Paul could withhold my dowry until I reach twenty-five. St Clere may even contest that he's entitled to some of it. If you would rather wait to ensure our financial future——'

'Your fortune can be given to the parish for all I care,' Luke growled. 'I'm not marrying you for your money.'

'Then you will marry me—today. It could be our only chance. If Paul discovers how I escaped, he will ensure it does not happen again.'

'Kate, you know I want you, but this goes against my principles.'

She pushed back from him. 'Then take your principles to your bed, curse you. For I shall be sacrificed to St Clere's lechery.'

At the vision of Kate in St Clere's arms, Luke capitulated. Life without Kate was unthinkable. St Clere would never revoke the contract, he knew that. It was a matter of pride that his chosen bride should not cast him aside in favour of a soldier. And how in truth could a dragoon legally contest the rights of a viscount? St Clere would win in any court of the land.

To win Kate he must marry her today and face the consequences. It would be a *fait accompli*. If St Clere did not wish to become a laughing-stock, he would have to accept the marriage.

By the same token Luke did not doubt St Clere would be his lifelong enemy. That did not unduly trouble him. But he knew better than to underestimate the Viscount.

The hurt in Kate's eyes as she suspected his rejection shed the last of his misgivings. She had made plain by her enticement that she held no such qualms. All that was passionate in her nature had pleaded with him. And she was right. Man to man he had faith in his abilities to outmanoeuvre, or outfight St Clere. As dragoon against a nobleman of the realm, Luke knew that all the advantages were in St Clere's favour. If he did not marry Kate now he could lose her.

'There's no time to waste. I must change. My uniform will call too much attention to us on the road.' He went into the bedroom, returning quickly wearing black breeches and a dark green coat. He nodded for Katherine to follow him to the stable. Moments later they rode away from the cottage both mounted on Crusader's broad back.

Luke leaned forward and kissed Katherine's cheek. 'Are you sure this is what you want, Kate?'

'I have never been more sure about anything in my life.' She took the pouch from her waist and pressed it into his hands. 'Use all of that if you must.'

His expression hardened. 'This is a loan, Kate. I don't like using your money—especially for this. But as a soldier I keep only a few pounds on my person. Had I more time I would have drawn funds from my London banker's agent in Chichester. Whatever it costs will be returned to you.'

She knew better than to argue with him where his pride was concerned. Instead she gave Luke instructions on how to reach Paghurst by cutting across country and avoiding the main tracks near Ferncombe. As they cantered onwards she smiled back over her shoulder at Luke. She felt light-headed and happy. The adoration she saw mirrored in his eyes took her breath away. Within an hour they would be man and wife. Last night there had seemed so many obstacles, until she had remembered the disreputable parson. Now all at once it all appeared so easy.

Too easy, an inner voice cautioned. She pushed it aside. The love and pride shining in Luke's eyes made everything else pale into insignificance.

Everywhere Katherine looked it seemed nature had bedecked herself to celebrate their wedding. With heightened awareness she noticed the gold, vermilion and rich russets of the autumn leaves beginning to cover the woodland path. As the trees thinned, to be replaced by hedgerow, the hawthorn bushes were garlanded with scarlet berries and the snow-like clusters of old man's beard. A dozen pink-breasted bullfinches dined off the black elderberries. The air was fresh and crisp, carrying the sweet scents of pine cones and meadowsweet which hung like incense in the air to bless their journey. Above them, the constant coo of the wood pigeons was accompanied by the trill of a song thrush—all adding to the spell which was weaving itself about her.

The autumn sun bathed her with its sensuous warmth and with a contented sigh she leaned back against Luke's chest, his lips possessive as they kissed her temple. Cocooned in a magical world, she drifted along in a dreamy haze which stayed with her as they approached the old vine-covered Vicarage.

A shrunken woman with an arm bent and crippled from a badly healed break answered Luke's knock.

'Parson's asleep. He can't be disturbed,' she squeaked, and made to shut the door in their faces.

Luke put his foot in the opening and pressed a gold coin in the woman's hand. 'Tell Rudd we shall await him in the church. There will be more of that if he attends us within ten minutes.'

The woman's jaw sagged. 'Yes, sir. I'll wake him at once.' She rubbed the gold coin on her grubby apron, her tone ingratiating. 'He were up all night tending a dying parishoner. Be assured he'll attend you directly, good sir.'

Katherine and Luke exchanged conspiratorial glances as the door was closed on them. Luke took her hand and led her across the overgrown garden snared with bramble runners.

'Will Rudd come?' Katherine was suddenly fearful. The church was covered in ivy and half the steeple was missing. It was an unprepossessing place which sent a shiver through her.

'If he is as greedy for gold as you say—he'll come.'

Luke paused in the church aisle. A gaping hole in the roof allowed the sunlight in, and Katherine wished she had been spared the dilapidated sight. The ancient lime-washed walls were green with mildew. The rood screen looked as if it had been smashed during the time of the Commonwealth. Its jagged remnants had neither been dismantled nor repaired. There was a sound from the direction of the bell-tower and Katherine saw a goat and her two kids trot out and run into the garden. From the piles of droppings it was obvious the goat often took shelter here.

It was more like the Devil's house than God's, and Katherine's courage almost failed her. She looked towards the altar and was relieved to see the wooden crucifixion on a faded and tattered altar cloth.

Katherine pushed aside her disappointment. This was hardly the style of marriage she had dreamt of. But one look at Luke made everything else unimportant. It was the man she was marrying who was important, not the place they were married in.

'What's your business?' a sharp voice demanded.

The short, bearded parson stood in the doorway.

'We wish to be married.' Luke opened his palm to reveal three gold coins. 'Without delay.'

'Can't be done. Not without banns being read.' Luke added another two coins to his hand. 'You'd be needing a special licence.' Rudd licked his large flaccid lips.

'This is my special licence.' Luke added another two gold pieces to the pile in his hand.

'Two witnesses.' Rudd eyed them belligerently. 'Must have witnesses. If'n it's to be legal.'

'Your wife and a servant will suffice.' Another coin joined the collection.

'How do I know one of you bain't married already? Or that the law will be down on me?'

Luke clamped his hand shut over the coins. 'You have our word on it.'

Still Rudd wavered, but his gaze remained on Luke's shut fist. The silence strained between them. Katherine glanced anxiously at Luke, willing him to offer the man more. It was nothing short of robbery, of course, but if it meant they would be wed. . . She said nothing. It was for Luke to conduct the matter his way.

Rudd finally nodded, accepting there would be no more money. 'I'll fetch the witnesses. But the consequences of this be on your heads. I'll say you threatened me at pistol-point if the authorities threaten to prosecute me.'

He shuffled out and returned in a few minutes with his wife and an equally ill-used maidservant who grinned toothlessly at Luke and Kate from under a large linen cap.

Luke took Katherine's hand as the parson began to speak the service.

As Luke spoke his vows Katherine gazed up at him, love misting her eyes. He sounded so confident. When his ardent gaze burned into hers, the longing which welled up within her made her own voice husky. Only when he released her hand to pull a gold signet-ring from his small finger to use as a wedding band did it all seem real. She stared at the gold ring, her throat working with pride and joy.

There was nothing insubstantial in the strength of Luke's embrace, and she swayed against him when he released her.

He turned to the parson and took one more coin from the purse. 'We will wait until we see you enter the marriage in the parish register.'

Luke left nothing to chance, Katherine was delighted to observe, and he had spent only half the coins in the purse. He returned them to her now. 'I am in your debt for ten gold pieces, Mrs Ryder. It will be returned to you on the morrow.'

'With interest, Captain Ryder.'

He raised a brow. 'And what would that be, Mrs Ryder?'

'A hundred kisses.'

'A fair bargain, Mrs Ryder.' He laughed softly. 'Would that I could begin to repay them now.'

Captivated by the love and desire of Luke's sable gaze, Katherine walked in a gossamer haze of contentment to where Crusader was cropping the wayside grass. While she was held in the warmth and haven of Luke's arms, the ride back to the cottage passed in a sybaritic daze.

'No regrets?' Luke questioned as he lifted her from Crusader's back. His arm remained about her waist as they led the horse into the stable. 'You deserved a better ceremony.'

'We are married—that's what matters, not the trappings.' She stopped outside the stable and put her arms around Luke's neck. He dropped Crusader's reins and the horse moved past them to drink from his stall.

The urgency of her husband's lips, firm and demanding upon her mouth, enslaved her mind and body until she clung to him with a fierce passion. Trembling, she drew back from him, her lips tingling from the possession of his mouth, her breathing shaky.

'A moment while I tend to Crusader's needs,' Luke murmured against her hair.

Katherine watched while Luke worked. She doubted if Crusader had ever been stripped of his harness and rubbed down in such haste.

Then with a laugh Luke swung her up into his arms and strode in to the cottage and through to its bedroom.

'Mine at last, sweet Kate.'

'Luke, your bruises—take care.' Katherine remembered the beating he had received yesterday, even if he ignored the pain he must be suffering.

'They are a slight inconvenience, nothing more.' He laughed against her hair.

Then the dominance of Luke's mouth moving expertly over hers brought a fever to her body as he lowered the length of her slender body against the hard strength of his own. The pins were drawn from her hair, and with unconscious sensuality she shook the fair tresses free to tumble in riotous curls down over her breasts to her waist.

Slowly he unfastened her gown, the touch of his lips against her throat igniting a sizzling trail of sensations. When he eased the thin straps of her chemise over her bare shoulders and kissed the hollow of her neck she moaned softly. There was a whisper of cool air upon her feverish flesh as he pushed her gown and chemise over her hips to fall about her feet. She felt no shame as his hands lingered with soul-searing lightness upon her skin, arousing a craving deep within her.

A tremor of anticipation rippled through her at the touch of the mattress beneath her back. The years of independence she had guarded so fiercely were an empty void behind her now. She was enslaved, helpless against the onslaught of her own desire.

When he eased back from her to remove his clothing, she sat up. Brushing his hands aside, she unfastened his jacket. The tunic discarded, her hands slipped beneath his shirt, moving over the hard smoothness of his chest. Luke sucked in his breath and stripped off the last of his garments. For an instant she gazed upon the splendour of his naked body, her throat drying at the proud evidence of his need for her.

She pressed her lips lightly to a bruise on his ribs, her hair spreading across his hips. Then he was bending over her, removing her silk hose—the last barrier between them. He lifted her foot and kissed every toe. Each kiss sent a thrill twirling through the length of her body. She caught her breath and stretched back on the pillows, moaning softly as his lips travelled with deepening fervour along her legs and thighs.

A quiver of pleasure ran through her at the searing gentleness of his touch. She moved against him, her pliant form savouring the feel of his muscled back, revelling in the glory of his lovemaking. The heat of his lips discovering the secrets of her body inflamed her to an uninhibited wildness, a need and craving for fulfilment.

Kiss for kiss, touch for touch, she responded to Luke's caresses and as her world exploded in a heatwave of passion her body arched, her nails digging into the flesh of his back as they moulded into one. An exquisite ache throbbed through her as the rhythm of their bodies created havoc with the sane world she knew.

Slowly, she drifted back to sanity, exhausted but replete. Through lids drowsy with contentment Katherine gazed up at her husband to find him smiling triumphantly down at her. She blushed. Would he think her abandonment unseemly in a wife? The heat in her cheeks spread, tongues of fire licking her neck and breasts. She had acted shamelessly, thinking only to give him pleasure. A wife should be decorous, meek and submissive.

His soft laughter added to her despair.

'Darling, Kate,' he forced out through his amusement. 'You cannot think I'm displeased. In my wildest dreams I never hoped. . .believed I would find such perfection for my own.'

Her answering grin was mischievous as she reached out to touch the strong line of his jaw. He twisted his head, kissing her hand as it passed across his lips. Then with a sigh he levered himself on to an elbow, his expression serious.

'It will be dark in an hour. Your brother must be told of our marriage.'

Katherine shivered. The glow of happiness faded, replaced by a chill fear. 'What have I done, Luke? I

thought only of myself. But St Clere will be furious.'
Her eyes widened in horror. 'What if he should call
you out?'

'Then I must meet him.'

She sat up. 'No.'

Luke frowned. 'The consequences must be faced,
Kate.'

She threw her arms around him, holding him tight,
her lips seeking the bruise on his cheek. 'What if St
Clere was behind the attack upon you?' Tears sparkled
in her eyes. 'Why did I not stop to think? I was so
angry that they would force me to marry St Clere when
I loved you that I saw only the means of thwarting
them. Now your life could be in danger.'

Those black eyes searched hers for a long moment.
A tear spilled from her lashes to fall upon his lips. He
licked it aside. Thick black lashes lowered to shadow
the expression in his eyes and her heart jolted at the
tension which was apparent in his body.

'*You* may not have considered the consequences,
Kate. *I* knew the risks.'

CHAPTER SEVEN

'CONFOUND you, Winters. Can't you even keep your sister under control? Where the devil is she?'

St Clere's furious voice greeted Katherine and Luke's arrival at Ferncombe Place.

'I am here, my lord,' Katherine said from the doorway. 'I had no intention of remaining a prisoner in my own home—as I had no intention of being forced into an unwanted marriage.'

'You will do your duty as your father bade,' St Clere snarled. 'I've been tolerant so far, Katherine. But I saw the Bishop at Chichester today. We will be married in the cathedral on the twenty-second of the month.

Luke stepped into the room. 'That will not be possible. Katherine became my wife this afternoon.'

St Clere's jaw sagged and he snapped it shut with a hiss of venom. 'How so? Without banns—without even a special licence? It is a sham—no marriage at all!'

'I am Luke's wife in every sense of the word. We were married by a parson and the deed registered in the parish records.'

'It is a whore you became this day, not a wife,' St Clere shouted. 'The contract signed by your father is as binding as a marriage. It will be upheld in any court of the land. You've been taken in by this. . .this scurrilous fortune-hunter.'

The hall echoed to the sound of Luke's gauntlet slapped against St Clere's cheek. 'Name your seconds,' he pronounced with lethal finality. 'You'll answer for having insulted both Kate's virtue, and my honour.'

St Clere's lips drew back into a haughty sneer. 'I do not soil my sword with the blood of an inferior.'

'Then cry craven and renounce the marriage contract,' Luke jeered.

St Clere stiffened, his blue eyes freezing to an arctic coldness. 'Paul will attend me. Dawn tomorrow on the heath.'

'No!' Katherine screamed. 'Luke is not a fortune-hunter. He loves me, and I love him.'

'Then he is an arrant knave and deserves to die for his presumption,' St Clere responded.

'Stay out of this, Kate,' Luke said in a voice so deadly that it sent a shiver of fear through her. 'It will be a pleasure to teach St Clere that he cannot govern your life like a feudal overlord.'

St Clere laughed cruelly. 'She'll weep at your grave more like.'

The atmosphere in the hall crackled with tension. Katherine stared anxiously at Paul, silently pleading with him to intercede. His gaze slid away from hers. He was on St Clere's side; he would do nothing to stop the duel. Her gaze was drawn to Luke, whose bruised face was set in haughty lines. The sable eyes narrowed with rage were those of a stranger. One hand tightened over his sword-hilt, while the other touched his blackened eye.

'We have unsettled business, St Clere. This time at least we face each other man to man, instead of my being set upon by your hired ruffians.'

'This madness will stop!' Katherine rounded on the two antagonists. 'I will not have you fighting over me.' She swung round to face St Clere, her eyes blazing with contempt. 'You dare call my husband a fortune-hunter. This show of affronted pride is not because you love me. It's because you see my dowry slipping from your grasp.'

'You common little whore.' St Clere's eyes bulged with rage.

A blur of white flashed before Katherine's eyes. Then her head snapped back, her cheek smarting from the force of his slap. Caught off balance, she staggered backwards and clutched at a chair for support.

Seconds later the floorboards creaked as the Viscount lay spreadeagled on the floor, blood spurting from his cut lip. Luke crouched over him. 'For striking Kate alone I will take pleasure in running you through.'

He stepped back from the blustering Viscount, whom Paul was helping to his feet. There was an embarrassed cough from the doorway and Sergeant Hopkirk entered.

'Not wishing to intrude, Cap'n. But there's an urgent matter that's come up. The men are outside waiting.'

'Can't it wait, Sergeant?' Luke questioned.

''Fraid not, Cap'n. Concerns a fugitive. He's been seen over——'

'Very well, Sergeant,' Luke cut in before the sergeant was indiscreet. 'I'll be with you directly.'

Ignoring the two men, Luke turned to Kate. 'I have to go.'

'I'll await you at the cottage,' she said, moving to the door.

'Sister, you'll go nowhere until this damned matter is settled.'

Katherine regarded her brother with mounting hostility. She had thought he would stand by her and at least have tried to understand her feelings. 'This is no longer my home. I live with Luke now,' she said.

'Paul's right,' Luke said heavily. 'You will be safer here.'

He shut his mind to the disappointment on her face. He had seen the lascivious gleam in St Clere's eyes. Kate had withheld herself from the Viscount for so long that he would see it now as an insult to his manhood. Luke did not want Kate spending time alone in the cottage. He did not trust St Clere. In exacting his vengeance against her, a reprobate like the Viscount was capable of forcing himself on her.

When Kate opened her mouth to protest he smiled wryly. 'A wife's duty is to obey her husband. It's better this way, just for tonight. I need a clear mind for the morrow.'

He touched the red weal on her cheek and his eyes

burned into her face as though he was memorising every detail of her features. His face blurred through the mist of her tears as she stared up at him.

'You cannot fight St Clere; your injuries from yesterday place you at a disadvantage.'

'Right is on my side.'

In the face of such assurance argument was pointless. He had to know she had faith in him. Katherine closed her eyes against her pain and leaned against Luke. He must not see her fear. She swallowed against the ache in her throat. It would be useless to try and reason with him and her pleas would only make it harder for him. Opening her eyes, she allowed only her love to shine through.

She mustered a brave smile and stood on tiptoe to kiss his lips, uncaring of St Clere's outraged snarl. 'God be with you tomorrow.'

Her voice broke, and so that Luke would not witness her tears she turned and ran from the room.

Accompanied by Sergeant Hopkirk, Luke rode through the morning mist to the heath. The chill air helped clear his wits. The patrol last night had not ended until the early hours of the morning when the suspected Jacobite spy had been caught and taken to the nearest bridewell at Arundel. His duty done, Luke had returned to the cottage for a brief four hours' sleep. After the duel, the prisoner would be escorted to Chichester for questioning by the authorities.

Luke straightened in the saddle and rolled his shoulders to ease the stiffness from his bruises.

Sergeant Hopkirk swore roundly. 'You shouldn't be duelling after that beating. And as it happens you shouldn't be duelling at all. If the commander hears of it——' Hopkirk whistled between his teeth. 'You know what that means? Your career will be over. I never thought you'd fall for an heiress. You always reckoned they were poison.'

'My wife is different,' Luke replied, taking no

offence at Hopkirk's familiarity. They had known each other for many years, fought too many battles and shared too many flagons of wine together for that. Years ago Luke had saved Hopkirk's life. Not that he would ever call the man to account for such a debt. But it meant Luke could trust him to keep his mouth shut and not discuss this incident with anyone.

The sky was smudged with streaks of pink and gold, the landscape taking on ghostly black shapes as the light brightened. The mist swirled about Crusader's hoofs and hung like thistledown over the trees, distorting their shapes. The grass was wet with dew and would be slippery and dangerous when he fought St Clere.

Luke felt no fear. Despite the disadvantage of his injuries, which would stiffen some of his movements, he was an accomplished swordsman. It was said St Clere had killed three men in duels and severely wounded several more, but Luke was no preening fop who duelled to assert supremacy over another.

Six years ago he had fought his first battle at Malplaquet under the great Duke of Marlborough. It was Marlborough's last and bloodiest battle. Luke had been twenty, and the horror of the magnitude of the carnage still nauseated him today. Other minor skirmishes had followed and Luke lost count of the number of men who had died screaming at the end of his sword. Then he had killed to survive. Would he be forced to do so again today? He suspected St Clere would not be content with the mere drawing of blood.

St Clere was already at the appointed place, wrapped in a long black cloak against the chill of the dawn. Paul Winters stood next to the Viscount, and placed ostensibly in the foreground was a wagon with a plain wooden coffin on it.

Was that supposed to strike fear in him? Luke grimaced with bitter humour. If St Clere was as good as his reputation, what need he of such histrionic contrivance?

Luke dismounted and stripped off his cloak and

uniform jacket. St Clere faced him. The Viscount had removed his wig and his scalp showed pink beneath his short-cropped blond hair. Without the large periwig, St Clere's features were coarsened, the lines from a life of excess and dissipation beginning to form at the sides of his mouth and nose.

Paul Winters stepped forward and bowed curtly to Luke. In his hand were two long rapiers with ornamental silver basket-weave hilts. They were longer and lighter in the blade than the officer's sword Luke always carried. Another ruse to trick him, Luke suspected. He smiled inwardly. The Viscount could not know that during his years in Europe he had alleviated many hours of boredom by perfecting the fencing techniques of such weapons.

Luke took up both blades. They were a perfect pair with nothing between the two either in weight or, as he discovered as he slashed the blade down and across him, in the whip and strength of the blade. Having made his choice, Luke stood in readiness as St Clere brought up his weapon.

Malevolent blue eyes met with those of darkest pitch. Luke saw the Viscount's eyes narrow a fraction before he lunged. Forewarned, Luke parried the blade with ease and launched into attack. Steel rang against steel as Luke forced St Clere to retreat in defence. Brief surprise at Luke's agility and skill registered in the older man's eyes, then a guard slid over their expression and St Clere's mouth tightened.

The duel began in earnest. St Clere retaliated with lightning speed, but Luke was there before him, parrying each thrust with an expert riposte. Soon the sweat was running down St Clere's face, and Luke felt his own perspiration covering his spine. St Clere was no novice. He cunningly feinted and then lunged, and if Luke's reflexes had not been those of a trained soldier the point of his blade would have sliced through his gut. Luke leapt back and saw an opening in St Clere's guard. Bending his knee forward, Luke extended his arm and felt the tip of his sword enter the flesh of St Ciere's shoulder. He stepped back and saw the blood seep across the Viscount's shirt.

'Blood is drawn, St Clere. Honour is satisfied,' he pronounced.

'Fight on!' St Clere shouted, circling Luke, his sword flashing in the watery sunlight penetrating the grey mist.

Luke jumped back, and as he did so his boots slid on the wet grass. He went down on one knee, his teeth clenched as his arm was braced against the weight of St Clere's body when the Viscount's sword pressed down upon his own. His bruised muscles were betraying him, quivering with the exertion straining upon them, Luke gritted his teeth, summoning all his strength as the sword-point was poised an inch above his heart.

The muscles in his arms protested as St Clere's weight continued to bear down. The blue eyes above him blazed his death sentence.

'Die, Ryder! Before the night is out, Katherine will be mine.'

The Viscount's crow of triumph gave Luke the chance he needed. He could feel the tremor through the steel which showed St Clere was weakening, and drew on his reserves of strength. There was no spare flesh on his body. Hours spent in the saddle had refined his muscles to a wiry strength, which even in his weakened condition gave him a stamina which far surpassed his opponent's. He pushed upwards and with a dexterity forged from long years of soldiering he overthrew St Clere.

The Viscount cried out in fury as he stumbled backwards, his foot catching in a bramble runner. Luke rolled aside and came up on his feet in a single movement. St Clere lay sprawled on the wet ground, panting, with no strength left to rise. Breathing heavily, Luke stood over him, and pressed his sword against his throat.

'You deserve to die, but I would not taint my

marriage to Kate with your death. Acknowledge you are fairly beaten. Renounce the marriage contract signed by Kate's father before the witnesses present and you may live.'

Every vestige of colour had fled from St Clere's face. His shirt was covered in blood from shoulder to waist and down one sleeve. His bloodless lips drew back in a malicious snarl.

'Take Katherine. If she'll have you. I doubt it. She's fond enough of you—but this sham marriage——' St Clere laughed harshly '—it was an afternoon diversion. Katherine knows her duty. Even she, wild and undisciplined as she is, would not sacrifice so much. Accept it was an exciting peccadillo. Katherine knows I'm prepared to indulge her headstrong lapses. She will not forget her duty to her father. Nor is she so foolish as to cast aside her position in society to become a nobody with a husband living on her income.'

Luke tossed aside the bloodied rapier and strode to his horse. St Clere's words rang in his head. They echoed his deepest fears. As he rode he clenched and flexed his hands to ease the tension building in him. St Clere's taunting had cut deep—as the Viscount had intended.

A week ago he would have vowed that marriage was not for him. Not for several years, or so he had thought. That was before he had tasted the torment a woman like Kate Winters could inflict on a man. Her image was seared into his mind. The provocative curve of her mouth promised paradise, and the unconscious sway of her hips when she walked set his blood aflame. She was beautiful. Not in the accepted sense, like a fragile painted doll, but her high cheekbones and green eyes which turned to emerald fire when she was angry had an earthy, sensuous quality few women possessed. She moved with the grace of a swan, yet always below the surface was the unpredictable leashed power of a tigress.

Kate was special. He had known many beautiful

women and accomplished courtesans, but none had held his interest for long. Yet from the first meeting he had desired Kate, and each encounter served only to inflame him more. She was a woman made for loving. That she remained a virgin when experienced woman-isers such as St Clere paid court to her proved she was remarkable.

A familiar ache of longing tugged at him. Wanting her had become an obsession. No woman could match her. Over the years seduction had come easily to him, but with Kate he knew that would never be enough. Virtue in a woman was not unique. Yet in a woman such as Kate it was astounding. Her strength of char-acter alone tempered her natural wildness—a wildness which made her snap her fingers at convention. His Kate would not forsake their love for a title and entrée to Court.

He swung Crusader into the drive of Ferncombe Place. They would leave here today. He wanted Kate away from her brother's and St Clere's influence. He was due a fortnight's leave from the army. He would take her to Somerset to meet his family, then they would go to Rochester to look for a suitable house. On his return to duty he would request an interview with his commander and resign his commission.

In buoyant spirits he leapt from his horse—but they ebbed as he saw the great studded oak door closed against him. In all the time he had stayed at the house the door had never been closed during daylight hours. His knock was answered by Sanders.

'I have come for my wife. Kindly fetch Mrs Ryder,' Luke demanded.

'There is no one here of that name,' Sanders declared in a high, pompous voice, allowing his gaze to travel over Luke as though he were mud beneath his feet.

Luke checked his anger at the man's attitude. 'I refer to Mr Winters' sister. We were married yesterday.'

When he made to stride forward, his entrance was

blocked by Sanders's stout figure. Three more menser-
vants appeared behind the major-domo.

'*Miss* Winters is unavailable to your call, Captain
Ryder. She asked me to give you this.' He held out a
sealed letter and Luke snatched it from him and tore
open the seal. The missive was short and to the point.

Luke
    Forgive me.
    Our marriage was a mistake. How could it possibly
be legal? My duty is to obey my father's wishes. I'm
leaving Sussex for some weeks.
    Don't try and find me.
    Forget me.

Katherine

Luke crushed the letter in his fist. Kate had betrayed
him. Like all her kind, she had diverted herself at a
dragoon's expense.

'Where is the treacherous bitch?' Luke grabbed
Sanders by his lapels and shook the major-domo.
'Where?'

'Miss Winters left at first light. I was not informed
where. Just that she would not return for some weeks.'

Luke released him with a snarl. 'Tell St Clere the
day he tries to marry my wife will be the day he goes
to his grave.'

He strode away, his heart locked in granite while his
mind whirled in a tempest of white-hot fury. Kate
could not stay away forever. One day that haughty,
treacherous bitch would learn that she had picked the
wrong man to play her heartless games with.

The clock in the old hall began to strike. Drowsily,
Katherine counted the strokes. When they reached six,
she groaned in dismay. By eight she had thrown back
the bedclothes with such force that it set her head
pounding. At the stroke of ten she staggered up,
massaging the steel band which seemed to be garrotting
her skull.

How could she have slept so late? And today of all days! She had intended to be up at five and at the heath. She shook her head to clear her fuzzy vision, and the pain stabbing at her temple made her clutch hold of the bedpost with a groan. She swallowed against the bitter taste in her mouth and with a start realised that her tongue was coated and dry. She had been drugged to keep her from the duel.

Paul had tricked her! She remembered him coming to her room last night, a cup of chocolate in his hands, urging her to drink, telling her everything would be fine. He had dabbed at her tear-reddened eyes, telling her the duel was just a formality to soothe St Clere's pride. Reassured, she had drunk the chocolate he had pressed on her. When she had lain down Paul had pulled the covers to her chin.

'It will all turn out for the best, Kat,' he had said gently before leaving her.

Katherine picked up the hand-bell and rang for Tilly. She was already dressed by the time the maid appeared.

'What kept you?' she demanded, her fear for Luke fraying her temper. 'Has Paul returned? Is Captain Ryder with him?'

Tilly did not meet her gaze. 'Master Paul is in the study. Let me arrange your hair before you see him.'

Something was wrong. Tilly was white-faced and nervous. Katherine snatched the brush from the maid's shaking fingers and threw it on the bed. 'What's happened?'

Tilly backed away. 'I can't say. It's best if you speak with your brother.'

Fear made Katherine grip the maid's narrow shoulders and shake her. 'Tell me! Has something happened to Luke?'

Tilly's long face crimped with emotion. 'Oh, Miss Katherine. How could the captain have so deceived you? Those dragoons are all alike—so handsome and so treacherous.'

'Luke is safe.' Katherine sighed with relief. 'But what are you saying? Treachery? What is this?'

'It's best if Master Paul explains.' Tilly burst into tears. 'How could that dragoon have played you so false?'

Katherine ran from the room, her heart scudding with a profound dread. Tilly's blabbering made no sense. Luke was apparently safe, but what had happened?

She found her brother in the study. He looked ill at ease.

'Did Luke and St Clere fight?' she demanded.

'Yes.' Paul stood up and, turning his back on her, walked to the window. He clasped his hands behind his back and stared out across the garden. 'Your lover was unharmed. St Clere was wounded in the shoulder.'

'Then where's Luke? Why isn't he here?'

'Because the man's a treacherous dog. He was just what St Clere said he was—a fortune-hunter. I paid him off. Five thousand pounds was all it took for him to forsake you.'

'That's a lie. Luke loved me.'

'He played you for a whore.'

'That's not true. On the day of the storm he could have——' She broke off, her face reddening.

'He could have what—lain with you?' Paul rapped out with derision. 'I suppose he played the gallant and made some excuse about waiting until you were wed? How noble. He'd know you were too proud to wed a man who had allowed you to be compromised. And you fell for his sweet talk. He wanted you to believe his intentions were honourable. What better way to lull your suspicions that he was after your money? Where did this so-called wedding take place? Did you go to Parson Rudd at Paghurst?'

At encountering Katherine's tight-lipped defiance, he sneered. 'I see you did. How convenient for Ryder. A bribe to equal the one to perform that false wedding service would just as easily erase it from the records.'

Paul allowed his scathing glare to travel over her body. 'And of course Ryder had his way with you—just to ensure that we would pay a higher sum to ensure his silence.'

Katherine spun on her heel and ran to the door. 'Where are you going?' Paul demanded.

'To see Luke. I don't believe one word you've said.'

'He's gone, Kat,' Paul shouted after her. 'He left the district as soon as I handed over the money.'

Katherine ran out to the stables. She did not stop to pin up her hair or change her morning gown into a riding habit. Neither did she wait for Cassandra to be saddled. She had to see Luke to confront him. She did not believe he had played her false. But then why wasn't he at Ferncombe Place? Why hadn't he come for her? Oh, she knew well enough the reputation army officers had. Each year there was always gossip of some silly heiress who had become infatuated by one and risked elopement or, worse, found herself pregnant and disgraced. She would not believe Luke was capable of that.

The moment her mare's bridle was on, she hoisted herself on to the bare back and set off for the cottage.

Luke returned to his cottage in a furious rage. He would stop at nothing to bring St Clere and Paul Winters to justice for their Jacobite sympathies. And if Kate was involved with their plots then God help her, for he would not. He did not have enough evidence to condemn St Clere yet. But in a week or two he would. He would call for reinforcements and have both St Clere and Paul Winters watched night and day.

And Kate would not escape his vengeance. She would pay for every lie, every deceit she had used against him. He had a very particular score to settle with that haughty bitch.

As he drew near his cottage he was surprised to see six army horses tethered outside. None of them belonged to his troop, and the fact that they were splashed with mud and their heads drooped with tiredness warned Luke that they had been ridden hard and for some considerable time.

'Gentlemen!' he said as he stepped through the door. He stiffened as he saw his saddlebags, packed with his belongings, on the table.

A stout major in a large powdered campaign wig stood up, the five soldiers rising with him.

'Captain Luke Ryder?'

Luke nodded.

'I am Major Riggley. And I arrest you, Ryder, for duelling,' he said in the high nasal tones so often affected by the sons of noblemen. 'You will answer the charges against you in London. I must ask you to hand over your sword.'

Grim-faced, Luke handed over his weapon. This bore the stamp of St Clere. The man took no chances.

'Have you nothing to say for yourself, Captain?' the foppish major whined.

Luke studied him with barely concealed insolence. Riggley was the type of officer he despised. Money, not ability, had brought him his commission. He was overweight, overbearing and over-indulged in every excess. His hooked nose and bulbous eyes showed a cruel and bullying trait in his nature. But like all bullies he did not have the backbone to hold Luke's piercing glare.

'I will answer to my commanding officer—not his lap-dog,' he asserted.

The major's fleshy features contorted and his prim mouth almost disappeared within the folds of his jowls.

'From the looks of his battered face, Ryder makes a habit of brawling,' he grunted. 'Sergeant, bind his arms; the man's clearly dangerous.'

Luke suffered the indignity of having his wrists bound and was pushed out of the cottage towards his horse. 'You must have been attended by a second. Who was it?' Riggley demanded.

Luke remained silent.

'No mind. My men will discover who attended you.

There was a Sergeant Hopkirk missing from his quarters this morning.' The major heaved his ungainly weight into the saddle. He turned to a young captain whose face was peppered with smallpox scars. 'Basset, take over Captain Ryder's duties here. Move the patrol further on to Petersfield. There's nothing to be gained by our presence in this district——'

'With respect, sir,' Luke interrupted, 'Highclere is the centre of Jacobite plots in this district.'

'You have a personal feud with St Clere. It does you no service, Captain Ryder, to slander his good name.' The major regarded Captain Basset pompously. 'Nothing of this incident must be spoken of. Should you be asked you will not mention this incident. You need only say that Captain Ryder has been recalled to London to take up further duties. There is the good name of His Majesty's army to consider. There's ill-feeling enough in this district for King George without a scandal making it worse.'

Luke rode away from Ferncombe in silence. St Clere clearly had friends in high places. He had thought of everything. Except that St Clere had seriously under-estimated his adversary. Luke was unimpressed by the Viscount's title and wealth. Neither was he intimated by the nobleman's threats. This was but one more score to add to the reckoning.

Katherine arrived at the cottage to find it deserted. All of Luke's possessions were gone. Still she did not believe Luke had betrayed her trust. She rode into the village, where she was told that the soldiers had ridden out under the command of a Captain Basset. Captain Ryder had been summoned to London.

The news shocked her. Luke *had* left without leaving word. She walked slowly back across the village green, leading her mare. Paul was right. If Luke loved her, he would never have left without sending word.

Her head bowed and she clenched her fist to combat the pain enclosing her heart. He had never been interested in her as a woman; it was her money which had led him to pay court to her. And she, gullible fool, had believed him.

'Good day, Miss Winters.' Parson Goodbody tipped his wide-brimmed hat in salute to her.

Her head came up and the expression in her eyes made the gentle preacher grow pale. Her green eyes burned with a luminous brilliance, an unholy fire which sparked iridescent flames—but it was a fire without heat. The parson shivered. The look in Katherine Winters' eyes was as icy as the Devil's breath.

Katherine did not acknowledge Parson Goodbody's greeting; she had not even seen him. She was numbed by Luke's betrayal. Her pride was cut to shreds, and all her passionate nature rose at the injustice. Now pain was fast turning that passion to loathing. The arrogance of the man smote her. Did he think he could just ride out of her life without paying the consequences?

It was time that arrogance of his was humbled. When next they met. . . She ran her tongue over her lips in anticipation: there would be a next meeting. Her lips curved into a mirthless smile. In the future both a meeting and a reckoning would be made.

CHAPTER EIGHT

ON HER return to Ferncombe Place Katherine was annoyed to discover St Clere waiting for her, but she was too wretched over Luke's betrayal to wish to confront the Viscount. Whether the marriage ceremony was legal or not, Katherine regarded her vows as binding. In her eyes she was still Luke's wife.

'My dear Katherine.' St Clere stood up as she entered the parlour. One sleeve of his purple brocade jacket was pinned over a white silk sling.

She felt guilty that he had been hurt. 'My lord, I'm sorry to see you were wounded.'

The Viscount was pale, but his expression showed no animosity. To her surprise, he looked concerned for her welfare.

'It was a small price to pay to save you from that fortune-hunter,' he said gallantly. 'The man was a rogue.'

'I see it has not occurred to either Paul or yourself that I may not have wished to be saved. I love Luke Ryder. He is my husband.'

'That was no marriage,' said St Clere testily.

'Vows were spoken, my lord,' she answered icily. 'In God's eyes, if not the law's, I became Luke Ryder's wife.'

'Your pride is hurt. We all love unwisely at some time in our lives. Ryder has betrayed and deserted you.' His tone was soft and coercing as he moved closer. 'Katherine, we have known each other too long to let this unfortunate *mésalliance* come between us. For your own good you must put the regrettable episode behind you. In time you will realise how caring your father was of your welfare. I wish our marriage contract to stand, but I am prepared to give you time.

I was wrong to try and force you.' His expression was tender but without passion. 'I have a very deep regard for you, more so than I have felt for any woman. We both spoke in anger yesterday.'

She shook her head. 'Now more than ever I know the folly of marriage. I will never wed again. Please accept my decision, my lord.'

St Clere smiled and waved a hand in denial. 'I would not abandon you so heartlessly. Events are moving fast in the Pretender's cause. Paul is about to leave for Scotland, and but for my wound I would go with him. I will remain in the south to persuade other peers to support our rightful King. In the meantime I would like to think we remained friends.'

Katherine's guilt intensified. He had every right to admonish her; instead he was being charming and considerate. It soothed her wounded pride. 'I wronged you once, my lord. I would not do so again. Only if you believe that I mean never to re-marry can I accept your offer of friendship. If you will forgive me, my lord, I would like to be alone.'

St Clere watched Katherine as she mounted the stairs to her room. Her pride was crushed, but her shoulders remained unbowed. He had seen the resilient glitter in her eyes. She would never forgive Ryder for his betrayal.

St Clere smiled with satisfaction. The abandoned way she had entered into an affair with the captain proved she was capable of great passion. Such a woman could not live long without a man's attentions. The thought of Katherine in his bed excited his jaded palate. She would make an unforgettable mistress, but as his wife she would bring with her the dowry he needed to rebuild his family's fortunes.

And he would have Katherine Winters' dowry. He would kill any man who tried to steal it from him. Luke Ryder had escaped lightly. He was only alive now because the young fool Winters refused to have any part in the dragoon's murder.

St Clere began to whistle as he walked out of the house. It was better this way. The letter he had written copying Katherine's hand had worked. Ryder was furious, believing he had been betrayed. The message sent to Major Riggley—a secret Jacobite—would ensure that Ryder was dismissed in disgrace from the army. Apart from his interest in Katherine, Ryder had begun to delve too closely into Jacobite affairs. St Clere had laid enough charges against the dragoon to have him cool his heels in prison for many months to come.

As for Katherine. . . St Clere contemplated his triumph over her. The riches of the Winters family would be his. Paul was a rash adventurer. If he fell in battle, Katherine would inherit everything. It was also time she learned humility towards her superiors. There was more than one way to get Katherine in his bed and the Winters fortune in his coffers.

Luke spent the first night of his arrest in Guildford gaol. He paced the tiny cell for hours, working off his anger and resentment. From outside in the street he heard the night-watch call two o'clock. There was a jangle of keys and his cell door opened.

Four brawny men came in, one holding a lantern. The set of their faces was disquieting. Luke tensed. He looked at the ginger-bearded man who was nearest to him for an explanation. Ignoring Luke's querying glance, the man jerked his head towards him. Luke found his arms grabbed and he was overpowered before he could stop them.

'Where are you taking me?' he demanded as they dragged him outside.

'Riggley requires the pleasure of your company,' the ginger-bearded man grunted sarcastically.

Luke was hauled through the gaol and into the dark street. He was taken across the road to a private house, and as he was roughly shoved down the cellar steps he

saw Major Riggley standing in the circle of light from
a candelabra.

'Good evening, Ryder.' Riggley grinned cruelly. The
major stood with his hands behind his back and from
his flushed face he had been drinking heavily. The
cellar was empty except for a large barrel lying on its
side.

'What's the meaning of this?' Luke demanded. 'I'm
answerable to Colonel Peters—no one else.'

'St Clere said you needed a lesson in respect towards
your superiors,' Riggley drawled. He turned to the
men holding Luke. 'Get his coat off and shackle him
to the barrel.'

Luke started back as he saw the chains attached to
iron rings set in the wall.

Riggley smirked and, bringing his hands from behind
his back, cracked the cat-o'-nine-tails he was holding
in the air.

Fury gouged through Luke, and with a snarl of
outrage he kicked out at the men holding him. At the
same time he twisted his already bruised body in a vain
attempt to heave the men off his arms. One man
loosened his hold, but the others held fast. His jacket
was wrenched from his body along with his shirt as
they hauled him, still fighting, over the barrel. He
received several punches to his ribs and head before
they finally succeeded in locking the manacles over his
wrists.

'God rot you, Riggley,' Luke swore. 'This is infamous. I'm an officer of the King. I demand a trial.'

The handle of the whip cracked down across Luke's
mouth. 'Silence. You're a disgrace to your uniform. A
seducer. A fortune-hunter.'

Luke spat out a chipping from a front tooth, the
blood from his torn chin dripping down the barrel in
front of his face.

The four men who had brought him slunk out. None
had been in uniform. This was then a private vendetta
and nothing to do with the army.

'You won't be so handsome after I've done with you.' Spittle sprayed from Riggley's mouth. 'Nor so likely to run off with another's bride.'

Luke raised his head, his arms straining as he craned back to vent his contempt. 'St Clere put you up to this. Have you Jacobite sympathies as well, Riggley?'

The first blow of the whip caught Luke unawares. He caught back a gasp as the pain bore through his naked back. He clamped shut his teeth, braced for the next strike. His face contorted as the flesh was stripped away, but no sound came from his lips. Not once did he cry out, but he could not control the writhing of his body, or the muscles knotting in his shoulders as the blood began to run down his spine. There was only the pain, excruciating and hate-generating in its agony.

He heard an enraged shout from some distance behind him. The blows ceased and the shouting dimmed to a drone as he lay gasping, slumped over the barrel. A groan was torn from him as he was lifted, the pain so terrible that he lost consciousness.

A week later, with the fever barely cleared from his brain, Luke was court-martialled.

He was found guilty and dishonourably discharged from the army. That humiliation was a greater torment than the whipping. When Luke left the courtroom, gallantry and chivalry were dead within him. His pride could not be broken and, to appease it, his hatred festered for those who had brought him to this.

Upon his return to his room to collect his possessions he was surprised to find Colonel Peters seated before the burning fire. Sergeant Hopkirk hovered awkwardly by the window.

Luke acknowledged the sergeant's presence with a softening of his rugged features. Hopkirk had saved his life. On hearing of Luke's arrest, Hopkirk had guessed St Clere was involved. He knew enough about the Viscount to have learned that he was a friend of Major Riggley. Hopkirk also knew, from a soldier who had

served under the major some years ago, that Riggley
was in the habit of whipping a subordinate on the
flimsiest of excuses. Hopkirk had ridden to Major
Grant, a friend of Luke's, who was commanding a
garrison at Dorking. Grant had been appalled at
Hopkirk's story. It was known to him that Riggley had
a house in Guildford, and since it was likely Riggley's
troop must stop for the night it was possible they would
find Luke in Guildford gaol. They had arrived at the
major's house just in time to prevent Luke's being
beaten to death.

Colonel Peters indicated the chair opposite him. 'Sit
down, Ryder. I suspect your disposition towards the
army at the moment is not very charitable, but I would
have you hear me out.'

Luke sat opposite the colonel, who had not been
present at the court-martial. He had known him since
he had joined the regiment as a young cornet, nine
years ago.

The colonel regarded him with a forthright stare.
'What got into you, Ryder? You were one of my best
men. I never had you down as a fortune-hunter, or
even a philanderer for that matter. To risk your career
upon a duel over a woman was the height of madness—
especially a woman who's reputed to become the next
Countess of Brent.'

Luke faced his commander's censure stiff-backed
and head high, as he had faced every charge at his
court-martial. He did not deign to answer. He would
make no excuses for his conduct.

Colonel Peters shook his head. 'Hopkirk tells me
you actually married the woman.'

Luke's eye narrowed as he regarded the sergeant.

'Hopkirk told me in your best interest,' Colonel
Peters remarked. 'Have you learned nothing from your
fellow officers? Did you think her family would allow
such an heiress to wed a soldier? Or that a man of St
Clere's standing would stand by and allow himself to
be ridiculed? The damned man wears that sling over

his wound like a banner proclaiming your guilt.' He paused and looked at Luke steadily. 'St Clere would keep a foot in both camps. With his wounded arm, he can offer his sympathies to the Pretender, while actually being unable to fight for him. He's often at Court now, toadying to those ministers who have the King's ear.'

'St Clere is a Jacobite,' Luke said harshly. 'Had I more time I would have proved it. Riggley's in with them too.'

'Ay, that much has been proven.'

Luke sat up, his eyes bright with interest as he leaned forward on the chair.

Colonel Peters smiled at Sergeant Hopkirk. 'Hopkirk's loyalty to you goes further than saving your life. He was party to your plans to hunt down the Jacobite leaders. On information you had already given him he put the pressure on an informer. Riggley was already under arrest for his treatment to you. When he learned we had discovered his treason. . .' the colonel's voice hardened '. . .the snivelling milksop had a pistol smuggled into him. He blasted his brains out.'

'That was convenient for St Clere. The major was in his pay. With me out of the way, he thought to keep secret his Jacobite sympathies,' Luke commented.

'Not to mention his pursuit of Miss Winters and her estimable dowry.'

Luke sat back, his voice clipped with loathing. 'Had I died at the hands of Riggley, St Clere's interests would have been well served.'

'Have you wondered why I did not speak up for you at your trial?' The colonel tapped his fingers together as he studied Luke closely.

The proud tilt of Luke's chin told him that the colonel had likely consigned him to hell for deserting him.

Colonel Peters shrugged. 'For that I apologise. St Clere has influential friends and they were set upon your downfall. My word against so many would have been useless. What say you if I offered you a chance to

redeem your name, and bring St Clere and all
Jacobites to justice?'

'Whatever needs be done. I will do it,' Luke assured
him.

'It will mean a new identity. There will be funds to
recruit as many men as you need. You will report
direct to me. I, in turn, am answerable to the Secretary
of State.'

Luke took the colonel's hand to seal the bargain.

The next morning Luke stepped back from the
mirror to study his reflection critically in the mirror.
The long, curling black periwig changed the outline of
his face, and the silk mask partially concealed his eyes.
But what was most effective of all in changing his
appearance was the indented scar on his chin and
chipped tooth where Riggley had slashed him across
the mouth. Once the dark line of stubble above his
upper lip had grown for another week into a sleek
moustache, the disguise would be perfect.

Satisfied, Luke marched out of the house to begin
his new role as a man called Hunter. God have mercy
on his prey, for he had no room but for vengeance in
his heart. Unlike Hal Penrose, he had survived a
misplaced love-affair with an heiress bitch. What he
did now he did to avenge Hal's death and teach a
lesson to those who believed their fortune put them
above justice.

November gales battered the Sussex landscape, stripping bare the last of the autumn leaves, uprooting trees
and shredding the thatch from the village cottages.
Each day Katherine rode over the estate supervising
repairs to the barns, walls and labourers' cottages. She
welcomed the long hours of work which stopped her
dwelling on Luke's betrayal.

During the last month St Clere was regularly at
Ferncombe Place and despite her earlier qualms he had
become a welcome visitor. Paul was in Scotland and

without St Clere's companionship Katherine would have found the evening hours lying heavily upon her.

Since Luke's desertion St Clere had proved himself a good friend. It was agreed no mention would be made of marriage, and Katherine began to relax and enjoy his company. He spared no pains to charm her out of her melancholy, hiring strolling players, minstrels and even tumblers for her entertainment. After the estate business was completed, they rode or went hawking every day. If the weather was bad St Clere rode over in his carriage and they exercised by walking in the long gallery which ran the length of the third storey of the house. On these days St Clere would sing to her and she would accompany him on the harpsichord.

Gradually the pain of Luke's betrayal eased, but it was always there fermenting. In St Clere's company she found she could be happy again, but at night the demons returned to haunt her, her hatred for the dragoon growing until she knew she would never be whole again until he had been made to pay for the way he had abused her love.

Today she had ridden over to Highclere Hall. It was a rare sunny November day, the sky cloudless—a day to be savoured before the mists and dreariness of winter turned the landscape grey and uninviting. Peacocks strutted across the lawns of Highclere, and with amusement Katherine watched them as St Clere came out to greet her.

'Let us stroll awhile in the gardens,' he suggested. 'I must leave in an hour for a meeting, I'm afraid.'

A light breeze ruffled Katherine's fair ringlets and the crisp late autumn air brought a glow to her cheeks.

To make up for his departure, St Clere was at his most witty. He lampooned King George with cutting asperity, neither did he spare the King's two bizarre and rapacious German mistresses. They, in St Clere's eyes, were only remarkable because they were both so incredibly ugly. At his anecdotes Katherine laughed so

hard that tears ran down her cheeks until finally she
was forced to hold on to St Clere's arm for support.

Taking a scented handkerchief from the deep cuff of
his jacket, St Clere tenderly dabbed the tears of
laughter from her cheeks. They stood very close, her
face almost on a level with his own.

'It is good to hear you laughing again, Katherine,'
he murmured.

She did not move away, but took his hand to remove
it from her cheek. He smiled and pulled her hand so
that it lay against his heart, before he raised it to his
lips. When she would have drawn back, her eyes
saddened as her gaze rested on the sling he still wore.
The muscle of St Clere's shoulder had been penetrated
by the sword and was slow to heal. It made his sword
arm useless, and was a reminder of all she wished to
forget.

In the distance she heard a dog barking. She peered
to see if she could see it, and before she turned her
attention to St Clere she saw a horseman outlined
against the sky on the low crest of the hill.

'Are you thinking of Paul?' St Clere said, close to
her ear. 'You must be missing him. Would that I could
have been with him when King James's standard was
raised at Braemar.'

There was no recrimination in his voice that his
useless sword arm prevented him fighting in the Rising,
but Katherine blamed herself. She hung her head.
'Because of me, you cannot fight for the cause you
believe in.' The restraint of the past weeks broke
without warning and her body began to tremble violently. 'How could Luke have played me so false?'

She was drawn into the circle of St Clere's arm. 'Cry,
my dear,' he soothed. 'Don't hold back.'

Gradually the warmth from his embrace eased her
sobs. Embarrassed by her weakness, Katherine finally
drew back from him.

'Your pardon, my lord. I'm not usually so weak and
foolish,' she apologised.

'Your tears are understandable, my dear.' His face was inches from her own. 'It's time you forgot Ryder. You are young. Would you deny yourself happiness?'

Uncomfortable at their closeness, she pulled back from him, but his arm remained firm around her shoulders. It was an embrace without passion, meant to comfort her. Unwilling to talk about Luke, she voiced her other fears. 'I worry about Paul. And your safety, my lord. In the last months of Queen Anne's reign your voice was one of the loudest in urging Her Majesty to name her half-brother as successor. Even if you cannot fight, your name is linked with that of James Stuart's cause.'

His fingers dug into her shoulders as he regarded her grave face. 'The plans for the Rising in the south of England go slowly.'

The indolent gallant was gone. Instead she was looking into the face of a man implacable and dedicated to his ideal. As heir to the Earldom of Brent, he stood to lose far more than her brother should the Rising fail. Her fears focused upon St Clere's safety.

'You will take care, my lord,' she urged.

He laughed softly. 'I've waited weeks to hear you speak with such concern.' He cupped her chin in his fingers, tilting her head to meet his taunting gaze. Guessing his intention was to kiss her, she placed a hand upon his chest and pushed back from him.

'Come, now, Katherine, 'tis unlike you to be prudish,' he teased. 'A kiss. Is it too much to ask? Tomorrow I go to London to rally recruits for King James. I could be gone for some weeks. Would you refuse an injured warrior?'

Katherine offered him her cheek to placate him, but she should have known he would not stop at that. His fingers gripped her chin and turned her face to meet his lips. He kissed her long and with masterly thoroughness, but she remained stiff and unresponsive until he finally drew back. Once his kisses had been capable of stirring her, though never with the soul-searing inten-

sity which Luke aroused—even now the memory of
Luke's kisses was too strong for her to respond to the
Viscount's ardour.

Their walk had led them to the fountain and she
wished their steps had taken them elsewhere. The
fountain reminded her of the night of the reception
when Luke had first kissed her. It was in the shadow of
this hedge that he had begun the seduction which had
stolen her heart. She turned away to stare down the
long walkway leading to the far end of the garden and
her gaze lifted to the rolling downs behind the boundary wall.

She frowned. The horseman she had seen earlier was
motionless, watching them, his figure black and forbidding against the blue sky. The boundary wall was low
here, and behind rose the slopes of the heath. For an
instant her heart catapulted at the way the horseman
held his head to one side, reminding her of Luke.

Instinctively, she put out a hand towards the rider.
But he wheeled his horse about and disappeared over
the brow of the hill.

Of course it would not be Luke. He was in London,
no doubt gambling and whoring away the five thousand
pounds which Paul had paid him to abandon her.

She blinked aside an angry tear. Her hand went to
her throat where her wedding-ring hung on a gold
chain beneath her gown. She had taken it from her
finger on the day of Luke's desertion, but had never
been able to discard it. She told herself it was a
reminder of the folly of love—of bartering something
as precious as her independence.

'Is anything wrong?' St Clere asked. 'You look
flushed. You've not caught a chill, have you?'

She turned to face him and put her hand lightly upon
his sling. 'I'm not worthy of your concern, my lord.'

St Clere gave a low chuckle. She should have fore-
seen he would take her remark as a challenge. 'You
are most worthy, my dear. Now, regrettably, I must

attend my meeting. I will ride with you back to Ferncombe.'

Throughout the short ride St Clere flirted with her outrageously. Had he guessed something of her thoughts? He was showing her she must not pine her life away, and it was impossible not to respond to his irrepressible charm.

Back in the courtyard of her home, Katherine dismounted and looked up into his handsome face. There were lines of pain around his mouth as he eased the discomfort of his arm and she wished then that it were in her power to love him. But her heart was dead.

'Thank you for another enjoyable day, my lord,' she said.

For a man with a wounded shoulder he moved quickly, taking her by surprise. He leant down from the saddle and kissed her, but his horse side-stepped, parting them. She was about to upbraid St Clere for his boldness when a movement by the gates caught her attention.

Her heart jolted and a prickling at the nape of her neck alerted her to danger.

The rider who fleetingly reminded her of Luke now studied them from the village green. The man was cloaked and his three-cornered hat was pulled low over his brow, obscuring his features. A shiver whipped through her body. There was something about the rigidness of his tall figure which made her feel he was passing judgement on them.

Katherine stiffened. Throwing back her head, she looked coldly back at him. It was as though he was awaiting a reaction from them. How dared he spy on them?

'Do you know that man?' she asked St Clere. 'It's the second time today I've caught him watching us.'

'What man?'

'The rider on the green.'

St Clere smiled indulgently. 'There's no one there, my dear. What did he look like?'

Katherine saw that he was right. The horseman had gone. 'I could not see his face, but there was something about the way he sat his horse which reminded me of Luke.'

'You need not fear it was Ryder,' he said, so emphatically that Katherine looked askance at him.

But St Clere had gathered up his reins and prepared to leave. 'That scoundrel will not have the effrontery to show his face in Ferncombe again. Take care while I am away, my dear. When I return I may have news of Paul for you.'

Luke stood by the village millpond and watched St Clere ride out of Ferncombe Place. Hatred scoured him at the touching scene he had witnessed between Kate and her lover. The second today. It confirmed all he believed of her. She was a born coquette. She had amused herself with him. From those tender scenes it was obvious she now saw herself as Countess, when the Viscount inherited the Earldom of Brent.

Not that Luke intended St Clere should live that long. The price of treason was death. Luke adjusted the mask he wore over his face and eased the still tender whip-cuts on his back. St Clere had many crimes against him to answer.

Unfortunately it had not been easy to find the evidence to denounce St Clere as a traitor. The Viscount was covering his tracks well. Since the injury to his shoulder he had played a double game. He had taken to cultivating staunch Hanoverian friends, while Luke could only suspect that some of his other exploits were linked with the Jacobites. But he would find that link. And when he did St Clere would pay for his treachery.

As would all Jacobites, Kate included. The cause was doomed, Luke was certain. Since the Pretender had raised his standard, there had been no great army of discontents flocking to his banner. In the south Jacobite recruits were even scarcer. Even the Catholic lords were playing a waiting game, and such indecision would cost James Stuart any chance of the throne.

Once St Clere was behind bars he would teach Kate Winters the lesson she deserved. Because of her he had been whipped like an animal, ignobly dismissed from the army, his name blackened, and he had brought shame to his family. The vows spoken in the hamlet church bound Kate to him as his wife. Her dishonour was his dishonour. She would rue the day she had dismissed him as if he were a serf.

Luke watched St Clere ride away from the village, and when there was a discreet distance between them he followed. As he passed Ferncombe Place, he saw Kate walk out of the stables. She was swinging her riding hat by its ribbon, and his insides clenched. She looked so beautiful and desirable that for a moment he was tempted to ride up and snatch her into his arms. But then a bleak look entered his eyes and his fists closed. He cursed himself for allowing her to breach the defences he believed he had built against her wiles. Forewarned, he would make himself immune to her beauty—a cool head and not hot blood was needed to teach Kate Winters her place.

It was seeing her come out of the stable which had destroyed his control—the stable where she had given herself so ardently to his kiss, her body moulding pliantly against his. From that moment he had been touched with a madness to possess her, to make her completely and forever his.

Passion had blinded him. Never again. Especially to a woman like that. . .a selfish, spoilt heiress. She was as bad as the rest of her kind. . .

CHAPTER NINE

WHEN one was alone and living on a dagger's-edge of fear for a loved one, each hour became a day, and a week dragged by with the slowness of a season. Or so the next two weeks seemed like that to Katherine. St Clere had contrived to send her a letter by messenger, and it had contained no word of Paul, but proclaimed his devotion to her. She had sent the messenger away without a reply. The Viscount's letter disturbed her. He had broken his word not to speak of love, or marriage, and it was news of Paul she hungered for. All she heard was the rumours of the Rising. And they grew more alarming with each day.

It was said the Pretender had landed in Scotland and his Catholic army were slaughtering and torturing any Protestant who refused to fight. Those tales she discounted. Had the Pretender even left the safety of France? she wondered. Rumours always conflicted. The most frequently heard was that the Pretender was still at St Germain. That added to her fears. How could he expect others to risk their lives for his cause while he remained safe in exile? Even the Scots were reluctant to support their tardy King. Only a handful of Scottish lords had come out with their men.

If the Pretender's cause was so poorly supported in Scotland, the land of the Stuarts, what hope had it in England? From what she knew of the pragmatic George of Hanover, he would show no favour to any rebel. What then would be Paul's fate? At the least they would lose Ferncombe Place. What worried Katherine was that Paul would lose his life. And there was nothing she could do to halt the consequences of her brother's deeds.

Faced with another sleepless night of worry,

Katherine did not retire. She sat on the Persian rug before the fire in the parlour.

Her bitter reverie was shattered by a thunderous knocking on the door. Without allowing time for a servant to have answered the knock, there was the stamp of booted feet marching across the hall. There was a threatening ring to the sound. Alarmed, Katherine stood up. Her hand touched the dagger which was permanently in a sheath at her waist, but was hidden by the folds of her gown. It reassured her. She only hoped there would be no need to use it.

She heard Sanders shout a protest. It was answered by a West Country voice snapping out an order.

Angry that someone had stormed into her house and was ordering her servants, Katherine hurried to the hall. There was no one there. She frowned. Had she imagined the danger?

The silence should have reassured her. Instead a premonition of danger remained, snatching away her breath. The library door was open and a light flared from within as a candle was lit. From the back of the house Tilly screamed. Katherine was outraged into action.

'Who dares molest my servants?' she demanded.

Three men armed with pistols were in the dimly lit hall. Two were pushing Sanders and Grimshaw down into the cellar. Another man, wearing a long woollen cloak and a muffler over his lower face, stood outside the library door.

'What's happening here?' she cried, though she had a sickening dread that the men were robbers.

'Bring the woman in here,' the West Countryman commanded.

The man on the door nodded for Katherine to obey, and her hand tightened over the dagger-hilt. She needed no second bidding; her temper was roused that anyone had dared to invade her home. The candle illuminated the library desk but cast the alcoves of bookshelves into black shadow.

'Be seated,' the terse, clipped voice ordered.

She spun round to face its owner, too outraged to give in to her fear. 'I demand an explanation for this intrusion into my house. Who are you, sir? If you are thieves. . .'

'*Sit down!*' the voice rapped out from the darkness. It was edged with threat. There was a huskiness behind the heavy accent which tugged at her memory. 'You will demand nothing. We are not thieves. I am known as Hunter. My purpose here is to learn the whereabouts of your brother.'

The man was a government agent sent to find Paul. Katherine's blood turned cold, but she allowed nothing of her fear to show on her face. She gripped hold of the chair-back, refusing to be ordered like a servant in her own home. Her head lifted as she glared defiantly into the darkness, seeing a tall, cloaked figure outlined against the moonlit window.

'My brother left Sussex some weeks ago to settle business affairs in London. After that he intended to visit friends in Berkshire. I do not expect him to return to Sussex for at least another month,' she said.

'You are a liar, madam, and an accomplished one at that. Your brother is in Scotland, is he not?'

Katherine braced herself against the accusation in his tone. She drew herself taller, her glare venomous as it pierced the shadows. 'You insult me, sir.' Her cheeks burned as she stirred her anger, knowing that it was her only defence. 'You break into my house like a sneak thief in the middle of the night. There are laws to protect innocent citizens. Be assured that the full weight of them will be brought upon your head.'

Her defiance was met with a harsh laugh and the stranger moved out of the shadows. As the candle-light fell across his face, Katherine saw that he was masked. In London it was common practice for men and women of quality to hide their identity behind silk masks when they travelled the streets. Here in the country it was generally Tobymen intent on robbing travellers who adopted such disguise.

'In this matter, madam, I am the law.'

Katherine stood her ground, haughty and defiant, though her stomach quaked with fear. There was something very sinister about this whole episode. She gripped her hands together to still their trembling. She would not be intimidated. Exercising rigid control, she resolved to remain calm and bluff her way through this encounter. 'No man is above the law, Mr Hunter.'

'It's just Hunter.' The black silk mask covered the upper part of his face and through the eye-slits dark, satanic eyes glittered as he regarded her without pity. 'You have much to answer for.'

With deepening fear Katherine recognised him as the man who had watched her and St Clere on the Viscount's last day in Sussex. But it was more than that which alerted her to danger. The voice was that of a stranger, but his stance and manner reminded her of her husband. It destroyed her composure. She took a steadying breath. Her imagination and overwrought nerves were playing tricks with her mind. Both men were of similar height and build, that was all. Luke always wore his hair tied back in a queue and was clean-shaven. Hunter wore a full-bottomed black wig and had a narrow black moustache. The strong jaw was also similar, but Hunter had a scar across his chin which Luke did not. Even so, the resemblance was unnerving and she found herself staring at his full lips. Then his mouth twitched, the lips curling back into a wolfish grin. The illusion was gone; a chipped front tooth changed his appearance entirely.

He indicated the chair. 'If you are not prepared to answer my questions you will be arrested and taken to a place better served for such purposes.'

There was a ruthlessness beneath his cool exterior which frightened her. He meant exactly what he said. Reluctantly she spread her skirts to sit down. He watched every movement, his dark eyes blazing behind the mask.

Refusing to let him see how badly she was shaken, she demanded, 'What have you done with my servants?'

'They are safe under guard in the cellar. I shall speak with all of them before I leave. They will know your brother's activities since his return from France.' His lips drew back into a bitter smile. 'Now give me the dagger I know you always carry—handle first and no tricks.'

Was there no secret safe from this devil? she seethed. Her hand hesitated upon the jewelled dagger-hilt. For an instant she was tempted to draw it and use it against this demon who had forced himself into her home. His lips drew back into a grim smile. Had he guessed her thoughts? There was a glitter in his eyes which dared her to act against him. He lifted his head, challenging her in an assured manner which was so like Luke that she faltered.

Too late she realised her mistake; his hand shot out, closing over hers, and with a flick of his wrist he wrenched the dagger from her fingers.

'Try anything so foolish again and you'll regret it!' He released her abruptly. His look was so filled with hatred that Katherine flinched.

She stood up, refusing to remain at a disadvantage with him looming over her. 'I don't like being threatened, Hunter. This is my house and you are an uninvited intruder. I have a right to defend myself.'

For a brief moment Katherine thought she detected admiration glinting in his eyes at her defiance. Then his lips set in an uncompromising line. If he was a government agent he could have her arrested and taken away for questioning. She suppressed a shiver. Once his prisoner, she would be at his mercy.

And just how much did he know about Paul's involvement with the Jacobites?

He sat on the edge of the desk, his hands folded

across his chest as he studied her with leisurely thoroughness. 'You are adept with words. But are they in defence of innocence, or a clever ruse to avert your guilt?'

Beneath the mask his jaw was as unyielding as rock, the full lips uncomfortably close to her own twisting into a sardonic leer. Glaring up at him, Katherine encountered the blazing fury in his black eyes. A stab of familiarity halted her words. Why did she keep confusing his image with that of Luke? The pain of Luke's betrayal remained a raw and aching wound. Would she never be free of the humiliation he had heaped upon her? Must every man of similar stature and build remind her of her faithless lover?

Hunter moved back into the shadows, his voice pitiless. 'This house is known to have entertained Jacobite supporters. Just this week a Jacobite messenger brought a letter here. I weary of your lies. I want the truth.'

Katherine gripped her hands together until her knuckles showed white. It was disconcerting to realise that her movements had been spied on. Her first instinct was to respond with anger—but that would be foolhardy. A level head was needed to deal with a man of Hunter's scurrilous breed. He must be referring to St Clere's letter, for no other messengers had come to Ferncombe. Had nothing missed the vigilance of this man?

'The letter to which you refer is from a close family friend,' she said.

'From the man you would take as your future husband.' If his voice had been cold and impersonal before, now there was a lethal chill to it. 'St Clere is a fervent Jacobite.'

Katherine held her tongue against denying her relationship with St Clere. If the man did not know of her marriage to Luke, she would not enlighten him. She did not wish to explain to such a man the humiliation of her husband's desertion. Besides, if he believed that St Clere was her betrothed, what was more natural than the Viscount's writing to her?

She raised a brow, regarding him with wry mockery. 'What can a government agent of your standing find sinister in a love letter?'

'Because I know you capable of deceit and treachery.' The tilt of his head was unmistakable, even before his voice returned to normal, his West Country accent dropped as he poured out his scorn. His dark eyes were bright and as merciless as the devil's.

Her mind must be playing her false again. It could not be true! Her eyes widened in disbelief as she stared at him.

'You have a conveniently short memory,' he jeered as he reached up to untie the silk mask and lowered it from his face. Katherine swayed, her mind buffeted with shock. She had not been mistaken.

'So, Kate!' he murmured with deceptive calmness. 'At last you deign to recognise me. Did you think I would just ride away and forget your treachery? You should go on the stage for the performance you gave to draw me off any Jacobite scent. You were a worthy spy, above and far beyond the call of duty.'

Shocked by the unexpectedness of Luke's reappearance, the pain of his betrayal reopened. She leapt to her feet, her eyes wild as the weeks of anger bubbled from within her. 'You dare talk to me of treachery? You knave!' She raised her fist to beat his chest, but both her hands were taken by his and forced down to her sides. They stood chest to thigh, both breathing heavily as their hatred consumed them.

'I see it all now. You were using me to find out more. . .' Suddenly through her rage she saw the precipice into which she had so nearly plunged. In her fury she had almost blurted out that Paul and St Clere were involved in the Jacobite rising. She clamped her lips shut.

Luke stared into her lovely face now frozen into a mask of hatred. This was the real Kate Winters. That she had taken so long to recognise him proved his memory had been easily cast from her mind. He had meant nothing to her. Their marriage was an afternoon's diversion to a spoilt and indulged heiress.

She had as good as told him she meant to wed St Clere. Because of her treachery he was an outcast from his family and friends, his career was in ruins, and he had been branded a reprobate and mountebank. Once those green eyes now glaring at him with loathing had shimmered with passion. She was wanton and corrupt as well as treacherous. The stubborn set to her chin warned him that she would tell him nothing here tonight. Once away from her pampered environment, in a place where she could not contact her influential friends, she would soon talk. He thrust her from him before his iron control snapped.

He marched from the room and gave an order to the man by the door. 'Find the prisoner a cloak. I'm taking her for questioning. If she puts up a fight, bind and gag her.'

They rode for just over a mile to an old rambling farmhouse. Katherine knew it well—too well for her peace of mind. It had been deserted for several months after the farmer, his wife and four children had all perished last winter from the sweating sickness. It was a place viewed with superstition by the locals—a place of ill fortune. The isolated dwelling was built around a fourteenth-century church tower, which was all which remained of an old village which had been wiped out by the Black Death.

Katherine was not superstitious, but whenever she had ridden this way she had always felt a coldness about the place. Now, in the eerie light thrown up by the lanthorns carried by Luke's men, she felt her skin prickle and a shudder quivered down her spine.

Throughout the ride Luke had ridden at the head of their party, while she had been surrounded by his men. It gave her the time she needed to assess her situation.

In the role of Hunter, Luke was a different man from the dragoon who had paid court to her, shown her kindness and consideration during the storm. But that had been the Luke Ryder bent upon seduction and blackmail. And she had fallen for that cold, calculated charm. Hunter was the real Luke—ambitious, mercenary, heartless. But why, when he had succeeded and been paid so handsomely by her brother, did he hate her so virulently?

As the men around her dismounted the night sky was suddenly lit by a flash of light. There was a storm out at sea and it was coming inland. Katherine felt the panic rise in her. She slid to the ground and as a low rumble of thunder rolled across the sky she clung to the saddle. Her heart pounded with the force of her old terror which turned her flesh to ice.

Luke took a lanthorn from one of his men and moved towards the old tower. 'Bring the prisoner to the tower room.'

Katherine was given a push in the middle of her back, which goaded her to retaliate, 'Don't push. I can walk without you mauling me.'

'Regular hell-cat Hunter's caught for himself,' her captor chuckled to his companion walking behind them.

The man snorted. 'Hunter won't take no nonsense from the likes of her. He's no time for fancy women—'less they warm his bed.'

At their further burst of laughter Katherine's temper began to rise. By the time she reached the room on the second storey of the tower it was brimming over. Luke stepped back to allow her to pass. She paused in the doorway, her glare accusing as she stared up at him. 'This is no government prison. Why have you brought me here?'

'To learn the truth.'

'You'll learn nothing from me, Hunter. This is abduction. You won't get away with such conduct towards a woman of my class.'

'A man will not be condemned for reclaiming his errant wife.'

Rage exploded in her skull. 'Is there no end to your infamy? What is it you want this time? A ransom to save my reputation? I thought it was agreed that sham ceremony was not legal.'

His mouth lifted in a sardonic twist. 'That's what you'd like to think, isn't it, my faithless spouse?' His cold voice scythed through her. 'It's legal. While I live you can forget about becoming a countess. And I would not count on your lover St Clere risking his craven hide to rescue you. Now that the English army is marching north, to defeat the rebels, his lordship has turned his coat. He's at Court ingratiating himself with King George.'

She checked her retort. It was on her tongue to say St Clere was no turncoat—but that would prove he was a Jacobite. Luke was deliberately goading her. She must consider every word before she spoke. 'Where else would a loyal nobleman who had sworn allegiance to King George be, other than at Court?' she flung back at him with all the derision she could muster.

'Like all your kind you would perjure your soul to protect your own interests.'

Lightning lit the tower room with a blue-silvery light, showing the hatred carved into Luke's handsome face.

'You dare accuse me of that? Wasn't your pay-off high enough last time? What more do you want. . .?' Her angry words tumbled out but they were drowned by a crash of thunder directly overhead.

Choked by her fear, Katherine pressed her knuckles to her mouth as her body began to shake. She took a step back and stood rigid against the stone wall. Her eyes were wild and her breathing heavy as she summoned the fortitude to overcome her fear. She despised herself for being unable to control this weakness, and was humiliated that Luke should again witness her terror. As the thunder faded she had conquered her trembling, but all the colour had fled from her face.

She held his stare as she mastered her terror. For an instant their gazes clashed.

Memories of that other storm at the cottage confounded her. Surely that was concern in Luke's black eyes? Hope irrationally soared. He lifted a hand to touch her and she found her breathing slowing with anticipation. Then abruptly his eyes hardened and he snatched his hand away.

The spell shattered, its demise bringing a sour gall to her mouth. It was his tender concern during the storm which had captivated her heart—a false tenderness to win him a fortune. The man was a mercenary. Lies and deceit were second nature to him. He would do anything for money. Even make love to a women he despised. She knew the truth of it now.

Holding her head high, she plucked her skirts aside so that they would not touch him as she swept into the tower room. Luke put the lanthorn down on the floor inside the chamber, its light showing her that the window was barred and the only furniture was a narrow truckle bed. The door banged shut and a key clicked ominously in the lock. She was a prisoner.

Luke paused outside the cell door until he knew his temper was once more battened down. He had thought himself immune from Kate's beauty. Didn't he know her for a scheming, selfish baggage? But each encounter stirred his desire.

He had never met a women like her! She was poison. It was time he freed himself from her siren's web. What had possessed him to abduct her? If only he'd not been so damned angry that she hadn't recognised him. It proved how false her love had been.

A madness had driven him since the night of the storm when he realised he loved her. No woman had fascinated him as Kate did. That same madness drove him still. Thank God it was tempered now, fashioned out of disillusion and the need to settle a score.

And settle it he would!

So far St Clere had escaped. The Viscount had known when to sit tight upon the fence and when to leap down into the Hanoverian camp. One of Luke's men constantly followed St Clere, but it would be a matter of time before the Viscount betrayed himself. Fortunately there had been other successes. Colonel Peters had been loud in his praise, but they did not ease Luke's anger. He remained an outcast from his family and friends. Until his name was cleared of the taint of blackguard, he would remain as Hunter.

Another flash of lightning brightened the tower. At hearing the strangled cry from behind the door, he fingered his chin. The ridge of the scar blotted all reason from his mind. Kate's betrayal had robbed him of the ideals he held sacred; now it was Kate's turn to learn how it felt to be used. After tonight he would be free of the images which plagued his dreams and unguarded moments—visions of a whore playing at being in love.

As the thunder continued to rage overhead, he unlocked the door of Kate's room. She was hunched on the floor, shuddering with terror. He rubbed his hand across his moustache and smothered the impulse to comfort her. A touch was all it would take to inflame his passion. He could not forget the ardour of her response to his lovemaking.

Strength of will controlled his desire. Damn the wench and his own hot blood for wanting her! He had brought her here tonight to use her as she deserved, not to become a slave to his own senses. Deliberately he recalled how she had betrayed him. Their passionate encounters had been a sham. Kate had never loved him. The pain bit deeper. Kate had amused herself at his expense, playing the harlot while St Clere and her brother plotted to raise an army for the Pretender.

And he had been taken in by her lies. It was time he broke the power of the wench over him.

The lightning flashed again. Katherine crossed her arms, hugging her body close as she braced herself against the battering of thunder to follow. Alone, she allowed herself to give in to the tremors which ripped through her body. She was huddled on the floor, her eyes squeezed shut, trying to blot out the lightning and the horrific image it conjured.

It was impossible. As the ghostly apparition filled her mind, she screamed. She had been a girl of ten when the power and magnificence of a storm had drawn her from her bed. Then she had loved its violence for its splendour. To view it better she had left her bedchamber and gone alone to the long gallery at the top of the house.

A thud above her head from the servants' quarters had drawn her interest. Their cook was elderly and sometimes had fainting fits. Katherine had run up the narrow stairs to the servants' quarters to investigate. The cook was snoring soundly in her bed, and as Katherine had turned to retrace her steps lightning had lit up the garret rooms. The door opposite her was open.

She had found herself staring up into the hideously contorted face of her governess, and the hanging body had kicked twice in its final death throes. The eyes had bulged grotesquely and the swollen tongue protruded like a bloated maggot from the gaping mouth.

Her screams had raised the household and since that night storms had filled her with terror.

Later, she had learned that the young woman had been turned out of her last position because the eldest son had seduced her. The governess was four months pregnant.

When the thunder rumbled away, Katherine tasted blood in her mouth. To stem her cries she had bitten deep into her lip. Jerking a handkerchief from the pocket of her gown, she held it to her mouth and rose shakily to her feet.

'At least your fear of storms was no act,' Luke's hard voice came from behind her. 'Unlike your other play-acting.'

He must have unlocked the door and entered under cover of the noise of the thunder. She whirled to face him, the passion of her anger parrying the terrors of the storm. 'It was you who played the tender lover. I was the fool who fell for your treachery.'

'*I* was the one betrayed!' Luke countered.

'Why was the money my brother paid you not enough? I loved you.'

'What money, woman?' His anger matched the vehemence of the storm. 'Your letter was clear enough. Why should you sacrifice becoming a countess to be a mere captain's wife? Don't start your lies again. I saw you kiss St Clere in the garden at Highclere, and again at your home. Once I was out of the way, clearly your marriage vows meant nothng to you. In the arms of your lover I doubt you gave me a second thought. If you had loved me, you would have recognised me before I removed my mask.'

Katherine stared at him incredulously. What he said made no sense. She had sent him no letter. Her suspicions were aroused. St Clere had been too willing to discount her marriage. Had events taken place that morning of the duel of which she was unaware?

She moved towards Luke, her gaze searching his for some sign that he still loved her. 'I sent no letter, Luke.'

His expression did not change. It remained bleak and unyielding. 'Your wiles will not work on me a second time, Kate. I'm immune to them. No woman is worth the disgrace you wrought upon my career and family. It was a clever ruse of St Clere to have me arrested for duelling. He took pains to ensure I was unable to act against him for some time. The imprisonment before my court-martial kept me out of the way while he dabbled in treason and made love to the woman I had believed different from others of her kind.'

There was no mercy in his eyes. Luke was convinced she had betrayed him. His fierce pride, which she had always admired, was now turned ruthlessly against her. While still unaware of his true identity, to cover for St Clere and Paul she had led him to believe that she intended to marry the Viscount. By shutting her mind against the resemblance between Hunter and her lover she had damned herself in his eyes.

'I saw a resemblance in height and build to the man I loved. But it was more than the scar on your chin which has changed you. The man I loved was chivalrous and honourable. You are a stranger, a mercenary bent upon revenge.'

'Do not speak of love, Kate. On your lips the word is a profanity.'

Each word knifed through Katherine's heart. She set her head stubbornly as her imagination filled in the gaps of his story. If it was true, it was small wonder he hated her. He had made no secret of his low opinion of heiresses. Had St Clere tricked them both?

From the set of his handsome face he would listen to no explanations of her conduct. Careful that her own expression betrayed none of her inner pain, she asked, 'What are your plans for me now, Hunter?'

'Why do you still call me Hunter?' His eyes narrowed.

Her tone was as contemptuous as his. 'It's what you've become. I am prejudged without even being allowed to answer your accusations.'

Lightning and thunder simultaneously bombarded the room. Katherine sprang back, the figure of the hanged governess dangling before her eyes.

'Go away!' she screamed at the image, her hands beating the air.

Luke heard the words and saw the revulsion in her lovely face. His anger fired as he believed them thrown at himself. He grabbed her shoulders and jerked her hard against him. 'Dismiss me like a lackey, would you? You're not a countess yet, though St Clere's likely no stranger to your bed. Now it's my turn.'

Katherine twisted her head away as his lips sought hers, and his mouth laid siege to the hollow of her throat. A wave of heat passed through her, but she was too angry to feel desire. This was not Luke. This was Hunter—her sworn enemy. She would never submit to him. As she squirmed in his hold, her fists struck his chest and her feet kicked against his shins. His long boots protected him from her feet, and to her fury her arms were caught and clamped down at her sides. His hands, like steel bonds, trapped her against him.

There was no tenderness in that fierce grip. His kiss was savage as he forced her backwards to the bed. The low mattress caught her at mid-calf, sweeping her legs from under her. They both toppled over and Luke put out a hand behind her to cushion their fall. He landed on top of her, the length of his muscular body pressing her into the mattress.

In the yellow light of the lantern she saw the angular planes of his handsome face tighten with desire. For a moment she remembered the tender intimacy of the cottage, and was aware of the musky scent of his skin that was uniquely his own. She drew a deep, shaky breath, and lay still as she stared up at him.

In the wake of the accompaying thunder her body began to quiver—not with terror this time, but from the devastation his nearness wreaked upon her senses. Desperate to free herself, before her body responded to the fervour claiming her blood, Katherine strained to push him away; but each movement increased the pressure of his thighs against her hips.

'Get off me,' she gasped, lashing at him with clenched fists. 'You're a disgusting, heartless lecher. I hate you.'

'The truth at last!' he rasped, his hand tugging at the hem of her skirts. His bitter laugh muffled against her ear. She increased her struggles as he continued to mock her. 'I want you, Kate, not your false words of love.'

'No—Luke, stop!' she panted, her flesh burning where his hand caressed the inner length of her thigh. Her body arched in revolt, horrified that he meant to take her whether she wanted it or not. She had to stop him. If he took her now, like this, another part of the Luke she had loved would be lost forever.

They were both breathing heavily. 'How can you believe I would betray you?' she gasped. Her voice was hoarse, the pain in it so real that it penetrated Luke's rage. Suspicious, he looked down at her. Her hair had come loose and spread with sensual abandon over the pillow. This was the Kate of his dreams, tantalising, provocative, her magnificent green eyes daring, even now, to flash their challenge. He regarded her in silence. She was his wife. He would take nothing that was not his by right.

Katherine lay unresisting and unresponsive. To take her like that would be a hollow victory. He restrained the aching need to possess her. He had not yet stooped so low as to resort to rape. She was by nature wanton and abandoned; he wanted her to acknowledge her depravity. She would yield to him willingly. He would touch the core of her passion, hear her cry his name at the height of her pleasure. He needed to prove she was the wanton he believed her. Only then would he be free of the obsession which haunted his nights.

Assured of his triumph, he began a slow, ravishing assault on her senses. His tongue teased the hollow of her neck, his breath hot as his teeth gently nipped the lobe of her ear. Hearing her stifled gasp, he tasted the sweetness of her mouth. Beneath the insistence of his kiss, her lips warmed and finally parted, her body beginning to move in supplication beneath him. When his lips travelled lower to kiss the wild pulse beating at the base of her throat, she moaned softly against his cheek. Suddenly she stiffened, a hand firm and insistent pushing against his chest.

'No, Luke.' She turned her head to avoid his kiss. 'Not like this, while you hate me.'

At her stricken expression he raised a mocking brow, refusing to give way to the nagging doubts which suddenly plagued him. He had once thought Kate so honourable. What a superb actress she was. She had duped him once. He would not give her the opportunity to do so again.

A light flared briefly in her emerald eyes, her tortured gaze leaving him uncertain.

'The Luke Ryder I loved would have listened to reason. Only Hunter, the law unto himself, would take a woman by force. Do you relish so much what you have become? If hating me eases the injustice you've suffered, so be it. But don't let it destroy all that was so fine in you.'

Luke sat back on his knees and looked down at her. He had meant to humiliate her, to prove she was powerless to deny him. There was anguish in her voice, but not pleading. Her eyes were over-bright, her high round breasts straining against the material of her gown as she breathed deeply. There was softness and beguilement in her parted lips. She was the seductress and he the seduced—to take her now would appease her need for satisfaction, not his.

He left the room without a word.

The door slammed behind Luke with a force which shook the floorboards, and Katherine turned her face to the wall. The storm outside had finally died away, giving her the peace she needed to think. Luke had not betrayed her, but clearly he was in no mind to listen to her story. That he had not forced her tonight, when she was at his mercy, proved him an exceptional man. A man worthy of her love. She admitted it freely. Although she found it hard to believe that St Clere had tricked her, she accepted that he had.

It was Luke she wanted. Luke she intended to have.

He had loved her once. She believed that under the pain of betrayal he still did.

She slid the wedding-ring from the chain at her neck and set it in its rightful place on her finger. She would move heaven and earth to rekindle that love.

CHAPTER TEN

'KATE is poison!' Luke addressed his reflection in the mirror as he shaved the next morning. Return her to Ferncombe and forget her, an inner voice counselled.

On waking that been his intention. She had been here for two days and despite his constant attempts to trick her or rouse her anger to win a confession from her, her agile wits had kept pace with him. To those she loved she was steadfast and loyal. But not so towards himself.

Why then could he not forget her? She had almost destroyed him once. And he knew better than to trust her. He felt his anger rising at the memory of her betrayal. It was rare that he allowed his temper to become his master, but the injustice he had borne could not be swept aside in a moment.

He smiled sardonically. His lovely tormentor would be tamed, he reflected with pleasurable anticipation. She had no scruples. He had seen the way she had been playing up to St Clere—to his cost he knew how effective her seductive wiles could be. Still, there was no other woman who could match her spirit. This time he would harness that wildness. The thrill of battle lightened his step as he approached the tower room.

When he entered he found Kate asleep. There had been another storm last night and she must have slept little. She lay on her back, her unbound hair spread over the pillow. An arm raised over her head drew tight the silk of her shift outlining the fullness of her breast. It was a sensuous pose and Luke felt his desire stir. He steeled himself against her beauty.

'Kate.' He was startled at the huskiness of his voice as he called to her.

Her eyes opened, dreamy with sleep. 'Luke, my

darling,' she answered drowsily. The radiance which lit her face faded as she held his stony glare. For a moment he had almost believed she was glad to see him.

Annoyed at the ease with which she aroused his passion, he made his voice deliberately cold as he addressed her. 'Get up. We're leaving.'

Her face paled. She looked as if he had dealt her a mortal blow, then her green eyes sparkled with a challenging fire.

'We must talk.'

'What have we to say to each other?' he taunted.

'The truth of what happened the morning of the duel.'

His anger inflamed, he was in no mood to listen to a repeat of her lies. Already he could feel his hold upon his temper slipping. Indeed they had to talk. But not now. If his temper got the upper hand, he might say more than he intended. The news from London had not been good. He might have his own account to settle with Kate, but he was not vindictive. Until he had learnt the truth behind the rumours about the Rising, he would not inflict unnecessary pain on her.

'What are you afraid to hear, Luke?' Her voice throbbed with anger. 'The truth?'

He spun on his heel, his stare hostile as he fought to curb his rage. 'Your vision of the truth is always entertaining.'

Katherine threw back the bedcovers and swung her legs to the floor. He was favoured by a glimpse of slender calf and thigh before she flicked down her skirt. As she slid her feet into her shoes, her hair fell forward over her face, hiding her expression from him.

Katherine chewed her lip to control her pain. She had awoken at the sound of his voice calling her name. Her dreams had been filled with his presence. In the half-world of waking and sleeping she had cried out her longing and need and, coming awake with a start, she was dismayed to discover not the Luke of her dreams, but the cold, implacable Hunter who glared down at her.

Katherine pulled on her jacket before looking at her husband to answer his taunting. Despite her mounting tension she caught her breath, her heart racing as she stared at his tall, commanding figure dressed in black.

'We do have to talk, Luke.'

'Does your conscience trouble you?'

Katherine inwardly flinched at the gruffness of his voice. As she beheld his desolate expression Luke appeared more remote to her than ever. He meant to make this difficult for her. The proud set of his jaw warned her it would be pointless trying to reason with him in his present mood. But she had to try.

'I never betrayed you, Luke. I loved you.'

A bitter laugh came from his lips. He pulled her to him in a crushing embrace. 'Is this what you mean when you talk of love?'

Guessing his intent, she tried to pull away, but he was too fast for her. His mouth swooped down over hers, his moustache grazing her upper lip with the roughness of his kiss. She clamped her teeth shut against the invasion of his tongue and her fists struck his chest. As she pushed against him she felt his muscles tense at her resistance. The pressure of his lips was relentless and his fingers tightened, holding her head rigid. As she was unable to twist her face away, her struggles became frantic to escape the humiliation he was inflicting upon her.

'You can't fight me and win, Kate,' he said hoarsely.

Then her lips were again claimed by his. At her refusal to respond, his kiss changed. Now he was deliberately taunting her, demanding her surrender as he had that first night here. His mouth played with expert thoroughness over hers as she continued to struggle in his arms, and the deepening sensuality of his kiss was as provocative as a caress, causing a fever to explode through her.

The tautness of Luke's arms gentled, though she

remained crushed against his body. There was fire now in his kiss as his passion rose. His hands slid down her spine, moulding her to his hard frame. When his tongue parted her lips to explore the softness of her mouth, her senses spun, shivers of pleasure setting her body aflame in answering response. Beneath her hand trapped against his chest the powerful rhythm of his heart matched the pounding of her own.

She felt a shudder travel through him and his expression hardened.

'What are you bartering your body for now?' His face was dark with contempt as he flayed her with his gaze. 'Your freedom? That's the only love you understand. You and St Clere are well suited. He's sold out his Jacobite friends to save his own hide now that the Rising has failed.'

'Failed?' she gasped, and tried to draw back, but he held her fast. 'What happened?'

'On the same day the rebels were routed at both Preston in England and at Sherrifmuir in Scotland. They surrendered. The Pretender had not even landed to support his own cause. The rebel prisoners will be brought to London.'

She bent her head as the enormity of his news hit her. 'What will happen to the prisoners?'

'Because you fear your brother is among them?'

To admit that would be to admit Paul was a Jacobite. Was this another trick by Luke to get her to condemn her brother? She had only his word that the Rising had failed.

'I have said my brother is with friends in the country,' she said.

When she refused to meet his gaze, he tipped her chin up with his finger, his voice gentler than it had been since her abduction. 'The prisoners will be tried. Some will be transported to the colonies. In such cases a token number are always hanged as a warning to insurrectionists. Their leaders will face death on the scaffold. But since your brother is in the country with friends you have nothing to fear.' His voice became harder. 'Your lover St Clere wore his sling at Court like a badge, proclaiming he was unfit to enter into any fight.'

At his scathing tone, Katherine overcame her anguish for her broher and retaliated. 'A wound you grieviously inflicted on him. He was lucky to escape with his life.'

'It was a flesh wound,' Luke jerked out, his fingers digging into her shoulders in his anger. 'It would not have inconvenienced him for more than a day or two. I dare say he cut a romantic figure in his silk sling, though it must have hampered his exploits in your bed.'

'St Clere was never my lover,' Katherine defended with heat, and pushed against him to break his hold.

She was abruptly released and he stepped back from her. 'Lies, lies and more lies. Don't you ever stop?' He flung his scorn in her face.

'The truth, Luke.' She pointed a finger at him as she began to pace the room, her skirts swirling out at each turn from the force of her anger. 'You are so prejudiced against heiresses that you won't give me a hearing.'

He leant against the wall and folded his arms across his chest. Lifting a brow in mocking accusation, he said, 'Then answer my questions about your brother and St Clere.'

'I want you to hear the truth about the morning of the duel. All you seek is to trick me into saying anything which may incriminate Paul. You learnt very little about me in our time together if you think I would ever do that.'

Luke studied her with cynical admiration. Nothing cowed her; her eyes were as bright and defiant as ever. And he knew her well enough to know that she must be in torment over the fate of her brother. He also knew that if Paul Winters was a prisoner she was not a woman to sit at home with her embroidery while fate

overran her brother. She would not rest until she had
done everything in her power to help him.

Armed with that knowledge and his inbred distrust
of her kind, he was prepared to let her speak. Just how
far would she go to convince him that she was
innocent?

'And what of us, Kate?'

'Of yourself I cannot speak. I know only what St
Clere told me about that morning. He said you had
been recalled to London; that you demanded the sum
of five thousand pounds to agree not to see me again.'

She saw his brows draw down and his full lips whiten
but when he did not speak she rushed on, 'I slept late
that day. I'd meant to go to the heath to try and stop
the duel. Paul had drugged my drink the night before.
When I awoke it was too late. When I was told you
had left Sussex, I went to the cottage. I could not
believe you were the fortune-hunter they claimed. The
cottage was deserted. You'd left Sussex without sending me word—what was I supposed to believe?'

They were the words Luke craved to hear. But trust,
once broken, was slow to mend. It was a plausible
story, but he had seen the way St Clere had kissed her.
She had not been fighting off his attentions. At this
stage he could not afford to believe her. But he was
prepared to give her the benefit of the doubt. Time
would prove whether her words were true or false.

Katherine stopped her pacing to stand before him.
Her eyes searched his and she swallowed convulsively,
but did not speak. The fresh fragrance of her wafted
over him.

'Kate I. . .' he began gruffly.

'Luke.' A wealth of longing was in her voice as she
moved closer so that their figures touched, and the
warmth of her body destroyed his calm. His arms went
round her. At the pliant sweetness of her mouth
opening beneath his lips the need to possess her
completely became a throbbing force, obliterating
anger and distrust from his mind. There was only the

bewitchment of her answering passion, the feel of her hands as they entwined in his hair, and the touch of her breasts and hips which inflamed him to a fever of longing.

'I want you, Kate.'

He took her face in his hands. His sable eyes compelled her to submit, but without the words of love Katherine yearned to hear. He had not even denied that he had taken the money to leave her alone. The hunger in his kiss had robbed her of resistance. Her breathing slowed when his face again lowered to hers. Tenderly, his lips explored hers, then he drew back, watching her reaction.

The desire was dark in his eyes and she saw her own rapturous face mirrored in those dark, demanding depths. Why did his touch devastate her reason—lay waste her will? Even as she summoned her strength to deny him she knew the battle to control her senses was lost.

The urgency of Luke's kiss was a masterpiece of seduction. It brought a pulsating melody to her blood, a piquancy in all her senses. The jacket slid from her shoulders, her skirt unhooked to fall unnoticed to the floor. Luke ran his fingers through her pale golden hair, and, lifting its silken curls, he buried his head in its scented softness. This was the tender lover she remembered. She luxuriated in the caress of his fingers on her neck, their skill arousing as they moved to the ties of her shirt. The heavy tresses of her hair were lifted aside, his mouth exploring in a heated trail across her shoulder, easing down the delicate barrier of silk which covered her breasts.

Katherine sighed, her neck rolled back and through half-closed eyes she met the passion carved into Luke's handsome face. His head dipped lower and when his tongue teased her breasts she moaned softly, her body swaying sinuously against him. A shimmering glow bathed her flesh as his hands caressed her, its heat spreading through her veins, melting her limbs to boneless supplication beneath the sweet enticement of his assault.

Luke laughed throatily, his words forced out between the fervent kisses which tantalised her burning flesh. 'You are a very desirable woman—beautiful and passionate enough to send a man to hell in his need to possess you.'

'Luke, my darling, I——' He stopped her words of love with a ravening kiss which left her swooning in his arms. He lifted her up and carried her to the bed, and she was surprised to find she was wearing only her shift. Self-consciously she drew it back over her breasts as he stripped off his clothes. But she felt no shame. She loved Luke and believed that despite his anger the tenderness of his lovemaking proved he still loved her.

She lifted her arms to welcome his as he covered her with his naked body. At the touch of his warm flesh, the potent proof of his desire pressing into her hip, a delicious quiver sped through her limbs, to concentrate its fiery source low in her stomach.

There was a subtle change in the way he now made love to her, a tenderness to each caress which stroked her undulating body, knowing every sensitive hollow and silken curve. She was besieged by his lips, the tip of his teasing tongue, his breath fanning her seared flesh until she arched and writhed, abandoned to the gathering forces of her passion.

Where Luke's lips touched, her skin became a furnace of sensations which swept through her entire body as she surrendered herself to the ecstatic sweetness of his lovemaking. Realising that the touch of his hands and lips which gave her pleasure would bring the same fever to his blood, her lips became as demanding as his.

Even in her inexperience she sensed the restraint in Luke. He was rousing her to a hot, mindless passion. Her cries of pleasure caught in his mouth, muffled but not stilled, the turbulence of her senses building, craving release from the scalding tempest of sensation which threatened her sanity. Consumed by the frenzy which carried her in its wake, she was subjugated by the mastery of Luke's passion.

When it was over, she lay too exhausted to move. Luke's face was buried in the pillow, his breathing gradually returning to normal. She held him close, knowing the spell would soon be broken, and she wanted to savour this moment for as long as possible. Her hand moved languorously across his back over a raised ridge and then another, and she gasped, feeling several other weals criss-crossed over his flesh.

'My God, Luke. What did they do to you?'

At her cry Luke pushed himself on to his elbow and looked down at her, his expression so bleak that her arms fell to her sides.

'Many would think that a whipping was no less than a seducer and fortune-hunter deserved. It was just one of the many crimes for which St Clere will pay.'

'No wonder you hate me,' she said brokenly.

'Hate implies emotion, Kate. Do not flatter yourself I feel anything for your treacherous hide.'

He sounded so dismissive that Katherine sat up, pulling the sheet across her to cover her nakedness from his gaze. His eyes narrowed as she saw the wedding-ring on her finger. Surely he would see the ring as proof of her love? A pulse pumped along his jaw and for a moment she thought he would speak. He did not.

'I don't believe that what happened between us meant nothing to you.' Her voice crackled with her shame.

He shrugged and resumed dressing. 'The Rising has ended. After I've settled my affairs in London, I've a new life planned.'

'The life of a sea-captain wandering the seas.' She recalled the future he had spoken of in the cottage. 'It was a life we planned together. I'm your wife, Luke. Take me to London.'

'Are you now prepared to barter your body to ensure you are close to the Jacobite prisoners?' he demanded.

He sound so cold—so final. But she could not believe he would walk out of her life. It was his pride talking—not his heart.

Without a backward glance he strode from the room. His departure left her heartsick and dejected. She picked up her discarded clothes and pressed them close to her chest, hugging them for comfort as she had her wooden doll as a child. Luke had taken her today to punish her. She crushed the pain the realisation brought. There was no point in allowing her pride to build further barricades between them. Did not wanting come very close to needing? And needing was an intricate part of loving.

If Luke still burned with thoughts of vengeance, he was too proud to admit that he still cared for her. Did he then have no insight into his own heart? His last kiss had held all the tenderness he had shown her during their courtship. In the meantime she should use every weapon known to woman to reclaim the love she was convinced lay dormant but was not dead.

Luke was not as immune to her as he believed. But he could be so obstinate in that pride. Would he take her to London?

Katherine leapt to her feet and began to dress quickly. While Luke had been making love to her she had forgotten her brother's fate. Each of the problems facing her were awesome, but neither, with courage and resilience, would be insurmountable. She had both in abundance.

Luke rode at the head of their party as they left the farm. Katherine was kept penned in by his men, unable to speak with her husband. Before they rode out he had refused to answer her pleas to take her to London, and now her mind wrestled in torment as they reached the crossroads.

Luke veered towards London, turning his back on the road to Ferncombe. He looked over his shoulder, his expression dark and unfathomable. But he had allowed her to travel with him. Katherine vowed it was the first step on the way to regaining his love.

Three days later they rode into a London which was cloaked in a thick fog. As they crossed London Bridge the shouts of the wherrymen on the river below were loud as they transported their passengers through the jumble of tall-masted ships riding at anchor. Linkboys ran with flaming torches beside sedan chairs along the crowded streets. In Cheapside the market stallholders huddled over braziers for warmth; their customers, hurrying their purchases, were muffled against the chill dampness.

Preoccupied with her fears for Paul, Katherine was glad Luke made no attempt at conversation. The usual sights which delighted her were distorted by fog, and when they turned from Cheapside into St Paul's churchyard to cut through to Ludgate Hill, the great dome of the cathedral was barely visible in the greyness.

Katherine turned to study Luke's silent figure. Earlier, as they passed through Southwark, his men had dispersed with instructions to send their reports to him at the inn in the Strand. Although Luke's expression was stern, there was a roguish quality now about his sardonic countenance which tugged at her heart.

After the rain of the previous weeks the streets were deeply rutted and their journey was slow. More than once a hired carriage had stuck fast in the mud and they were forced to divert from the main thoroughfare along foul-smelling side-streets. A beggar tugged at her skirts. When she looked down into his pinched young face and saw his lips blue from the cold, she put a hand in her pocket and tossed him a coin. There were so many beggars that she knew it was not wise to encourage them, but the starving faces of the children always upset her.

An eerie atmosphere pervaded the streets which was

not caused by the fog. There was a heaviness in the air, a sullenness which Katherine had never noticed before. London was not the merry capital she remembered. Or was it her imagination? Her fears for Paul were making her morbid. Often from the open door of a tavern a song would be heard. Usually it was the same one, its jeering tone sending a shiver through her: the song of the Jacobite defeat.

'And we ran and they ran
And they ran and we ran
And we ran and they ran awa' man.'

The song was always accompanied by sneers and derisive laughter. No one now admitted to Jacobite sympathies, none dared show compassion for the rebels.

They turned into the courtyard of an inn. As their horses were led into the stables a stout man, who was obviously the landlord, bustled forward to greet Luke.

'Hunter! Your room is ready. Will you be wanting a meal sent up?' The landlord's eyes flickered knowingly over Katherine. 'A meal for two, sir?'

'My wife would like a bath prepared in our room.' There was a sharpness to Luke's voice which wiped the leer from the landlord's face. 'Later we will require a hot meal and your finest wine.'

Luke took Katherine's arm and led her across the galleried square courtyard, up an outer staircase and along a covered walkway. When he opened the door of their room for her to enter, she hesitated.

'What's wrong? Now that you've achieved your aim to be in London, do you regret your choice of companion? Perhaps you would prefer St Clere to be your protector?' His black eyes were bright with anger.

'No. I don't want St Clere. I never wanted St Clere.' She moved into the room and with a defiant toss of her fair curls eyed him boldly over her shoulder. 'One day you will learn that I never go back on my word. I am your wife, Luke, but I know you brought me to London to use me as your whore. That's your revenge upon me, isn't it?'

Luke regarded her gravely. 'There's much to be settled between us, Kate. But it must wait. I have to go out.'

'You're leaving me so soon?' she blurted out without thinking.

The cynical lift of his brow was infuriating. 'Are you inviting me to stay?' He pulled her against him, her hip pressed against the proof of his desire for her. 'I'll wear no cuckold's horns. You are a woman capable of great passion—a woman who is ultimately desirable and whose sensuality few men could resist.'

'Now you mock me!'

Luke gave a cynical laugh. 'Perhaps I mock myself. You have that effect on me, Kate. God knows why, for I don't trust you, and I have long despised everything you stand for.'

'But you don't hate me?' She put her hands on his chest. 'Say you don't hate me; I could not bear that.'

He stared down at her, their breath mingling, but his lips remained provokingly out of reach.

'No, I don't hate you, Kate.' There was resignation in his voice and the expression in his eyes was carefully guarded. 'Neither do I love you. You are my wife, and, God help me, I want you. Suffice it that as a mistress you have no equal. We are two people who are drawn together by a mutual need.'

She drew a deep breath and smiled, concealing the pain within. 'You have left me with no illusions. And if I were guilty of the crimes you believe then I would deserve none.'

He cocked his head to one side, regarding her thoughtfully. 'You always had a damned uncomfortable way with words.'

She put her arms around his neck and offered him her lips. 'Can your meeting not wait another hour? Let me prove that you are the only man I ever wanted.'

'There's not a courtesan to match your wiles,' he

said and, unexpectedly, he grinned. As he lowered his mouth to hers, the proud assurance which had first stolen her heart was back in his eyes. 'How can I refuse such an offer?'

Katherine gave herself up to the ecstasy of his kiss. Each time she glimpsed the old Luke and not Hunter she knew another barricade between them was breached, and her heart rejoiced.

During the next two weeks Kate spent much time alone. When Luke was with her she could not fault his attention or manner, but he had many business affairs to settle in connection with his ship soon to dock to Rochester. To his credit, he also spent hours trying to discover what fate had befallen Paul after the surrender at Preston. All he knew for certain was that Paul had not returned to Ferncombe.

The waiting and the not knowing were torment. Her mind raced round in endless circles. Who could plead on Paul's behalf if he was a prisoner? And if that were the case, how could she help him? She pulled her thoughts up short. This was getting her nowhere. She must concentrate on one thing at a time. Until Luke had definite news of her brother she could do nothing.

A shadow passed the window of their room and she ran to the door on recognising Luke's footsteps. When he did not enter she looked out of the window. Luke stood on the gallery, staring down at the courtyard in a preoccupied manner. She saw his hand moving across his moustache as it did when he was troubled, and when he entered the room and removed his hat his eyes were hooded by his long black lashes.

A stab of fear made her clutch her hands together over her chest. 'You've heard news of Paul!'

He nodded. 'He's among the prisoners being brought to London.'

'Where will they take him?' she asked, sinking down on to the bed as the shock hit her. Luke sat beside her and put his arm around her shoulders.

'Newgate, most likely.'

Katherine shuddered. Any confinement would be torture for Paul, who was always so restless.

'Newgate?' she groaned. 'Dear God, how will be endure it? Isn't the prison a cesspit of squalor and degradation? I've heard the turnkeys inflict unnecessary cruelty upon the prisoners.' Tears stung her eyes and she blinked them back. 'That will be just the beginning of Paul's suffering. What if he's condemned to be hung, drawn and quartered as a traitor?' Her voice broke at the horror of that fate.

Luke brushed the tears from her cheeks. 'Don't allow your imagination to leap ahead of itself. I can ensure that Paul will be relatively comfortable in Newgate with money sent in for a single cell, good food and wine. He'll not be shackled, and he'll not be abused. If he's found guilty he could be transported. That has happened to some of the Scottish prisoners. Only a few were hanged as an example.'

Hanged. The grotesque vision of the governess filled Katherine's mind. She began to tremble and threw her arms around Luke's neck. 'Not hanged. I couldn't bear that. Not for his face to be twisted in agony, his eyes bulging, his tongue. . .'

Her shoulders were taken and she was given a hard shake. 'Kate. Stop it! What makes you talk like that?' Luke sounded shocked. 'It's not like you. Take a grip on yourself.'

Katherine continued to tremble, her voce crackling with terror as she shook her head wildly from side to side. 'He must not be hanged. I've seen what it can do. Why do you think I'm so terrified of storms? Our governess hanged herself during a storm. I found her. Saw her face. . .the horror of it. I was ten.'

Luke hugged her close. 'Kate. Oh, Kate, I had no idea.'

The tenderness in his voice unleashed the weeks of pent-up misery. She began to sob, unable to control the stream of tears.

Luke continued to hold her, his voice soothing against her hair. 'They will not hang Paul. I promise you that whatever it takes will be done to prevent it, Kate.'

Gradually the strength and warmth of his arms calmed her sobs. The differences between Luke and herself were no longer important. She felt lost, helpless, like a child. Closing her eyes, she leaned her head against his chest. Paul's face hovered before her eyes, intensifying the ache which gnawed within her. It was so long since she had seen him.

'Kate!' Luke turned her to face him. He tilted her chin up with his finger and gazed into her tear-filled eyes. 'Promise me you'll do nothing rash.'

'Why should you care?' she retorted sharply, her fears now more for Paul than for her relationship with Luke. 'You brought me to London thinking to use me as a whore. You hate Paul and will be glad to see him punished.'

Above the high folds of his stock the muscles in Luke's neck corded with tension. 'Paul was a young fool carried along by an ideal. He's hardly more than a boy. How old is he—eighteen?'

'Seventeen,' she told him.

'His life has just begun.' Luke stood up, his step measured as he paced the room. 'St Clere was the ringleader I was after. To discover the extent of his involvement was why I was sent to Sussex. The duel discredited my evidence. But my quarrel remains with St Clere. I have no wish to see your brother hang.'

She licked lips which had suddenly gone dry. There was sincerity in Luke's tone. There was a difference in him today; even though there was no sign of the cold stranger who had become Hunter, he was still as remote from her as ever. A question burned in her mind; dared she ask it?

'Would you help Paul, if he needed it?'

The guarded look returned to his eyes. 'If I refuse, would you go to St Clere? If it does not jeopardise his own position, St Clere may speak for him. He's the one with influence and friends.'

Her anger matched his that he should think she would turn to the Viscount. 'I want nothing more to do with that man,' she said with her cheeks flushing. 'Not after what he did to you.' She pressed her brow against the carved post of the bed, her anger subsiding to be replaced by fear. 'If you will not help, I must find some other way.'

'I gave you my word that I would not let Paul hang. I will do all I can.'

She stood up and held out her arms, her voice imploring. 'Hold me again, Luke. I'm so frightened for Paul.'

When their bodies were almost touching, she reached up, pulling the pins from her hair, then shook her head so that the curls tumbled in wild abandon down over her shoulders to her hips. Desire and suspicion was in Luke's eyes as he watched her. Her love for him was her lifeline, her link with sanity. She needed him now more than she had needed anything in her life. She would not speak of her love, but she could show it.

Luke held back, distrustful of Katherine's motives. Was she offering her favours to secure his help for her brother? When he looked deep into her eyes, he saw the fear, the uncertainty, the need to be comforted, the need to combat her feeling of frustration and helplessness—the need for forgetfulness.

He took her into his arms. 'For all your treacherous ways, there's not a woman who can hold a candle to you, Kate.'

When he took her face in his hands, he felt her tears scalding over his fingers. They burned his lips as he kissed them away, tears more searing than all his distrust and anger at her betrayal. He felt the heat of tears in his own eyes, her pain becoming his pain. He wanted to say the words to give her peace, but they refused to form, leaving him as bereft of comfort as herself. His embrace held her with the veneration he could not speak, cradling her pain and sorrow.

Her mouth parted beneath his, her arms holding him so tight that he felt her desperation and longing. Her natural sensuality had made her an avid pupil to his lovemaking, and this she turned upon him now. Her body moved with the eroticism of an accomplished courtesan, beguiling, arousing, as she removed his sword-belt and dagger to lay them beside the bed. Her skilful hands were impatient upon his clothing as well as her own.

As her legs wrapped around him, he forgot their differences. He was aware only of the lovely, sensuous body moving rhythmically in response to his touch. Hungrily, he feasted his gaze on the perfection of Kate's figure. The jade depths of her eyes beckoned him to drown in the enchantment of her seductive charms.

'God help me, I want you. . .no matter how you've lied or cheated,' he confessed.

Giving her no chance to answer and destroy the delicate truce between them, he tasted the honeyed fragrance of her mouth. His flesh on fire from Kate's demanding caresses, he curbed his own desire to stroke and arouse her body and finally, with a cry of surrender, Kate rolled across him and sheathed him within the cascading heat of her body.

Afterwards, Katherine lay replete, floating in a dream world of sensation. She savoured it, bedevilled by the musky scent of Luke's skin and the firm body lying beneath her own. Languorously she snuggled down into his arms, her lips lightly playing over his throat. This was a stolen moment, recapturing the contentment of their wedding-day. She studied his face in repose. He was watching her with guarded intensity, nothing revealed of his thoughts. Whatever Luke felt for her, their bodies' response to each other had remained the same. If only everything could return to how it once had been!

But nothing stayed the same. The dream was blasted as Luke rolled her off him and left the bed. Hurt by his callous action, she watched him reach for his clothes. She sat up, drawing her knees to her chin and, with an enraged cry, snatched up the pillow and hurled it at his back.

'Damn you, Hunter!'

The pillow glanced ineffectively off his shoulder, and when he finished fastening his breeches Luke turned an amused expression upon her.

'What, no false words of love?' he mocked. 'At last you are beginning to show your true colours.'

Scrambling to her knees, she dived across the bed and grabbed at the dagger on the floor. Luke did not even flinch as she drew her arm and the blade embedded itself in the bedpost less than an inch from his head.

'One day,' she fumed, 'I swear you'll goad me too far.'

CHAPTER ELEVEN

KATHERINE'S eyes widened with pleasure as she looked round the saloon of the house Luke had taken for them in Jermyn Street. Like every room she had seen today it was elegantly furnished, its walls painted in soft colours and the plasterwork decorated with gilt.

'Does your new home please you?' Luke asked drily.

She smiled up at him, but his expression as usual was enigmatic, his dark eyes flashing with bitter humour. During the last ten days at the inn an uneasy truce had sprung up between them. Two chests of her clothes from Ferncombe were in the bedroom she was to share with Luke, brought by a carter on Luke's orders. Was this, then, to be a new beginning?

'It is a home any woman would be proud of. How came you to find it so quickly?' she asked.

'The fortunes of war, my dear. Its last owner fled the country to a life of exile.'

At the mention of the defeated Jacobites the smile faded from Katherine's lips. 'He was fortunate to have escaped,' she said heavily.

'You're still upset from seeing the prisoners paraded through London,' Luke said. 'I did warn you not to go and look for Paul. You would not listen.'

'I had to see he was alive,' she replied, and turned away to study one of the paintings. The bright reds and blues merged. Instead of the colourful hunt scene she saw Paul as she had last seen him in that terrible procession.

She did not know what she had expected that day. But it was certainly not the bedraggled column of men, tied to their horses and being pelted by rotting garbage from the people thronging their route through the City. It was a drizzling December day. Despite his bonds, and face nipped with fatigue and cold, Paul had sat tall in the saddle, staring straight ahead as though the jeering crowds did not exist.

When she had called out his name, he'd given no sign that he had heard, and she had laid her head against Luke's shoulder, unable to stop her sobs, as her husband had led her away.

She blinked aside the tears which threatened to destroy her calm now. Tears would not help Paul. Action would. 'Why won't you let me visit Paul in Newgate?'

'It's no fit place for a woman,' he said firmly. He stood by the fire, the lean contours of his face hollowed with tension. 'He's only been there a few days. The money I sent will ensure he's freed from his shackles and provide him with decent food and a single cell. For the moment nothing more can be done.'

'I can't stand by and do nothing while Paul suffers.' She paced the polished wooden floor, her high heels rapping out her agitation. 'Let me contact Mr Sewell, my father's lawyer. He had my jewels in safekeeping. I'll sell them to pay whatever bribes are needed to gain Paul his freedom.'

'Kate! I've told you before, leave your lawyer out of this.' The cold, implacable light was back in Luke's eyes. 'It will take more than bribes to win your brother's freedom.'

Katherine whirled to face him, the emerald of her gown accentuating the green fire in her eyes. 'The sale of my jewels could buy me an audience with the King,' she asserted.

Luke gripped the marble ledge of the fireplace, and looked at Katherine's reflection in the gilded mirror above his head. 'Do not place your hopes too high on the clemency of His Majesty,' Luke warned. 'He's not a man who forgives any slight against him. An example will be made of the Jacobites. While the Pretender lives, there will always been some idealist ready to take up arms for his cause.'

'But our German King has little love for England,'
Katherine persisted, her cheeks flushing with anger.
'He's not even troubled to learn our language. Why
should he care about a few rebels? He could have gone
back to his beloved Hanover had the Rising
succeeded.'

Luke kicked a log into place on the fire, then came
to put his hands on her shoulders. 'The throne of
England is a rich prize. His Majesty will not relinquish
that which he regards as his by right.'

Lifting her chin defiantly, Katherine clenched her
hands in impotent frustration. 'I must do something. I
can't bear the thought of Paul a prisoner in that
dreadful place.'

'Newgate is no place for a gently reared woman,' he
said less harshly.

She refused to be placated. 'It's no place for a
gentleman either. Especially for one as young as Paul.'
Her voice rasped with her anguish. 'He looked so ill
when the prisoners were marched through London. He
could be locked away for months without a trial. I have
to see him. He's all the family I have.'

'For the brother you love you would go to any
lengths to save him—you dare fling that in my face?'
Hunter glowered back at her. 'You betrayed me fast
enough when it suited your ends. I'd almost forgotten
what a hypocrite you are. You've put up quite a show
of passion these last nights.'

Katherine glared up at him, her heart aching that he
could change from lover to her enemy so rapidly. The
truce she had placed so much faith in had been built on
quicksand. He must never guess how deeply his words
had hurt her.

'Your mind is warped with thoughts of betrayal. I
risked my life to save yours at our first meeting. You
conveniently forget that,' she retorted.

When he heard Katherine begin to repeat the same
old excuses, something snapped in Luke. What was he
doing here in London with this lying jade? She was

staring at him, her green eyes flashing with the
brilliance of emeralds, showing no fear, only a wilful
and obstinate defiance. Yet there were times when they
darkened, reminding him of a forest glade in spring-
time. Then she would cling to him, her arms and legs
twining about his body as she matched the driving force
of his passion. What spell had this siren woven over
him, that he forgot duty, honour, everything in his
need for her?

But there were occasions when he almost found
himself believing her lies. She was staring at him now
with that haughty defiance he despised. It was not for
her to dictate the terms of their relationship. Whatever
madness drove him—it had been roused by her treachery, and the demon was far from laid to rest. As a
mistress Kate had no equal. He had brought her to
London knowing it was likely she would betray him
again. Why then did he not cast her out? Because she
alone of all women could make him forget reason and
lose his self-control?

Roughly, he jerked his mind back to what she was
saying.

'. . .I've already sent word to Mr Sewell.'

He put her from him, distrust making his voice gruff.
'Is there no end to your treachery? You've acted
against my wishes.'

'Because your pride was getting in the way of
reason,' she retaliated. 'It was not just to help Paul,
but to give a statement to clear your name about the
duel and our marriage.'

'I need no woman to fight my battles.'

Katherine flinched as the brittle voice condemned
her with a finality which made her heart contract. She
sat down on a scarlet silk-covered chair. She did not
look at Luke, but at a point above his shoulder, as she
made her voice as cold as his. 'You may as well know
everything. Mr Sewell accompanied me to Colonel
Peters' office. I gave him a written statement that St
Clere had forced the duel upon you, that you fought it

to protect my honour. That you were not a fortune-hunter, and had behaved with chivalry and the greatest respect and courtesy at all times. Actually he had already received a similar letter from Paul, who regretted his part in the affair.'

Luke eyed her with suspicion. That was why Peters had summoned him to the regiment's headquarters this morning and told him that his name was cleared and if he wished to return to his duties it would be with the rank of major. Luke had refused. It was upon the sea he saw his future. His ship had returned from the Mediterranean and its next voyage would be under his command.

'It would seem I am indebted to your family.' Luke spoke with such violence and loathing that Katherine winced inwardly. 'I'm not a lackey to be paid off. Peters knew the truth of the duel. Sergeant Hopkirk had given his statement. But St Clere's influence went above that of my commander. Soon I shall repay St Clere with the justice he deserves.' He bowed mockingly to her. 'Our bargain was implicit, madam. And it was upon my terms. I honour all my debts, even those heaped upon me against my will. By your deceit you have made me honour-bound to aid your brother. A clever ruse—but a treacherous one. I should have suspected no less.'

He strode to the door, but she was there before him, flinging herself against it to prevent his leaving. She was breathing heavily, the swell of her breasts rising and falling above the low neck of her gown as she glared her fury at him.

'Why must you be so hog-headed? I tried to make right a wrong by going to Colonel Peters. I don't want you indebted to me. I asked you to help Paul because I had no one else to turn to. But I wanted you to do it of your own free will—because I hoped that what was between us was more than a sordid liaison. Will your pride never give you peace? Isn't it obvious that you are the last man on earth I see as a lackey? You are the only man to whom I have given my favours. Even to save Paul I would not sell myself. I'm here because I love you. I have always loved you and you're too stubborn to see it.'

'Stand aside, Kate. I don't want to hurt you. But I will not listen to your lies. You think you can twist everything to suit your own ends. Life is not like that,' he told her.

When she refused to move he drew her away from the door, his eyes black with contempt. 'I'm sick of your wiles. You've got what you wanted. While I'm out, have my belongings moved to another bedchamber. Tomorrow I'll take you to Newgate. Not that your brother will welcome your visit. You know nothing of men. By seeing him so reduced, you will strip him of whatever dignity he has left.'

Luke strode out of the house, banging the front door behind him. So much for new beginnings, Kate fumed.

By midnight her anger had died and she sat on the chair at the top of the stairs waiting, praying for him to come home so that she could apologise. She saw now that a man as proud as Luke would resent any interference to clear his name. It was that pride she loved, and it was that pride which was turned against her, because of her background.

Katherine awoke to the early morning cries of milk-maids and orange-sellers shouting their wares. She gasped as she sat up, her neck and side aching where she had fallen asleep on the chair. Luke was walking up the stairs, having just returned home. He was unshaven and smelt of cheap perfume and brandy. The look he gave her was incredulous.

'You've a perfectly good bed to sleep in,' he said drily. 'What possessed you to sleep there?'

She rose stiffly and eased the crinks in her neck. Her glance was scathing as it travelled over his dishevelled figure. Her disillusion was complete. 'I had a misplaced idea that if I apologised I could salvage something from this mess. I was wrong. I see now that all you ever

wanted from me was a means to be avenged upon St
Clere. You found your solace quickly enough elsewhere. Now that your name is cleared, the debts
between us are wiped clean. I want nothing more from
you. I shall find my own means of helping Paul. I'm
leaving, Hunter. I call you that—for that is what you
have become.'

'No, Kate. You'll not leave.'

Her eyes flashed that he had the temerity even now
to command her. The coldness and mockery had gone
from his face, leaving that fierce pride which for once
had lost its forceful self-assurance.

'I found no solace,' he said. 'I sent the woman away
and got drunk instead. But I cannot forget what you
are. . .an heiress.'

'Whatever I am, you are my equal, Luke.'

'And you really think there is something worth
salvaging from the débâcle which our relationship has
become?'

She smiled wryly. 'If you are prepared to learn to
trust me, there is.' She gazed up at him, her eyes wide
and dark with emotion.

'And you are a woman who is used to getting her
own way.' He raised a brow in a way that made her
heart caper wildly.

'Not while you reek from another woman's perfume,'
she taunted.

'*Touché*,' he said and pouted in roguish contrition.
'Then I shall change at once. We will leave in an hour
to see this lawyer Sewell. I would know what he sees
Paul's chances to be, before we go to Newgate.'

She watched him stroll down the corridor to his
room, his step lighter than it had been for months. At
his door he turned back and leaned against the wall,
his grin devilish. 'Have the servants prepare me a bath.
And in this new role of equality you've discovered you
may come and scrub my back.'

'Then I fear that we would never get to Mr Sewell,
or Newgate,' she replied.

He laughed with a vigour she had not heard since their reunion. 'How very true. I shall restrain my baser emotions until this evening. With your permission, of course, sweet Kate.'

She bobbed him a mocking curtsy. 'Permission granted, my master.'

Newgate's towered gatehouse cast its gloomy shadow over them. Katherine held tighter to Luke's arm. Even from the outside the feeling of malevolence permeated from the prison.

'Are you sure you want to go in?' Luke regarded her solemnly through the eye-slits of his silk mask. 'I will visit Paul if you would prefer to remain in the carriage.'

She shook her head. 'I must see him.'

She had no illusions regarding the Jacobite cause. It was a shattered, ill-fated dream. She prayed that Paul would survive the consequences of his misplaced loyalty. For his sake she must let nothing of her fears show.

Once inside the prison, the stench of Newgate stung her nose and robbed her of breath. Coughing, she leaned closer to Luke, comforted by his strength and assurance. Even so, when a bandy-legged turnkey shuffled towards them her flesh cringed as he extended a greasy palm towards Luke.

'Garnish!' he wheezed, licking his lips in greedy anticipation of a rich bribe.

Luke dropped several coins into the turnkey's hand. Slowly the man counted them and sniffed deprecatingly, his small, watery eyes staring out of a pockmarked face slyly assessing whether or not they would pay more. The look in Luke's eyes warned him he would get nothing else from them, and the turnkey nodded towards the basket Katherine was carrying.

'What's in there?' he demanded.

'A bandage and salve for my brother's wound and some food,' Katherine answered.

The turnkey flipped back the linen covering, his greasy fingers picking over the fresh bread, meats and fruit she had bought to supplement Paul's diet. He picked up a chicken leg and bit into it, his laugh malicious as he backed away to let them pass.

'Bloody Jacks ain't nothin' but trouble,' he called after them. 'The sooner Jack Ketch starts turning 'em off, the better I likes it.'

At the mention of the hangman, Katherine shuddered. She kept close to Luke. The odour of unwashed bodies, excrement, vomit and fear hit them like a blast from Hades. Even with a nosegay pressed to her face, Katherine's stomach turned with nausea at the overpowering stench. The sights she turned her head from were even worse.

As they hurried across the courtyard, a loud roar from the crowd of prisoners at the far end drew Katherine's attention. Some of the creatures scarcely passed as human; their emaciated bodies were half-naked and covered with filth, their eyes, either blank with apathy, narrowed with cunning or wild with fear, stared back at her. They were massed together, their shrieks rising to fever pitch, welcoming any diversion which distracted them from their own misery. Too late, Luke stepped in front of Katherine to shield her from the brutality of the scene.

She turned away, appalled at having seen a naked woman bound to the whipping-post, her back a bloody pulp, her legs buckling as she sagged unconscious while the whip still continued to lay into her flesh.

Luke drew her aside to avoid a couple who, inflamed by the savage cries of the crowd, lay on the ground slaking their lust, oblivious to the whistles of encouragement thrown at them by their companions.

'I should not have brought you here,' Luke snapped, his voice muffled by his cloak pressed against his mouth.

'I would have found a way to come,' Katherine gasped through the stinging rawness of her throat which made speech almost impossible. She kept her eyes downcast as they passed through the lower ward. Even so, she was not spared the sight of skeletal arms covered in running sores which were thrust through the bars towards them. Nor could she shut her ears to the plea for alms, the rattle of heavy chains and the despairing wails of the suffering.

She barely checked an unladylike oath as her foot slipped in the overturned contents of a slops bucket and she fell against Luke's side. His arm gripped her waist, steadying her.

'Take heart, Kate. It's not much further.'

'I would endure far worse to see Paul,' she answered, her determination overcoming her misgivings.

Another turnkey barred the entrance to the middle ward where the Jacobites were held. Here at least it was quieter and the smell less overpowering. She contained her impatience while Luke handed more money to the turnkey.

'Let's see yer faces. There'll be no wearin' of masks in 'ere. Wouldn't want one of the Jacks thinkin' he could slip out undetected behind a mask,' the man growled. Then he hawked in his throat and spat on the floor, just missing Luke's highly polished boot.

Luke tensed but made no comment as he and Katherine removed their masks and moved on into a dingy passage.

''Arf-'our, no more. Winters is in the fifth cell on the right,' the turnkey shouted after them.

They climbed the flight of stairs leading to Paul's cell. At the open door, Katherine froze, shocked at the change in her brother. Paul sat hunched up on a truckle bed, his head cradled dejectedly in his hands, an empty gin bottle swinging between his grimy fingers.

'Paul!' She spoke his name softly.

He turned like a man in a dream, his sunken, darkly circled eyes staring out of a haggard bearded face. For a moment he did not move, then his eyes cleared with recognition. The gin bottle slid from his fingers, but he made no attempt to rise and greet her.

'Kat!' Self-consciously he raked his fingers through

his shoulder-length, matted hair. 'I was not expecting visitors.'

'Then it's as well I came.' She covered her alarm at the state he was in by her sharpness of tone. 'You look like a man who's given up hope. Where's your pride, Paul? This place may be a running cesspit, but you don't have to wallow in its degradation.'

Luke touched her arm. 'Kate! Leave him be. It's hard enough for him, you seeing him like this.'

Paul looked at Luke. 'Ryder!' he said with a snort. 'St Clere won't be too pleased you're back with Kat. Glad to see it. Serve St Clere right. Turned his coat to save his hide while I rot here.'

'Give me a statement that he was involved and I'll see he rots in the Tower,' Luke said drily.

Paul shook his head. 'I'll not stoop to his level by betraying my friends.'

'That's the spirit which will get you out of here,' Katherine encouraged. She sat on the bed beside him, appalled at how thin he had become. 'I know its hard, but you have to fight and keep up your strength. How's your wound?'

'Sore as hell.' He lifted his shirt and she saw a dirty bandage wrapped around his ribs.

She looked across at Luke. 'No one's tended this in days. Can you get some water? Once his wound is cleaned and he's been shaved he will feel better.'

Katherine took the soap, salve and fresh bandage from her basket and while Luke bribed the guards to allow water to be sent to the cell she worked on Paul's wound. It was a jagged bayonet cut. Fortunately it was not deep enough to have damaged any vital organs, but it oozed pus and the surrounding flesh was raw and inflamed.

Luke returned with the water and a bottle of brandy. He handed the bottle to Kate. 'Let Paul have several mouthfuls of that, then I'll hold him while your pour some of this over the wound,' he said. 'I've seen old soldiers use it on the battlefield to stop infection.' He turned to Paul. 'I'm afraid it will hurt like the devil.'

Paul grunted and gritted his teeth, his face breaking into a sweat as Katherine poured the brandy on his wound, then she applied the healing salve and bandaged it. He allowed her to wash his hair and shave him in a mutinous silence. When she finished she looked down at her handiwork in satisfaction.

'At least now you look like a young gentleman. We brought you clean clothes and some decent food.'

For the first time since her arrival Paul grinned at her. 'You always did fuss over me like a mother-hen. And this time I'm grateful.' He stood up and held out his arms to hug her. 'You were the last person I wanted to see me like this. But I do feel better. You're right— I was giving in to despair. It won't happen again.'

She stared into his gaunt face, which now it was washed and clean-shaven showed an unhealthy greyish colour. She pushed back a lock of brown hair which had fallen over his brow.

'You'll soon be out of here,' she soothed.

'At what cost? A journey to Tyburn!'

A jangle of keys from close by warned them that the turnkey was approaching.

'It won't come to that, Paul. I swear it,' Katherine whispered.

'Time's up.' Two turnkeys stood by the door to substantiate the order.

'You'd better go, Kat.' Paul put out a hand to Luke. 'St Clere wronged you. If you can make Kat happy then I wish you both well, and give my blessing to your marriage.'

Luke took Paul's hand but made no comment. And still in silence he led Katherine away. They did not speak until they reached the carriage Luke had hired.

As it pulled away from the prison, Katherine said heavily, 'Tell me truthfully, has Paul a chance of being pardoned?'

Luke squeezed her hand. 'There's always a chance.'

'I asked for the truth, Luke.'

'The King is demanding an example be made of the rebels. It is intended that the leaders will be tried first. Much will hinge on the fate of the Earls of Derwent Water and Kenmure. Their trials have not been set yet.'

'But Paul looked so pale and thin. And his cheek was hot with the beginnings of a fever.'

A numbness settled over Katherine as they rode back to the house in Jermyn Street. Though during her visit Paul had regained his spirits, it was obvious that he was ill. She hoped she had been in time to stop his wound becoming infected, but gaol fever struck down many prisoners, killing them before they were even brought to trial. That would not happen to Paul, she vowed. If everything else failed, she would find a means for him to escape.

Few prisoners escaped from Newgate and the Jacobites were more heavily guarded than most. So her hopes must first rest upon a pardon. For that she needed the influence of someone at Court, and the only person she knew was St Clere. And she had promised Luke she would have nothing to do with him. Nor did she wish to. She hated St Clere for his treatment of Luke.

Yet if Paul's life depended on it, what other choice was there?

The opportunity came a week later when Luke's ship docked at Rochester. The weather was stormy and the country so swept by gales that Luke refused to allow Katherine to accompany him. The roads were impassable and he took passage on a coal barge from the Thames to the River Medway.

Within an hour of his departure she had slipped out of the house and given an urchin sixpence to take a note to St Clere's house close by the Mall. To ensure its delivery she promised the boy that the Viscount would give him a further sixpence. The note asked St Clere to meet her the next day at the Royal Exchange. Here she hoped that as she strolled along the gallery of

shops accompanied by her maid any meeting would
look accidental.

The next day was cold but dry. Katherine stilled her
guilt at acting against Luke's orders, and her own
protestations against considering the Viscount could be
an ally, and she set off to the Exchange. Arriving there
early, she spent an uncomfortable half-hour examining
the contents of the market stalls and gazing into the
windows of the shops, every few seconds scanning the
crowd for sight of St Clere.

Just as she thought he would not come she saw him
approaching. She sent her maid into a shop to purchase
a yard of wide lace to replace a torn ruffle on a sleeve
of a gown. To her dismay St Clere was not alone. He
was accompanied by four courtiers, two of whom had
masked women on their arms.

'My dear Katherine,' St Clere greeted her warmly. 'I
had no idea you were in London until I received your
note.'

Katherine was glad the maid was out of hearing at St
Clere's blatant indiscretion. 'My lord, I would speak
privately with you,' she said.

'How can I refuse so charming a request? Dine with
me tonight at Brent House.'

'That is not possible, my lord.' She shot him a baleful
look. He was openly compromising her before his
companions.

'Then I cannot help you.' His blue eyes glinted
arrogantly as he bent to whisper in her ear. 'From your
manner it is obvious you have not come to ask my
forgiveness for the abominable way you dismissed my
suit. Why should I help you?'

'Once we were friends.' She took his arm and drew
him away from his companions. 'I have always been
honest with you. I ask nothing for myself, but for Paul.'

'I do not concern myself with the welfare of traitors,'
he told her.

'Take care, my lord. I know much which could put
you in the Tower. You recruited Paul to the cause.

You saved yourself by hiding behind a flesh wound and used that duel to bring shame upon an honest man. If you refuse to speak for Paul I shall have no qualms in speaking out all I know of the French spies who frequented Highclere. I doubt your position is so safe at Court that it could stand the scandal.'

'Is that a threat?' St Clere's lips curled back in a snarl. 'You'll regret it, if it is.'

She met his glare with coolness. 'I will not be intimidated, my lord. There's a sworn statement with my lawyer to be handed to the Lord Chief Prosecutor should anything untoward happen to me. Times, dates and descriptions are all written down. But as a friend I should not have to use it. All I ask is that you do your best for Paul.'

'You and your entire family can go to the Devil. Your brother knew what he was getting into. You insult me by refusing my suit, and then run off to London to live with Ryder.' He laughed at her startled expression. 'Do you think I would just come at your beck and call? Urchins are notoriously free with their information for a shilling or two. I had someone check out your address and the man you're living with. It's Ryder. You'll get no help from me. I've friends powerful enough to discredit any statement made by a woman of such low moral character that she denies her class to marry beneath her. It will be your name which will be lampooned in the streets, not mine.'

'But Luke *is* of my class,' she fumed. 'His family are revered in their county. They own a fleet of merchantmen and their income is the match of my father's. It was you who stooped to marry out of the nobility—because my dowry was vast enough to soothe your pride. You have no concept of loyalty or honour.'

St Clere leered at her. 'Perhaps if you had offered yourself to me as freely as you did to Ryder I might have found it in my heart to help Paul.' There was murder in his eyes as he glared at her. 'You have consorted with my sworn enemy and I shall rejoice in bringing you both down.'

CHAPTER TWELVE

Upon arriving at Jermyn Street, Katherine was surprised when a maid informed her that Luke had returned and was in the first-floor saloon. She had not expected him until tomorrow at the earliest. She pushed aside her guilt at meeting St Clere. It had been a humiliating experience and had not helped Paul. Rather it had intensified the Viscount's hatred for Luke, and she knew now that St Clere was a vindictive and powerful enemy.

The saloon door was open. Luke was standing by the fireplace, his face set with anger as he stared at a piece of paper in his hands. With an abruptness that startled her, he screwed the paper into a ball and flung it into the fire. She watched Luke as he stared down at the flames licking around the charred remains.

'Luke, was it bad news?' she asked anxiously.

He spun round, the fury in his eyes centred upon her. 'Proof of your treachery,' he accused. 'You've had an assignation with St Clere. That was a note from his lordship informing me of your deceit. You could not wait to go to him. Any help I could give Paul was not good enough for you.'

She was condemned before she started. Katherine searched Luke's face for some sign of understanding. There was none. It was the hated, intractable visage of Hunter who glared back at her. All the barriers she had tried so hard to breach were once more erected against her.

She opened her mouth to speak, but he cut across her words, his tone as unyielding as iron.

'I hope your assignation was worth it.'

Katherine's temper erupted that he had again judged her without waiting to hear her story. 'St Clere was the best chance Paul had of gaining a pardon. I had a means of bargaining with him, or so I thought.'

'I am well aware of your bargaining charms, madam.'

The insult goaded Katherine past caution. 'Damn you, Hunter. It was not like that.' Her hands clenched, she sprang at him, her fists striking against his chest. 'Why won't you trust me?'

Her wrists were caught in a rigid grip and forced down to her sides. Meeting Luke's glare, Katherine saw a muscle pulsating along his jaw as he strove to control his anger. Her stomach knotted with fear.

'Trust you?' he grated out, his lips twisting into a cruel, mocking sneer. 'I made that mistake once. Never again.'

Katherine swallowed against the agony piercing her heart. What demons drove him still? What did she have to do to convince him of her love? But convince him she must. If she did not speak now, she had the terrible feeling he would walk out of her life for good.

'I was wrong to go to St Clere, I admit that. But at the time I thought he would help Paul. It was because of St Clere that Paul got involved with the Jacobites. I thought also to spare implicating you. It's bad enough Paul has lost Ferncombe and could lose his life—I did not want the same to happen to you. . .'

Not by so much as a flicker of an eyelid or a muscle movement did Luke's expression reveal his thoughts, and her voice trailed into silence.

Katherine sighed. Whatever she said Luke would draw his own conclusions. But she could not just give up. 'That's the truth—believe it or not, as you choose. St Clere has proved he has no loyalty to Paul, or to any man but himself. You wanted dates of when St Clere met the Jacobite spies at Highclere. I'll give them to you.' Unfastening her cloak, she walked into the adjoining morning-room, remarking over her shoulder, 'Though if they should in any way implicate Paul I will not swear to them in court. I'll not condemn my brother just to bring St Clere to justice.'

The cynic in Luke, which had ruled his every action these past months, continued to question Kate's motives. Her story was what he wanted to hear. But was it the truth? That she now would give him the proof of St Clere's treachery also showed that she could turn on her friends. Not that St Clere deserved any loyalty.

He rubbed his hand across his scarred chin. It was unlikely he would ever resolve his doubts. He wanted to believe her innocent. Yet each time he began to resign his trust she did something like this. He'd be a fool not to be suspicious of her motives. She was wild, impetuous and independent. The very qualities which had first attracted him to her now condemned her in his mind. The impetuousness which had taken her to St Clere today was the same which had governed her actions when she saved him from the outlaws' bullet that first day.

Or were they outlaws? His thoughts ground remorselessly on. What if Paul had been behind that attack? Kate would do everything in her power to help the brother she loved.

Luke looked through to the morning-room to where Kate stood gazing out of the window. She glanced sidelong at him, her head thrown back, defiant and provocative. How often he had admired her indomitable spirit. If only he had not loved her so much—or once trusted her so completely.

Katherine turned at the sound of his footfall. 'Do you want me to leave your house?' she asked.

'If I said yes, that would release you from our bargain and you would be free to go to St Clere.'

'I don't want St Clere.'

'Then what do you want, Kate?'

I want you to love me again, her heart shouted, but the words remained unspoken. They were not what he wanted to hear. 'I need a friend, Luke. And I don't want to lose what is good between us.' She took a step towards him, a hand held out in silent pleading.

'If you remain, there must be no more running to St Clere,' he stated.

The anguish vanished from Kate's beautiful face, and with a soft cry she put her arms around his neck. 'I knew you'd not fail me, Luke.'

Even as Luke took her into his arms and his mouth met hers with rising passion a part of his mind still mocked him for his weakness in wanting her.

During the next two weeks events passed slowly for Katherine, but today at last something positive was happening. Luke had arranged a meeting with a crippled solider he had known when he had fought on the Continent. The veteran had fared poorly after his discharge—he had lost an arm at Malplaquet and had taken to begging on the streets to stay alive.

Since their visit to Newgate, Luke had advised caution in their plans to save Paul. If their activities were noted, a watch would be put on them, and they would then be powerless to help Paul should the need arise.

Bad weather during those two weeks had prevented Luke from returning to oversee the repairs to his ship now docked at Deptford. Despite Katherine's fears for Paul, it had been a time for coming to terms with the uncertainty of her future. At least the tension between Luke and herself had lessened. If they were occasionally guarded in their speech, they had at least begun to relax in each other's company.

Several times they had visited the theatre, or taken a river trip to Ranelegh Gardens, and Luke seemed determined to take her mind from worrying over her brother's plight. The happiest times for Katherine were when they spent an evening at home alone. Then she would play the harpsichord and Luke would stand at her side turning the pages of the music. Or they would play chess or cards, the teasing returning to their banter, and the house echoed to the sound of their laughter. After such an evening, when Luke made love to her, she would often catch a softening in his expression, and it gave her hope that he was regaining his trust and his love for her.

The hired carriage drew to a halt by the frozen Thames beside London Bridge. Katherine put her hand in Luke's as he helped her alight, and stared in astonishment over his head. The normally bustling river had been brought to a standstill by the coldest winter Katherine could remember. It had attracted hundreds of revellers to the Frost Fair held on the ice.

She wrapped her fur-lined cloak closer about her body and pushed her hands into her sable muff, seeking some warmth.

Luke took her arm and led her across the slippery ice to mingle with the crowd. 'I arranged for us to meet by the silversmith's booth on the south side,' he said, his breath steaming in the cold air. A slow, heart-stopping smile spread across his full lips below his mask. Katherine blushed, remembering the passionate demands of his lovemaking that morning. Then as she remembered the serious implication behind their outing her expression became grave.

'Relax.' Luke's fingers tightened over her arm. 'No one suspects why we're here. Enjoy the fair. Look at those two women squabbling like starlings over that absurd feathered hat on the milliner's stall. And there's the fire-eater. Come, there's time to watch him before our meeting.'

Katherine responded to Luke's light-hearted mood. She marvelled at the fire-eater, and laughed so hard at the antics of a troup of dwarf tumblers that she was forced to hold her side. They then paused to watch some skaters on the ice, and Kate looked at them with longing.

'Can you skate?' Luke asked, pulling her towards a man hiring out the skates.

'No, but I'd love to try,' she said.

Luke helped her to tie the straps over her boots and

as soon as she stood up her feet took on a life of their own, sliding away from her control.

'Ohh,' she cried, waving her arms like windmills to keep her balance.

Laughing, Luke caught her and held her tight against his body. 'Take it slowly. Relax. You'll love it.'

His hands were firm upon her waist as he pushed her forward. For several yards her legs wobbled and her arms circled to keep her footing as Luke gave her instructions. All at once she found she could stand upright and, with Luke's support, she relaxed as they sped around the ice specially cleared for the skaters. She could feel his breath against her neck, the strength of his arms warm and supportive around her.

'This is wonderful.' She smiled at him over her shoulder, feeling suddenly happier than she had been for weeks.

Luke returned her gaze and the laughter in his eyes made her gasp. 'Just don't get too confident—it can be fatal,' he warned.

Her love for him flowed through her. She half turned to place a kiss on his cheek, but the movement sent her legs slithering from under her and she toppled, pulling Luke down with her. They lay in a crumpled heap, their legs tangled and both laughing so hard that they had no strength left to rise.

'What possessed you to do that?' Luke wiped a smear of ice from his face and raised himself to his feet.

'Because I was happy and you were rather irresistible.'

She gave him her hand to help her up. He took it and, whisking the glove from her hand, raised her palm to his lips. His kiss ignited a fuse between them. Their gaze met, held by devouring flames, neither moving, each lost in the magic of the moment.

''Ere, why don't yer kiss her, guv'nor?' a rough voice sniggered from behind them. 'Don't stand there gawping at 'er.'

'If anyone is irresistible, it's you, my Kate,' Luke murmured. He looked away, the spell broken. 'It's time to meet Jem.'

Their skates removed, they strolled past the booths set up by printers, toy-makers and potters. Any conversation was impossible unless they shouted above the shrill cries from the pie-sellers and pedlars. Luke kept her arm firmly through his, locked possessively against his side. When they neared the silversmith's stall near the end of a row of booths, her feet turned leaden. There was no sign of the one-armed soldier.

'Have some hot suckling pig while we're waiting,' Luke suggested. He paid the woman standing over a turning spit for two pieces of the succulent spiced meat.

Katherine chewed it hungrily and licked the juice as it ran down her chin, then laughed and tossed the bone to a scavenging dog. When she turned back to Luke, his expression was sombre, and he looked away quickly, as though uneasy that she had caught him studying her.

From his superior height Luke looked over the heads of the crowd, then, taking Kate's arm, he led her away from the meat-seller. Apparently absorbed at the sight of some children being pulled over the ice on sledges, he halted.

The cold was beginning to seep through Katherine's boots and she fidgeted to keep warm. Her restless gaze roamed over the skyline until it rested on the forbidding square keep of the Tower. The happiness of the day faded.

Within those imposing walls the lords who had supported the Rising were awaiting their trials to begin. Her stare travelled along the riverbank, over the chimneys of closely packed houses punctuated by imposing church spires and towers. Her study stopped at the great dome of St Paul's Cathedral. Almost within the shadows of that most spectacular of England's churches lay Newgate and all its horrors.

'You must not torment yourself, Kate,' Luke said,

turning her away from the north bank. He pulled her
fur-edged hood closer about her chilled face. 'You've
done all you can to ease your brother's suffering. The
trials will begin soon. Yet delay could be a good sign.
His Majesty may decide to make an example of only a
few of the rebels. There's a chance many will be
pardoned.'

Katherine sighed wearily. 'It is the waiting which is
so hard.'

'And you are not renowned for your patience,' he
quipped, but there was no condemnation in his voice.

'Paul always said it would be my downfall. And he's
just as impetuous. Look where it's landed him.' She
put her hand to her throat to ease the raw ache within.

From near by a haughty voice rose above the noise
of the revellers. Katherine whirled around, her eyes
widening with a mixture of anger and alarm as she
stared across at a gambling booth. St Clere was there
with two masked female companions hanging on each
arm.

She darted back behind the hanging of a stall, pulling
Luke with her.

'Kate, what's wrong?' he demanded.

'It's St Clere,' she warned.

The laughter went from Luke's eyes. 'I hide from no
man, least of all St Clere.'

He turned to go back into the aisle. A hand was laid
on Katherine's shoulder from behind, and she barely
managed to stop a scream of fright.

'I don't mean you no harm, ma'am.' A red-haired
man appeared at her side, his narrow, pinched face
covered in freckles and scored with premature lines.

'It's all right, Kate,' Luke said. 'It's Jem.'

Katherine now saw that one of the man's sleeves was
pinned to his threadbare, patched jacket.

'What have you found out, Jem?' Luke asked.

'Newgate ain't a place to escape from less there's
outside help. Ain't no guard likely to turn a blind eye
either, if yer get me meaning. It'd mean 'is job an

likely a whippin' which would kill 'im. But I bin askin' round. But the fraternity of thieves and beggars, who haunt Alsatia and Southwark, are a close-mouthed breed. One loosened his tongue after a skinful of ale. Name of Dogsbreath. Years ago 'is brother were switched off at Tyburn for thievin'. Dogsbreath visited him on his last night before they took 'im to Tyburn. He said that the highwayman Black Ned had jus' walked out, disguised as one of the gallants who'd come to toast 'is health. Popular wi' the gentry, was Black Ned, especially the ladies. I ain't saying such a ruse will be easy. Too much at stake for the turnkeys— but then they're partial to a drop of brandy.' He winked slyly. 'And if it were to become a regular occurrence that you slipped them a bottle along with the garnish—say for a visit or two before the escape— they ain't likely to be suspicious.'

'You've done well, Jem.' Luke dropped a pouch of coins in his hand.

'You take care, Cap'n. If they catch yer, yer'll swing for it.'

Jem touched his battered hat and disappeared into the crowd, and Katherine clutched Luke's arm. 'It's too dangerous, Luke. I will not have you risking your life for Paul. Perhaps he'll be spared because he's so young.'

'The judge will see him as a man,' Luke replied hollowly. 'And his health is deteriorating. For the moment we will wait until the King has given an answer to our petition for Paul's pardon. An escape will be the last resort if there's no hope of clemency.'

'I have no faith in King George's showing leniency to the Jacobites,' Katherine said heavily. 'But this is not your fight, Luke. You've suffered enough because of our marriage. . .marriage to a woman you distrust and no longer love. Why don't you just go and leave us to our fate?'

'Words of defeat, Kate?' He tipped up her chin with his gloved finger. 'That's not like you.'

'You've suffered enough, Luke,' she said as they walked back along the main aisle of booths. 'It has to end somewhere. I can afford to hire men to smuggle Paul out of Newgate. If Paul and I must pay the penalty for that attempt, then so be it. I've never regretted our marriage, Luke. You do.'

'Regret is not the word I would have used to describe our marriage. It is——' Luke broke off, his body stiffening.

Ahead of them, blocking their passage, was St Clere.

'Strange company you consort with, Ryder,' the Viscount sneered. 'A one-armed beggar. Now what information could you be buying from the likes of him?'

'The man was a soldier in my troop; he was wounded at Malplaquet,' Luke answered in scathing tones. 'Old soldiers look after their own if they can.'

'The common men always did have a tendency to stick together. But I know intrigue when I see it. And if it concerns Katherine it concerns her brother Paul.' St Clere's blue eyes narrowed behind his mask. 'Those who help the Jacobites are as guilty in the eyes of the King as the Jacobites themselves. It will be the gallows for the lot of them. And as a loyal subject of His Majesty I know where my duty lies.'

He sauntered off, leaving his threat heavy in the air between them.

'He suspects something,' Katherine said shakily. 'Paul is doomed. We dare not act now.'

'I'll not cry off because of St Clere's threats,' Luke said.

Fear for him choked Katherine's breath. Couldn't he see the danger? Much as she loved her brother, Katherine would not let Luke throw away his life. Paul had chosen to support the Rising. If all else failed then both Paul and herself must resign themselves to the consequences.

As the cold winter days turned into weeks, those consequences looked dire indeed. Luke refused to break his word that he would help Paul. It strengthened her love for him, but by the same token her fears that she would be the cause of his death gave her no peace.

In February Katherine's hopes were crushed. The Lords Kenmure and Derwent Water had been tried and found guilty. They were to mount the scaffold on the next day, the twenty-fourth. When Paul had been told the news he had lapsed into despair, and the gaol fever which Katherine's medicines had so far kept at bay took hold of his weakened body. Several of the Jacobite prisoners in Newgate had already died from the fever. In desperation Katherine found herself considering Old Jem's plan. If Paul was to escape, she would not allow Luke to risk his life alone.

That evening, after they had dined and she had played Luke's favourite pieces on the harpsichord to put him in a mellow mood, she broached the subject.

'If Paul attempts to escape it will be without you being involved.' Luke was emphatic. 'It's far too dangerous.'

'I won't allow you to place your life in danger for my brother while I do nothing. If anything should happen to you and Paul my life would be meaningless. I've thought this through, and with me it will stand a better chance. They pay little heed to me now when I visit Paul. Beneath my cloak and gown I could be dressed as a man. Paul would take my clothes—such a disguise will cover his weakened condition. The turnkeys will pay little heed to a woman leaning heavily on a man's arm. They will think her overcome with grief after visiting her sick brother.'

Luke took her shoulders and stared into her eyes. 'Such a plan could work. But I'll not have you involved. One of my men will masquerade as a woman. It's too dangerous for you.'

Katherine clutched at Luke's arm, her voice desperate. 'I'm not afraid. Please, Luke. I have to do this.'

He rubbed a hand across his mouth. The moustache

had long been shaved off, another sign that the part of
him who was Hunter was slowly being eroded.

'You forget our bargain, Kate. It was agreed I help
you only upon my terms,' he reminded her.

'This is different. I don't want cosseting just because
I'm a woman. I didn't care about the danger when I
saved you from the outlaw's bullet.'

A guard slid over Luke's expression. Katherine
cursed her foolishness in mentioning the incident. The
companionship they had shared over the last weeks
had been as free and easy as that of friends. Now she
saw that the traps were there and still baited, waiting
to snare an unwitting comment.

But she ignored his withdrawal from her. Her plan
was so simple—it had to work. 'There will be little
danger,' she insisted. 'Several guests will accompany us
when we visit Paul. These will move about among the
other Jacobite visitors and prisoners in their cells, and
when Paul is disguised I will be among the first to
leave. Paul will follow with you. To allay suspicion
some members of the party will stay behind in Paul's
cell talking as though the prisoner is still there.'

Katherine caught her breath as she waited for Luke's
approval of the plan. His expression remained
uncompromising.

'It will work.' Her voice throbbed with excitement.
'I can't sit back and do nothing. It's not my way.
Please, Luke. . .' She put her hand on his knee. 'This
is something I would have us do together.'

Interminably, Luke's black stare burned into her.
'It's a plan ripe for bedlam. But it could work. The
turnkeys grow lax. I make a point of bribing them well.
They'll not notice an extra face among so many when
we leave,' he agreed.

He needed time to come to terms with both the plan
and Kate's insistence that she take part in it. He stared
into the fire, loath to involve Kate. He suspected Paul's
condition was becoming serious. If they waited any

longer for the trials to begin it could be too late. He could be dead of gaol fever.

Luke could feel Kate's gaze on him as she silently willed him to agree. The thought of her in danger pitted him. He had brought Kate to London to get her poison out of his system. He stared at her ethereal beauty, her fair skin flushed from the passion of her plea. Too often the guard of his hatred was penetrated, leaving him desperate to believe that her words of love were true, her passion unfeigned. Distrust was slow to die, but time would tell. Once Paul was free the truth would out. Until then he would not weaken, would not acknowledge what was tunnelling through the granite which had hardened his heart.

'You realise that if Paul escapes he must live in exile,' he provoked, his pain making his words brutal in his need to test her. 'You may never see him again.'

'Better that than he be dead. Or sent as a slave to the colonies,' she retorted.

'Even the weather is against us,' Luke persisted. 'Because the Thames has frozen over my ship can sail no further than Barking Creek. What of Paul's fever? Will he stand such a long carriage-ride? He'll need tending. There's the ship's surgeon but——'

'If anyone is to tend Paul, I shall,' Kate cut in.

Luke's misgivings increased. Yet even through his anger at Kate's reckless disregard for her saftey his admiration for her courage grew. Each day she showed more of the qualities which had won his heart. There was no sign of the selfish heiress in her concern for her brother. Would she seek to trick him and go into exile with Paul?

'First, we have to free him from prison,' he replied tersely.

'Then you agree?' Kate flung her arms about him with delight. 'I knew you would. We cannot fail. Together we shall triumph.'

'And if we fail, Kate?' He stared deep into her

shining eyes, adding curtly, 'Will we dance in hell together, or heaven?'

She sighed with contempt. 'If we are together, in this life or the next, for me it will be heaven.' She lay across his arm and searched his face for the answer she yearned to hear. His expression was enigmatic.

Luke heard her words with mixed emotions. He saw beyond the room to the danger of the future. There was much Kate did not know—that a man with an eye-patch had been following him ever since the Frost Fair, for one thing. Usually he shook him off before he visited Paul, or had any dealings with the Jacobites. The information Kate had given him concerning St Clere was being followed up. To bring St Clere to justice he must have the statement of one of the Jacobite spies who had attended the Viscount at Highclere. Such information could win the prisoner his pardon. Paul had given him several names which were all aliases, but Luke had yet to track any of them down. It looked as if they had all scuttled back to their master, the Pretender, and were safe in France.

Luke had put his own spies on the man with the eye-patch, and they had learned that the man was in the pay of St Clere.

It meant that St Clere was awaiting his moment to strike.

CHAPTER THIRTEEN

'GARNISH!' the turnkey demanded as their party passed through the prison gates.

Katherine kept her head down and, pressing a nose-gay to her face, leaned closer to Luke. She suppressed a shudder and tried to still the nervous fluttering of her stomach. Newgate was more oppressive than ever.

As Luke handed over the money, several members of their party, all dressed as fashionable and wealthy men, entered the prison. Luke held Katherine back from entering the outer ward. Ahead of them was a group of coarse-voiced women who, from the way they reeled, were obviously drunk. At Luke's reluctance to permit Katherine to follow behind the women, she realised that they were the whores brought in for the prisoners.

A glance at him showed her his face was taut as he scanned the courtyard, noting the position of the guards. Briefly, his gaze flickered over her and his eyes softened with encouragement.

Once the women ahead of them had disappeared into a building, Luke led Katherine forward. The stench within the prison was as bad as she remembered, but though it stung her throat and nostrils this time it did not fully penetrate her consciousness. Slowing her breathing to ease the pounding of her heart, she concentrated on what must be done before Paul could walk free from here.

She relaxed as she felt the pressure of the dagger against her shin where she had concealed the blade in her boot. At least they were not totally defenceless against attack should their plot be discovered.

At the foot of the stairs leading to Paul's cell, a muscular turnkey barred their way.

'No more visitors upstairs,' he stated sullenly. 'Too many already. You'll 'ave ter wait.'

Katherine's flesh flushed with alarm. The success of the plan depended on the confusion aroused by a large number of prison visitors. She held her breath as Luke produced a silver coin from his pocket.

'There are but two of us,' he said smoothly.

'That makes no odds.' The turnkey eyed Luke narrowly. 'This ain't St James's Park. Yer can't just stroll through as it pleases yer.'

Luke took one of the two bottles of brandy laid in Katherine's basket. 'It's the lady's birthday today; she wishes most particularly to share it with her brother.' He held the bottle out. 'Perhaps you would care to celebrate with us?'

The turnkey licked his lips, his bloodshot gaze fastened on the bottle. But there remained a stubborn, malicious set to his bearded features. He took the bottle and pocketed the coin, adding ungraciously, 'Can't just let any cove in ter see the rebels.' He thrust his head forward, leering at Katherine. The acrid smell of his unwashed body and rotting teeth made her flinch back, and the man's thick, bushy brows drew menacingly together.

Fear gripped her that the situation was slipping from their grasp. The turnkey was being deliberately obstructive. He planted his feet firmly apart and crossed his arms, barring the way up the stairs.

At her side Luke tensed. If he lost his temper and provoked the turnkey further, they might never get to see Paul—let alone get him out of the prison. Katherine laid a restraining hand upon her husband's arm. 'The guard is but doing his duty,' she reasoned sweetly. Her skin crawled at the way the man licked his lips as his gaze mentally stripped her naked, and the muscle in Luke's arm beneath her hand bunched. He was on the point of striking the guard. She made to move past the turnkey, but the man stood his ground.

'Bin complaints there's too many whores coming into the prison. The woman stays 'ere,' he said.

With a snarl of rage, Luke stepped forward, snapping out, 'I've just told you that this lady is sister to one of the prisoners. She is also my wife.'

'That's wot they all say——' The turnkey winked, unabashed.

'I am a respectable married woman,' Katherine cut in sharply.

The turnkey's eyes glinted cruelly as he jutted his chin forward, clearly spoiling for a fight. 'You 'aint so respectable if you're kin to a damned Jack.'

Another turnkey came into the ward from outside. It was a man Katherine recognised from her previous visits.

'Wot's the 'old-up 'ere, Ben?' he asked, his small eyes on the brandy bottle. 'The cove 'ere is a regular visitor to Winters. Generous, 'e is. We wouldn't want to antagonise a man who knows 'ow to show 'is appreciation of the favours we bestow.'

'Good day, sir,' Luke said curtly and held out two more silver coins which were palmed and pocketed by the turnkey with speed. 'The brandy is to celebrate my wife's birthday today. If your companion is not disposed to partake of it, I'm sure you will not insult us by refusing.'

'I won't indeed.' The second turnkey grinned. 'You be going up now, sir, and your good wife. Don't pay no mind to Ben 'ere. He's new to the job. Keen, like. Don't quite know the way we do things 'ere.'

Katherine hurried passed the guards, the encounter leaving her pale and shaken. She whispered to Luke, 'Will that new turnkey be a problem? He took a close look at my face. If he stops us on the way out. . .' She could not go on.

Luke squeezed her hand. 'With luck he'll be too drunk to notice. From the looks of him he's a man who likes a drink.'

Katherine was far from reassured, but she forced a

smile. If she showed any weakness Luke might stop the escape just to protect her. She suppressed a shudder. If they failed they would all end up within these accursed walls.

When Katherine and Luke entered Paul's cell, two of her husband's men who had gone on ahead excused themselves. Instead of passing out of the cell they stood talking to Luke in the doorway, effectively blocking the view inside from any passer-by.

Paul stood in the corner. He was freshly shaved and his face was flushed. She hoped it was from excitement, not a return of the gaol fever which was gradually wasting his body. She gave him a quick hug and a kiss on the cheek. His face was hot. Worried for his health, she looked into his eyes. They were over-bright—a sign of returning fever.

'Don't look so concerned, Kat,' Paul said. 'I'm fine. I only wish you were not involved.'

Katherine flashed him an encouraging smile which belied the fear gnawing inside her. Her hands were surprisingly steady as they unfastened her cloak.

'There's little time,' she said, flinging her cloak on to the straw pallet in the corner. Her gown, its lacings already loosened, quickly followed. She straightened from stepping out of a petticoat and Paul chuckled as he stared at her slim figure dressed in man's clothing. His movements were frustratingly slow as she helped him into her clothes. She took the plain black cocked hat from her head and pulled off the blonde wig she was wearing. Beneath it, her own hair was sleeked back into a queue.

The blond wig in place, Paul sat on the bed while she applied powder to his face, covering the tell-tale shadow of his beard-line. She put some carmine to his lips and cheeks and stepped back to survey her handi-work. Satisfied, she handed him the nosegay which would hide his features from the guards. To complete the disguise she lifted the deep fur-lined hood over the wig and pulled it as low as possible over his brow.

Luke stepped inside the cell and, removing one of the two black cloaks he was wearing, handed it to Katherine. Paul looked at him uncertainly.

'Do I pass as a woman?' he asked.

Luke grinned. 'You'll do.'

'Just remember to try and walk like a woman, not with great strides like a man,' Katherine warned.

Katherine stooped over the cold water in the washing bowl and, dipping a handkerchief into it, used it to scrub all traces of powder and paint from her own face. Then she pulled on Luke's cloak and pushed the peak of the black hat down over her face.

Luke nodded to the men by the door, who exchanged places with them in the cell. 'Give us as long as you can before you leave. I want as much coming and going between these cells as possible to confuse the guards.'

When Paul swayed and stopped for a moment to hold on to the wall, Luke linked his arm through his. 'Lean on me,' he said. 'The guards will think you're upset at leaving your brother. And keep the nosegay close to your face.'

Paul leaned heavily on Luke's arm and looked worriedly across at Katherine.

'Should this fail, Kat,' he said weakly, 'I want you to know I'll never forget what you've done. Both of you.'

'There's no time to talk now,' Luke dismissed Paul's gratitude. 'Time for that once we're out of here.'

Beneath the powder Paul had grown very flushed, and Katherine feared the fever was fast overtaking him. They must get him out of Newgate quickly, before his strength failed.

Outside in the corridor, Katherine heard Luke's men in the cell addressing Paul by name and speaking as though he were still present. Everything now depended on Paul and herself being able to fool the guards. She was joined by another of Luke's men as they began to descend the stairs. She affected a manly stride and deepened her voice as she spoke to the man at her side, her face turned from the turnkeys sitting on guard.

At the bottom of the stairs, her heart lurched. The turnkey who had challenged them earlier had stood up to block their path.

'Leaving so soon?' he jeered. 'I thought the lady wanted to celebrate her birthday with 'er brother.'

'My wife is upset, which is only to be expected,' Luke said with crisp authority. 'Allow us to pass.'

'Wot's yer 'urry? Ain't the pleasures of Newgit to yer liking?'

Standing behind her brother, Katherine could see Paul's stooped figure trembling as the fever gripped him.

Luke fixed the gaoler with a commanding glare. 'There are no pleasures, only suffering here.' He held out a pouch of several coins. 'I have an arrangement with the other turnkey. Winters is to receive the best food brought in from outside. This is to pay you for your trouble. There will be more next week, and every week, until the Jacobites are brought to trial.'

The pouch was grabbed in greedy fingers.

'Drink to the health of His Majesty,' Luke continued. 'I would know Winters fared well during his stay here.'

There was a guffaw of laughter from the direction of Paul's cell, and Paul was loudly addressed by name.

The turnkey shuffled back, weighing the pouch in his hand. 'I shall look forward to your weekly visits.' A broad, single-toothed grin split his face as he gestured for them to pass.

A stinging sweat broke out over Katherine's body as they moved across the open yard. At each step she expected to be challenged by a guard, and she kept glancing anxiously at Paul, whose feet were beginning to drag. Had they delayed too long in getting him out? Would her brother's weakness now prove their undoing?

She saw Luke stoop to say something to Paul, and

immediately her brother seemed to rouse himself and walk more steadily. Dear God, let Paul not pass out, she prayed fervently. Give him the strength for just a few more minutes. Then he would be free.

As they walked through the different wards towards the main gate, Katherine noted Luke's handing a coin to any hovering guards and, feeling more confident, she lengthened her stride to match his assured step.

Already the final barrier was in sight. Then, yards from the main gate, the heel of her boot slipped on a patch of ice and she went down on one knee. Biting back a cry as a sharp pain shot through her leg, she heard a snort of laughter from the guards by the gate. Luke looked back, but the diversion she had caused allowed him and Paul to pass through the gate unmolested. For a horrified moment her companion began to hold out his hand to assist her to rise. Her eyes flashed their warning. Such aid would destroy her disguise as a man. He quickly snatched his hand back. Had the guards seen his movement?

Katherine rose to her feet and dusted off her knee in a gesture of annoyance, then strode on. Her nerves were strained to breaking-point, her body alternating between hot then icy cold. They were level with the guards. Would they be suspicious?

But the fall had shaken her more than she believed possible, and as they approached the gate her trembling legs threatened to give way beneath her. The man at her side nudged her and she saw he held a brandy flask in his hand.

'Take a drink,' he said. 'It will give you strength. Besides, most of the young bucks who visit here do so on a drunken spree.'

She gulped down the fiery liquid and handed the flask back to him. Luke and Paul were already outside the prison, but her rush of relief was doused with sickening dread as she saw the guard by the gate watching her through narrowed eyes.

With a drunken-sounding laugh her companion

swayed against Katherine and drank from the flask.
Katherine took it from him and waved it in an expan-
sive gesture at the guard.

'Your health, my good man,' she slurred.

She pretended to drink but allowed no brandy to
pass her lips a second time. She would need all her wits
should Paul's disappearance be noted and the alarm
raised before the waiting carriage got them safely
through the city.

As they neared the gate a disturbance broke out in
the courtyard, and the guard who had been studying
them was called to assist. Looking across the open
space, Katherine saw a struggling male prisoner being
dragged towards a horse and cart. They tied the man
to the back of the vehicle.

Katherine strode out of the prison while the guard
was distracted. She looked back once as the prisoner
was led out behind the cart. A chaplain walked at his
side. There was a loud crack followed by a scream of
agony from the prisoner as the whip came down upon
his shoulders. The prisoner was about to be dragged
through the city and flogged.

She hurried on. Luke and Paul were already in the
coach, and as Luke held out a hand to help her inside
she gave a sign of relief. The first danger was over.
Now to get Paul safely aboard Luke's ship moored on
the Thames near Barking.

Overjoyed, she flung her arms around Paul. 'We did
it. You're free.' She looked across at Luke, and was
startled by the grimness of his expression. This should
have been a moment of triumph binding them closer
together, but he was looking at her and Paul with the
cold, assessing stare of Hunter. What did he suspect
her of now?

Paul slumped back tiredly into the corner of the
carriage and Katherine leaned forward to touch Luke's
arm. 'We could not have done it without you.'

Luke shrugged. 'We are not clear yet. We have to
get away through these crowds.'

She peered out of the window. The people who had gathered to watch the flogging pressed in around them. To try and move away would attract undue attention to the carriage. They had to sit and wait it out.

It was the most tortuous ten minutes of Katherine's life. She had chewed her thumbnail to the quick before the flogging procession moved slowly down the street, the crowd thinning as it followed it. Luke ordered the coachman to make a detour through the side-roads, then sat back in the seat, watching Kate as she pressed a vial of medicine to Paul's bloodless lips. She tenderly wiped the sweat from his brow, love and adoration obvious in every gesture she made. The old suspicions stirred, cutting Luke to the bone. Was Kate prepared to leave the brother she adored and continue her life with him? Or would she betray him yet again?

He bit back a caustic comment. Throughout the entire escape Kate had been superb. But then he knew her to be a clever actress. Had the role of dutiful wife been just that—a role?

Once out of the city the coach picked up speed as it travelled over the frozen ground. Luke tipped back his hat and rubbed his hand across his chin. Their ruse had worked. Paul Winters was free. Unfortunately St Clere had escaped the justice he deserved. That rankled. He frowned, his mind going back over the day's events. It centred upon the faces in the crowd pressed close to the coach during the flogging. One particular face had been glimpsed only briefly. How could he have dismissed it? The man with the eye-patch would have missed nothing. By now he would have reported to St Clere.

Lost in his thoughts, Luke remained silent and brooding; with each passing mile his antagonism against the Viscount grew. He studied Paul. The young man's face was no longer feverish, but grey with exhaustion. He turned to look out of the window as they passed through the village of Bethnal Green.

An hour later, as they crossed the marshland at

Barking, the view was becoming obscured by a gathering mist, but he had seen the twin masts of the brigantine as it rode at anchor in the river.

The *Sea Serpent* was their future. Ferncombe Place was lost to Paul, as was Kate's own fortune. All had been sequestered by the Crown as the estate of a suspected traitor. The petition to the King had failed. Even the charges Luke had brought against St Clere were discarded out of hand. The wily Viscount had saved his own hide by turning evidence against his fellow conspirators, Luke was certain.

When Paul was safely away from England, he would settle the old score with St Clere. They would set sail for Jersey within the hour, where Paul would regain his strength. With her brother free and recovered in health, Kate would no longer need a protector.

Throughout the journey Katherine's tension mounted. She glanced frequently out of the window, each time dreading she would see signs of pursuit. When they were out of the city she relaxed, but remained disheartened by the rigidness of her husband's frame. Luke's expression was shuttered and she could not begin to assess how his mind was working.

At a harshly indrawn breath from Paul, she dragged her eyes from her husband. With frightening weakness Paul clutched at her hand.

'Do you think the escape has been discovered? Are we being followed?' he asked.

Katherine glanced at Luke, who shook his head, and some of her disquiet eased.

'We're safe for now,' she soothed. 'We've already reached the marshes.'

The coach drew to a halt. Luke retrieved his sword-belt from the floor beneath the seat, where he had placed it before entering the prison, and got out. Katherine watched him as he stared towards his ship anchored in the river channel. He looked so remote and unapproachable as he stood with his cloak billowing behind him like a sail in the cold wind.

Her heart constricted. Was this change in Luke because he intended their relationship to end? She stepped down from the carriage to go to him. The icy air caught at her throat and she shivered as she stared about the desolate, flat marshland, the swirling grey tentacles of mist making her surroundings sinister.

Looking across the frozen marsh to reassure herself they had not been followed, she saw her husband raise a closed lantern. He opened and closed the shutter twice, signalling the brigantine. The tide was out but the longboat could come ashore in the creek. When he turned to stride back towards them, his voice was as wintry as the weather.

'Can Paul walk?' he asked.

'Yes,' Paul replied, appearing at the coach door. He fumbled impatiently with the fastenings of the hooded cloak. 'But first I would be rid of these clothes.'

'Then make haste. I don't want to linger here,' Luke ordered.

Katherine conquered a resurgence of alarm. Was it possible they still might get caught and arrested?

'Damn it, Kat, give us a hand with these laces,' Paul groaned.

Her brother's voice sounded weak. Looking at him, Katherine saw him sway, his face flushed from his exertions. With an exclamation of dismay, she ran to his side. She helped him out of the gown and petticoats and he shivered in his shirt and breeches as she once again drew the cloak over his emaciated figure.

'Here, give him my cloak.' Luke tossed it to her, then turned to dismiss the coachman.

Paul staggered as he tried to walk. Luke caught him and hooked her brother's arm over his shoulders, supporting him as they walked to where the longboat would land. Once there, he settled Paul on the bank of the creek and turned to Katherine.

'Will Paul be all right?' she asked fearfully. 'He's so much weaker than I realised. Will the money from the jewels I sold be enough to set him up in a new life? There are bound to be physician's fees.'

At the tremor in her voice Luke curled his fingers around her wrist, drawing her closer to him. For a long moment he looked down into her upturned face. The uncertainty in Kate's green eyes roused the old demon of distrust in him. But his need for revenge had died. She had not balked at selling her jewels, and when he had told her that her dowry was confiscated by the Crown she had shrugged, saying the dowry was a curse and she was well rid of it. They were not the words of a spoilt heiress.

But then, knowing Kate as he now did, she was too selfless for that. He had been wrong to allow his distrust to condemn her for the fickleness of others of her kind.

If only he could be sure with whom her first loyalty lay. Was it Paul? Or himself? And what was the truth behind that fateful dawn morning of the duel?

Raising a hand to brush a tendril of fair hair from the corner of Kate's cheek, he felt himself drowning in her beauty. At that moment he would have sold his soul to the Devil to believe in his wife. Her skin was smooth as velvet but icy to the touch. Was her heart as frozen as her flesh? Since the day he had returned from his ship to learn she had asked St Clere for help Kate had spoken no words of love to him. But then had he not flung her falseness in her face? Was it pride which kept her silent?

He crushed a rising ache to hear again her lips whispering endearments. He had vowed to be done with sentiment. But if she was innocent? The question cut into him as he gazed into the sparkling promise in her emerald eyes. He willed himself to remember Kate was a siren, luring him by her air of innocence on to hidden rocks which could still bring about his destruction.

But for once he did not care. He loved Kate. It was time he told her so.

'Kate.'

Even as her name formed on his lips, a distant sound alerted him to possible danger. His hand fell to his side and, looking over her head across the flat marshes, he saw through a gap in the mist that a group of riders was fast approaching.

CHAPTER FOURTEEN

'THE longboat will never reach us before the riders,' Luke ground out. 'Kate, get Paul to the water's edge and board it as soon as it comes ashore. If there's trouble, go without me.'

'No. I'll not go without you.'

'This is no time for false heroics, Kate,' Luke snapped.

Katherine stubbornly shook her head; she had recognised the lead rider. It was St Clere. She would not leave Luke to face the Viscount alone. It was because of her that St Clere was his enemy.

Luke also had seen St Clere. The men who rode with him looked an unsavoury band of cut-throats. He rounded on Kate.

'Is this your ultimate betrayal? My ship is out there waiting to take Paul to safety. All you need is a timely rescue by St Clere to prevent you leaving England. . . And, of course, my death, to leave you free to marry the Viscount.'

Katherine flinched back from him. Her throat worked but no words formed.

He was angry at himself for beginning to trust her, and it made his fury the greater. 'Has St Clere already begun proceedings at Court to regain Ferncombe Place in his future wife's name?'

Katherine backed away, her eyes round with shock. 'Still you believe me capable of such deceit?' she blazed. 'Devil take you, Hunter! Salve your misbegotten conscience and believe what you will. I no longer care. The Luke Ryder I loved is dead. I have only loathing and contempt for Hunter.' Spinning round, she staggered away.

'Ryder, have you taken leave of your senses?' Paul wheezed. 'Kate would never betray you.'

'Do you think I'm blind?' Luke rapped out. 'To Kate your escape was just another diversion—like our marriage. She turned her back on that fast enough when it suited her. She's using me now as she used me then.'

Paul's frail body sagged, his face grey and haggard like an old man's as he shook his head.

'My sister never betrayed you. St Clere wrote that letter you received. To my shame I went along with his plan. Kat was drugged and in her room when you called at the house. She was told you had been paid off with five thousand pounds.' Paul swayed, his confession draining his strength. 'It was I who wronged you, not Kat. I wanted her to marry St Clere and her future be assured. But from the first I saw Kat was drawn to you like no man before. From the night of the reception at Highclere I knew you had won her love. It's Hunter she hates, not Luke Ryder. She'll go to the grave loving him.'

Paul hunched over and shuffled away. Katherine ran to his side, her arms supportive as she lowered him to the ground.

Through his rage Luke realised he had made the most appalling error. He should never have allowed his anger and grief at Hal Penrose's death to drive him so far. His lack of trust of all heiresses had finally killed Kate's love.

Behind him the thundering of hoofs warned him that St Clere was almost upon them. He had no chance to apologise to Kate. When the riders drew to a halt, he turned to face them. Until his men in the longboat reached the shore he was outnumbered.

Luke drew himself to his full height. 'I doubt you've come to wish us Godspeed, my lord,' he said drily.

'You did not think I would let you escape without a reckoning,' St Clere drawled.

Before Luke could guess Kate's intent, she darted

forward, but with a sharp glance in her direction he cautioned her to be silent.

'Go and wait for the longboat to land,' he ordered in a low voice.

To his annoyance Kate did not move, her lips compressed obstinately. She was pale, but to her credit showed no sign of fear. When she took another step forward, he feared her about to intervene, and his hand on her arm jerked her back.

St Clere sneered. 'It's time you learned a lesson in manners. And that young lad too. He's got an insolent look.'

Rudely reminded of her disguise, Katherine stepped back. The mist was thickening. The angry way she wrapped her cloak about her figure showed Luke the effort it cost her to control her outrage.

He stared into the face of his enemy. St Clere's haughty face was frigid with hatred. Behind the heavy lids his eyes gleamed with an unearthly brightness. There were a dozen men with him, and they dismounted while the Viscount remained imperiously upon his horse.

With relief Luke saw that the longboat was now in the creek. There might only be five men on board but they were a match for St Clere's cronies. Paul was too weak to fight, so that made the odds two against one. All his crew were ex-soldiers whom at some time he had saved from starvation on the streets. To a man they were loyal to him.

'You again resort to hired assassins, my lord,' Luke jeered, the emphasis he placed on the title derogatory. 'They did not succeed in destroying me last time. Neither did you, on the occasion you were forced to face me man to man.'

Luke glanced at Kate, who was striving to remain calm. A tightness settled over his chest. She was his salvation. He knew now she had not betrayed him. St Clere, in his craving for her dowry, had used her as cruelly as he had him. Remorse speared him. He had wronged Kate—unpardonably.

He resisted the desire to draw his wife close to praise her for her courage. Shaken by the intensity of his emotions, he dragged his gaze from her. He could not afford to be side-tracked—St Clere's men were closing in.

'Get back to Paul,' Luke ordered her.

Luke drew his sword, balancing his weight on the balls of his feet as he prepared to meet the first attack. The sailors had two hundred yards to cover before the longboat was landed.

Like a pack of ravening dogs the assassins charged. His sword flashed, scything in an arc, cutting and thrusting as he held them at bay. His attack was without mercy. With consummate skill he ducked and side-stepped. His blade danced like quicksilver, parrying, turning upon each attacker with swift, accurate precision, then snaking under the guards of his attackers to keep them hesitantly out of the reach of its now bloodied edge. Two of the men were wounded, their screams of pain unnerving their companions.

The pace were beginning to tell on Luke. His teeth were clenched against the laboured breath scalding his throat, his arm beginning to tremble from wielding the sword.

'Hold on, Cap'n, we're with you!'

A heartening cheer came from near by. He dared not glance over his shoulder to see how close his men were. Two of his assailants were pressing him so furiously that he was barely holding his ground. Skill triumphed over brawn as stroke by stroke his sword parried their wild lunges, and he forced one attacker to his knees.

Then there was a cry of alarm from the assailants as his men fell upon them and began beating them back. Within moments three of the assassins lay dead, four others were wounded and had stopped fighting. Only one of the sailors was injured.

'Fight, you curs,' St Clere screamed. 'Fight, damn you! A hundred pounds to the man who kills Ryder. Nay, two hundred—to any man—that includes the sailors.'

'Show 'em we can't be bought,' a sailor shouted. 'To the captain!'

The fighting was fierce, easing the pressure off Luke's tired sword arm. Luke grinned diabolically, seeking a chance to turn his attack upon St Clere. When another opponent lay screaming in the marsh mud, his fingers clutching his pierced gut, the others began to retreat in haste.

'We yield,' one shouted. The man threw down his sword and fled to his horse. As he scrambled into the saddle, his actions were followed by all his companions capable of flight.

Katherine let out a long held breath. Luke was safe. Then a movement at her side caught her eye. St Clere was drawing a pistol from his saddle holster.

'Luke, watch your back!' she screamed. Heedless of the danger to herself, she hurled her body at St Clere's horse at the very instant the Viscount fired. The gelding reared, the pistol discharged into the air and St Clere was pitched over his mount's head on to the ground.

Katherine's fears were centred on Luke who had whirled and run towards St Clere, his expression murderous.

'Get back!' Luke yelled at her.

The warning was too late. Her attention fixed on Luke, she had not noticed St Clere coming to his feet. Suddenly an arm locked around her throat. The decadent nobleman intended to use her as a hostage. She twisted round, her nails raking at his face. With an oath St Clere lashed out, striking her in the stomach and doubling her over in pain.

'You bastard, St Clere!' Luke raged. 'Is your fight now with women? Leave Kate alone.'

St Clere looked at her with shocked surprise. When she had flung herself at the horse, her hat had come off, and now the Viscount's expression twisted cruelly as he recognised her. She was jerked brutally against his frame and his hold tightened about her throat.

'So it is you, you little bitch,' he growled in her ear as he fumbled inside his jacket with his free hand. 'I might have known you'd not be far from the side of that black devil.'

She kicked and writhed, but each movement increased the pressure against her windpipe which was slowly choking her. When a cold object was pressed against her temple, she saw Luke check his movement towards her, and the ominous click which reverberated through her skull turned her blood to ice. A pistol was cocked and pointed at her head.

Katherine was hauled backwards, the Viscount's arm like an iron vice as he edged away from Luke. The pistol stabbed against her temple.

'Stay back,' St Clere warned, 'or she dies!'

Katherine trembled as St Clere dragged her to his horse. His threat was no idle one.

'There's no escape, St Clere.' Luke's face was bloodless as he challenged the Viscount. 'Let Kate go.'

'She's my safe passage out of here.' St Clere ran the edge of the pistol barrel down across her body, daring Luke to attack him. 'And once away. . .' he laughed vindictively '. . .Katherine will be returned to you. After I've taken my pleasure of her, of course.'

The pistol slid downwards to press against Kate's stomach as he added with greater menace, 'Try and stop me, and I'll take great pleasure in shooting her before your eyes. Gut shot is a slow and agonising death. Call off your men.'

'It will be a merciful death compared to what you'll suffer if you harm my wife,' Luke responded with deadly quietness. He signalled for the sailors to stay back.

Katherine gulped for air, the pressure on her throat excruciating. She must not pass out. To escape she would need all her wits. So much had happened, so quickly. She did not delude herself that Luke acted through pride, not love. His accusations earlier had proved he did not love her. As for herself—her heart was dead.

Pride dictated that St Clere would not triumph over them. All around them the sailors stood tense and poised, awaiting Luke's command. Her husband was frozen into immobility. Only his eyes looked alive and they were as savage as a cornered panther's.

'Get on to the horse,' St Clere ordered Katherine. 'And no tricks.'

Katherine obeyed, her limbs shaking as she fought to control her terror. The pressure of the pistol against her side remained firm as the Viscount swung up behind her and kicked the horse into a gallop.

Fear threatened to overwhelm her as they pounded away, not just for herself, but because she knew Luke would follow. She did not fool herself that it was because he loved her, but because he owed her his life. Luke would track St Clere down out of duty.

After all they had accomplished, was St Clere to be the victor? Was it to end this way? Outrage and anger scalded through her veins. St Clere would not win.

'Are you frightened, Katherine?' he chuckled wickedly against her ear. 'You should be. Now you and Ryder will suffer for the trouble you've caused me!'

'Luke will hound you. You'll never get away with this. You've failed to kill him three times,' she reminded him.

'There are more ways than one to destroy a man.' St Clere jammed the pistol against her side. 'To see the woman you love ravished and then killed before your eyes will leave him a mental cripple. Oh, yes, Ryder will follow. You are my lure.'

St Clere was insane with jealousy and the need for revenge. And to think she had once called Luke's mind warped. He had condemned her with words. If she had not been so angry with Luke, she would have acknowledged long ago that all his dealings with her had been

tempered with tenderness. And the consideration of
love. . .

Luke did love her.

The knowledge exulted her, fired her intrepid spirits.
Her mind raced in rhythm to the horse's drumming
hoofs. Luke loved her. . . She must escape. . . But
how? St Clere would kill her. Stay calm. . .await your
chance, she told herself.

Another horse was gaining on them. Luke was in
pursuit.

St Clere kicked their horse to a faster pace, and it
shot forward into the thick mist. Then suddenly it
stumbled, its hoofs striking uneven ground. Katherine
was thrown forward, and when she gripped the horse's
sides with her legs to stop herself falling under its hoofs
a pain shot along her calf as the thin-bladed dagger dug
into her leg. Her pulses raced with excitement, tram-
pling her fear. She had forgotten she still had the
dagger concealed in her boot. Somehow, without
arousing St Clere's suspicions, she had to retrieve it.

While the Viscount struggled to keep the horse's
head up, she slipped further forward, as though caught
off balance, and, quickly drawing the blade from her
boot, she hid it under the folds of her cloak.

St Clere jerked her body upright. 'One more move
like that and you're dead.'

Fear prickled Katherine's spine. Had he seen the
dagger? But when he continued to curse the tiring
mount, digging in his heels to urge the beast to a faster
pace, she began to relax. St Clere needed to exact his
vengeance upon Luke upon his own ground. He had
no intention of confronting her husband face to face.

Their wild flight must have disorientated the Viscount's bearings on the marsh. Instead of rough terrain
they were now on the oozing river mud. The thick mist
obscured everything. The horse slowed, nervous of the
sucking mud beneath its hoofs. The hoofbeats behind
were closer. St Clere looked over his shoulder.
Katherine followed his stare and saw Luke's dark figure

emerging out of the mist. The arm about her waist
tensed and the pressure of the pistol was removed as
St Clere raised his arm to shoot Luke.

Rapidly the gap closed between the two horses. The
ears of Luke's mount were laid back and its hot breath
steamed dragon-like from its flared nostrils. Luke was
crouched low in the saddle, his cloak whipping back
behind him. He rode like an avenging demon.

When Katherine felt St Clere draw breath to steady
his aim, she lunged wildly at him with her dagger—but
the angle was wrong and the thin blade glanced off his
cloak to nick the side of his jaw and ear.

St Clere slammed the pistol butt against her head,
momentarily dazing her, and as she reeled forward in
the saddle the nervous horse stopped in its tracks,
refusing to go on.

'Release Kate,' Luke shouted, almost upon them.
'Fight like a man, you bastard!'

St Clere shifted his position, bringing his arm up to
fire the pistol at Luke. Katherine acted with the instinct
of a tigress defending her mate. She rammed her elbow
into his ribs, deflecting his aim as the pistol was fired,
and at the same time she kicked out, swinging her leg
over the pommel of the saddle and throwing herself
down on to the soft mud.

The dagger remained tight in her grasp and, unre-
stricted by hampering petticoats, she rolled and came
up on to her knees.

Seconds later Luke launched himself from his mount,
his arms circling St Clere as the impetus of his attack
brought both men to the ground. There was a tangle of
arms and legs as they struggled together, then Luke
twisted free and straddled the Viscount, pinning him to
the ground.

'It's just us this time, my lord,' he growled. 'None of
your villains are here to do your dirty work.'

To Katherine's horror Luke's body was levered
upwards as the heavier bulk of St Clere rolled him
aside. Both men swayed to their feet, swords drawn

and bodies crouched as they waited for each other to attack, and there were a few moments of stillness while both men sized each other up.

'Be prepared to die, Ryder,' St Clere snarled as he made his first lunge.

The ferocity with which the steel blades clashed made Katherine shudder. A murderous rage twisted St Clere's and Luke's face. Her blood gelled to ice. There would be only one survivor. With her nerves almost at screaming-pitch she continued to watch the combat. Luke, despite his tiredness from his earlier fight, moved with skilful grace, ducking and pivoting as he parried each stroke, but St Clere was also adept in evading Luke's thrusts.

The latter laughed cruelly. 'I've spent every day since my wound healed with my fencing master. I hope you've said your farewells to your wife, Ryder.' The speed of the Viscount's sword arm gave the lie to the injury he had paraded as the emblem of his loyalty to King George.

Both men were breathing heavily, their breath steaming in the chill air. St Clere continued to laugh as he pressed his attack. To Katherine the contest was frighteningly even. Luke had beaten St Clere before, but he had already fought one exhausting fight today, and she could see he was tiring. Even so, Luke pursued his attack with deadly accuracy until his opponent was forced to give ground.

Katherine stood tense, her heart thundering in her breast. The ground under their feet was no longer firm but slimy with oozing mud. It sucked at the men's feet, hampering their agility. The hilt of her dagger bit into her palm, the pain unheeded. She saw Luke feint, drawing St Clere's blade dangerously near her husband's heart, but with precision timing he nimbly twisted aside. With a dexterity which caught St Clere unawares, Luke then flicked his wrist, sending St Clere's blade winging through the air to land yards behind him in the river mud, but at the same moment

Luke's foot was sucked down into the mire, throwing him off balance, and he fell on his back.

St Clere was facing Katherine, the furthest from her. His eyes were glazed with blood-lust. Katherine saw him flip back the full skirts of his coat, revealing a dagger strapped to his hip, and as the Viscount's hand closed over its hilt Katherine snapped into action. Her hand came up, her eyes narrowed as she took aim, and with all her strength she threw her dagger.

Her shaking hands affected her aim; instead of embedding in his shoulder it struck St Clere's arm. However, the surprise of her attack halted the Viscount from plunging his own dagger into Luke's prostrate body long enough for Luke to recover and rise to his feet.

St Clere backed away, his head twisting from side to side as he searched for his sword. It was several yards behind him. He ran backwards with Luke in pursuit. The mist distorted their figures, and Katherine followed, unable to bear the suspense of not knowing what was happening.

With each step the men sank further into the river mud, which now wrapped around their calves. Luke froze and turned to shout back at Katherine, 'For the love of God, Kate, stay back. It's quicksand.'

Katherine stared at her own feet. The mud squelched over the toe of her boot but came no further. She was to the right of Luke. Here the ground was still firm.

St Clere shrieked as he went down, his body distorted by the swirling mist. Luke had managed to retreat several paces before the mud held him fast.

'Luke!' Kate screamed, placing each foot down tentatively before it took all her weight. 'The ground to your right is firm—can you reach it?'

'Not without help.' His voice was flat with finality.

She continued to edge forward but the solid ground ended several feet from where Luke was stuck fast. He pulled off his sword and dagger-belts and began to tie the leather straps together, then, holding one end, he threw the makeshift rope towards Katherine. It fell three feet short.

'No. Don't try and reach them!' Luke ordered

'I'll get the horse's reins,' she suggested. 'They will be long enough and the horse can pull you out.'

An unnatural calmness took possession of her as she ran back to where the horse cropped the frozen grass, then she heard St Clere's terrified shout.

'Help me!' St Clere screamed hysterically. 'I'm sinking!'

For the moment she could do nothing for St Clere. Perhaps it was already too late. She hardened her heart. Luke still had a chance. She would not think of failure. He had survived too much danger for death to claim him now. She had to concentrate on saving Luke. Then, if there was time, they would do what they could for St Clere.

The horse threw up his head at her approach and began to side-step.

'Don't be difficult,' her voice quavered. 'Here, boy.' The horse's ears twitched, but he stayed still as she grabbed the reins. 'I've caught the horse,' she called to Luke. The mist had thickened and she could no longer see him on the mud. 'I can't see you.'

'Over here,' his voice guided her.

'Help me!' St Clere called from further away. She could hear his frantic struggles, the noise intensified by the mist.

Fear scalded through her veins, making her sob with frustration as the nervous horse shied away from the mud. She must not communicate her own alarm to him. She took a steadying breath, and put her hand on his muzzle, stroking him as she urged him forward. 'That's it, boy. You can do it. Dear God, you have to do it.'

'That's far enough, Kate,' Luke ordered. He now lay flat on the mud. He took his dagger from its sheath and tossed it to her. 'Cut the reins—just leave yourself enough length to hold on to.'

Katherine picked up the dagger and sawed through the leather reins. As she did so Luke hauled in the belts he had earlier thrown towards her. The reins cut, she threw them to him, and felt her body begin to tremble as she waited for the makeshift rope to be thrown back at her. They landed at her feet with a plop. When she stooped to retrieve them the horse jerked back on the reins. Sweat broke out over Kate's body.

'Steady, boy, steady!' She edged forward again. Her fingers closed over the leather but as soon as she lifted it she knew it would never be long enough to hook over the saddle pommel. She wound it around her hand; the shortened reins were already tight around her other palm.

She lifted her gaze to Luke, who even now had the courage to give her a grim smile.

'You can do it, Kate. I'd stake my life on it.'

She swallowed against the lump his words brought to her throat. If she failed he was doing just that. Stretching out her arms, she braced her body to take the strain.

'Back, boy,' she commanded the horse.

Her arms felt as if they were being pulled from their sockets as the horse obeyed. The leather straps gouged deep into her hand, cutting off the flow of blood. She screwed her face up against the agony, her voice grating in her throat as she continued to encourage the horse, 'Back, boy. Back!'

At any moment she thought her arms would be torn from her body. The leather belts shuddered and gradually, inch by inch, her feet were pulled back by the straining horse. They were gaining ground. Another few inches and Luke would be free.

There was a last blood-freezing cry from St Clere, then an awesome silence. The Viscount must be dead— choked and consumed by the river mud. That must not happen to Luke. She called up all her reserves of strength and heaved on the straps, urging the horse to pull harder. Every blood vessel in her body felt about to burst and her arms shook with the effort.

Then suddenly the resistance gave and she shot back several paces. She fell to her knees and was dragged several more feet by the horse before Luke yelled at it to halt. Exhaustion blurred her vision, but she could see Luke rising to his knees on the firmer mud. He was safe.

Relief flooded through her and she took comfort that her husband was alive. But without Luke acknowledging his love her own life might as well be over. She was done with living on the dregs of his affection. She would sail with Paul to France and begin a new life there.

She let go of the reins and pressed her face against the ground, the cold reviving her, and Luke crawled to her side and slumped down beside her. He gently unwound the leather straps from around her fingers and massaged the circulation back into her numbed hands. The leather had cut the skin and he kissed the laceration.

'You saved my life. I am forever in your debt,' he told her.

'No, Luke. We have no debts to each other.' Too sick at heart even to look at her husband, she turned away. She did not want him staying with her out of indebtedness.

'What do we have, Kate?' he asked huskily. 'My God, when I think what that madman might have done to you!'

Something in his tone made her face him. When he would have reached out to touch her she closed her eyes against an onrush of pain. How would she find the strength to leave him and thus salvage what little pride was left to her?

The touch of his hand on her face brought her eyes open with a start. His swarthy complexion was dabbled with mud and his hands were thick with it; but it was not that which made her pull back, but the compelling intensity of his stare. The golden lights in his dark eyes pierced the fragile barrier she was striving to maintain against him.

'You haven't answered my question, Kate.'

'What would you have me say?'

'Don't you know?' He took her into his arms. Both their fine clothes were covered in mud, but neither seemed to notice their bedraggled condition. 'It would take a lifetime to right the wrong I've done you.'

'I don't want your gratitude,' she dragged out. Her body was stiff and unyielding in his arms, lest even at this moment she surrender to the fire coursing through her veins.

'It's not gratitude I would lay at your feet, sweet Kate——'

She shook her head, cutting across his words, 'I'm too tired to quarrel with you, Luke. I'm tired of your distrust and suspicions. Leave me in peace. I'll not ask for what you are too stubborn to acknowledge.'

Luke's fingers tightened over her arm. 'You talk in riddles.'

'Do I?' she flared, indignation stinging her out of her lethargy. 'I never wanted anything from you but your love.'

'But you've always had that!' he exclaimed in obvious astonishment.

'Have I?' she challenged. Luke was being infuriatingly oblique.

His lips twitched, the sharp lines of his face softening with self-mockery as he drew her close.

'What do you think has driven me these past months, if not love? Had I loved you less I would not have gone to such extremes to keep you at my side. I love you, Kate. I always have and always will.'

He crushed her to him and his mouth covered hers in a long fervent kiss until her lips parted and their breaths mingled with a sweetness she had thought denied her forever.

'Does that not prove my devotion, my darling?' he asked finally.

'Yes,' she sighed and, oblivious of the mire, wrapped her arms about him, and drew his head down to receive her kiss.

A shout drew them apart.

'They're over here.'

It was Paul. They both looked up to see him standing over them. 'My God, Kate, this beats the lot of your crack-brained capers. We near killed those cut-throats' horses riding after you. We feared you both dead at St Clere's hands. And what do we find? The two of you rolling in the mud like a couple of street urchins!'

Katherine looked at Luke and for the first time saw the extent of his muddied garments and face, and from the amused expression in her husband's eyes she must look a similar fright. They both looked up at Paul's aghast expression, the tension of the last hour snapped, and simultaneously they burst out laughing. Clinging to each other for support, Luke helped Katherine to stand.

'The pair of you are well suited, and ripe for bedlam.' Paul continued to stare at them, shocked.

'We were not rolling about in the mud for our pleasure.' Luke sobered and put his arm around Kate's shoulders. 'My wife risked her life to pull me from the quicksand. St Clere was not so fortunate.'

Paul blenched and stuttered an apology, but Luke waved it aside and lifted Kate on to the horse's back. 'If we do not hurry we shall miss the tide,' he said as he swung up behind her. 'Once your escape has been noted, Paul, it will not be long before the authorities learn of our presence here. A hue and cry will be raised. And it will be all our hides they will be after.'

CHAPTER FIFTEEN

THE gentle rolling of the *Sea Serpent* and creak of canvas as the brigantine ploughed its way through the open sea broke the stillness of the captain's cabin. From the narrow confines of the bed Katherine sighed contentedly as she snuggled closer against the warmth of her husband's body. They lay wrapped in each other's arms, both lost in contemplation as they stared out of the small window at the full moon which illuminated the cabin. It was six weeks since they had sailed from England.

Safely tucked in the haven of his arms, Katherine wondered at her own blindness over the past months. Though Luke had at times acted distantly towards her, on many occasions his consideration of her needs had been that of an ardent lover. He never ceased to amaze her. An hour ago when they had put her brother ashore on the French coast she had been surprised when her husband had presented Paul with a large pouch of money.

'It's this year's annuity from Kate's dowry,' Luke had told him. 'Mr Sewell, the lawyer, forwarded it to Jersey. Somehow he had managed to release it from the sequested estate. I never wanted Kate's money, and it will give you an income to live in comfort during your exile. But you will never be able to return to England. Once you have settled upon a banker, send me word. The future annuities will be paid into that account.'

'It's Kate security, not mine,' Paul had said stubbornly.

Kate had shaken her head. 'It has been the cause of all the pain and misunderstanding between Luke and

250

myself. I don't want it. I have a husband to provide for me now.'

'I'm only glad it seems your names were never linked with my escape,' Paul had said. 'Promise me, Luke, when you return to England you will fight to regain Ferncombe Place. That's Kate's birthright as well as mine. I would not have strangers living in the house built by our family.'

Their farewells had been brief. Away from Newgate, Paul had recovered quickly from the fever in Jersey.

'Are you content now, my love?' Luke broke through her thoughts now.

With Paul safe her fears were now all for her husband. 'Will it be safe for us to return to England?' she queried, but her voice held no sign of regret.

'Safe enough—if you're prepared to bluff it out. Questions will have to be answered about our visit to Newgate, but Old Jem sent me word that the gaolers have sworn that we left an hour or more before Paul was discovered missing. It's a mystery how he escaped, and one that the authorities will not make too much of. Since the Lords Kenmure and Derwent Water were beheaded, there is a danger that the Jacobites may be seen as martyrs, and that would be bad for the Hanoverian cause.'

He smiled, his teeth flashing roguishly in the moonlight. 'Have we not come this far and triumphed?' A spasm crossed his lean face as he drew her close and buried his mouth against her throat. 'So many misunderstandings, my darling. So many wasted months together. Never again shall I allow my stubborn pride to doubt you, or your love.'

On seeing the love and devotion glistening in Luke's eyes, Katherine's breath caught in her throat. Her hands moved over the warm, firm muscles of his chest, her fingers tingling as they traced the line of the dark, curling hair which tapered to his flat stomach.

'Show me again how much you love me,' she murmured.

His response was immediate. With an amused laugh
he drew the sheet from her nakedness. He had made
love to her countless times, and her response had been
all a man could have desired. But now there was a
difference in her passion. On the day of their wedding
she had given herself with abandon, but it had been
tempered by innocence. Afterwards in London she had
responded with a sensuality which had been more
satisfying than any woman he had known before. This
time there was a difference—a difference so profound
that he realised that throughout the time in London
she had been withholding an integral part of herself.

It shone out now like an aura around her. Her eyes
were softer, dreamier, her touch cherishing, venerat-
ing, robbing him of his own control. She was not
merely making love—her body was the personification
of love itself.

Katherine moaned softly as their bodies entwined.
No longer forced to curb her murmurings of love, she
found that his name was a constant sigh upon her lips.
There was a new reverence to his caresses. They were
no less insistent, but every kiss or touch brought a
rapture which transcended anything she had experienced before.

'So brave—so beautiful, my beloved Kate,' he
crooned against her ear.

The love burning so fiercely in his eyes was the only
accolade she would ever need. It filled her with a
delicious warmth, radiating from his strong male body.
A sense of wonder stirred in Katherine's subconscious
as he possessed her with a blend of tenderness and
hunger that aroused the fires of her passion. Lifted to
a plateau of explosive sensation, she found herself in a
world of enthralment and perfect harmony.

This was paradise surpassed. It was the merging of
twin souls.

'I am reborn.' She smiled drowsily up at him, and
the adoration in his eyes humbled her as he lovingly

ran his hand through her long hair, winding it into a golden rope about his neck to bind them closer.

'From now until eternity I shall prove my love, my beautiful siren. I shall love you all my days,' he vowed.

Katherine rolled across him. An all-consuming tenderness swelled her heart. Passion was but an infinitesimal part of her love for this man. Nothing could part them now. They had triumphed over the vagaries of fate, and that was all that mattered. Together they would ride the storm of the weeks ahead.

A year later Katherine smiled as she stepped from the coach on to the drive of Ferncombe Place. There was an air of neglect about the shuttered house and gardens, but it did not matter. Ferncombe Place was again hers. In a week or two everything would be as it was. She was home, their court battles to regain possession finally behind them.

She felt a moment's sadness that it was not Paul who was here taking his rightful place. But he could not return. Even though many of the rebels had been pardoned by the King, Paul was still in league with the Jacobite Court who continued their plotting in France. After a long legal battle Luke had paid the fines on the Winters' estate and the property had been returned to her family.

Now Katherine's waist was circled by Luke's possessive embrace.

'From this moment, my love, I vow you will have only happy memories of your home. You mustn't fret for Paul. He's determined to spend his life for a cause he believes just, no matter how misguided that may be. It's time there was laughter again within these walls. We shall hold a reception to celebrate your homecoming and we shall dance until dawn.'

Her teasing reply was cut short by a gasp as a sharp pain shot through her back. Instantly the smile drained from Luke's face.

'Kate! Are you all right? The journey was too arduous for you.'

'Help me inside. I was pampered and cosseted throughout our carriage ride, but in truth, my love, during the last few miles I began to fear our son would be born upon the roadside, and not his rightful home.'

'Kate, only this morning you told me there was another fortnight before the birth.' Luke raised his eyes heavenwards in exasperation. 'I'd never have allowed you to face the danger of the journey had I known.'

'That's why I kept quiet.' Her smile was bright with mischief. 'I wanted our child to be born here.'

She gasped as a pain sharper than the rest stabbed through her back. She was lifted into his arms and smiled into his worried face. 'It is as well you insisted the midwife travel with us. I believe our child is somewhat impatient to be born.'

'Stubborn minx,' he said as he placed her gently on to the mattress of the room prepared in readiness for their arrival. 'I should have known that in this, as in all things, you always get your own way. Will I never be master in my own home?'

She laughed softly and grasped his hand as the force of her love threatened to overwhelm her. 'You are master of my heart,' she told him.

Tenderly he brushed a golden tendril of hair from her cheek. 'As you are mistress of mine, my darling Kate.'

The other exciting

MASQUERADE
Historical

available this month is:

BREATH OF SCANDAL
Elizabeth Lowther

Cassie Haydon had always wanted to go to Austria, her grandmother's home, but not until the death of her mother was she free to do so. A liberated woman, after all, this was 1904, Cassie had no qualms about accepting a post working at the Kurhaus in Bad Adler.

Unfortunately, the first person she encountered was Count Petransky, who was convinced she would be delighted to be his mistress! His behaviour ruined her chances of a happy working life, for the Kurhaus director, Dr Anton Sommer, disliked the count and believed Cassie was a loose woman. How was she to make Anton see the truth?